# Shoot Your Shot

# Shoot Your Shot

## LEXI LaFLEUR BROWN

CANARY STREET PRESS

**CANARY STREET PRESS™**

Recycling programs
for this product may
not exist in your area.

ISBN-13: 978-1-335-01656-0

Shoot Your Shot

For questions and comments about the quality of this book, please contact us at CustomerService@Harlequin.com.

TM is a trademark of Harlequin Enterprises ULC.

Canary Street Press
22 Adelaide St. West, 41st Floor
Toronto, Ontario M5H 4E3, Canada
CanaryStPress.com

**Printed in U.S.A.**

To my muse, you know who you are.

# ONE

## Lucy

I don't need an online personality test to tell me I'm a bitch when there are plenty of men who do that for me without the hassle of entering my email address. Just my luck, because tonight the club is filled to the brim with willing and able potential.

"Turn that hockey crap off. The Emeralds are playing tonight," I say, ordering the bartender to change the station on the TVs mounted behind the bar. I don't necessarily follow sports, but my boss is obsessed with the National Women's Soccer League and maybe if Seattle wins, she'll be in a good mood for once. The Emeralds are down two goals in the final seconds of the game. With my optimism and the Emeralds' shot at a spot in the playoffs shattered, I scoop up my three beer bottles by the necks and brace myself for the crowd.

I push my way through the overstuffed club with my hands full, desperate to reach the booth at the back of the bar where my friends promised to save me a seat. I'm late, but at least I'm not empty-handed. Wiggling my way through unmovable bodies, I gasp for air that doesn't smell like cheap cologne. I try to shout, "Excuse me," but it's a waste of breath. Eventually, after being elbowed a few too many times for my liking, I bear down and push my way through the wall of people, a technique I perfected in the punk rock mosh pits that raised me.

The crowd opens up as I near the back corner, but before I can reach my friends, a giant behemoth slides in my way. I slam right into its rock-hard exterior and the impact practically knocks the wind out of me, and along with it, the beers out of my hands. They spill all over my shirt and fall to the floor; there goes an hour of pay. I look up to see what I've hit. It isn't a behemoth; it's just some guy. He flies forward onto a tabletop, catching himself before he topples over and falls on the floor.

"What the fuck!?" He stands and turns around with fists clenched and cocked up near his chest. He takes a step, but the crunch of broken glass prevents him from getting any closer. He looks around for the perpetrator until his gaze finally drops down onto me.

My look has always scared off guys like him: I'm covered in tattoos, and have recently cut, bluntly chopped bangs and box-dyed hair—a blue black that says all anyone needs to know about my current mental state. I'm only five foot something, but my tone is obvious: *Don't fuck with me; I'm not the one.*

Despite the fact that he stands at least a foot taller than me, my arms are tightly crossed over my chest as I proudly show off my long-serving resting bitch face, determined to scare him out of my way without a hassle. If looks could kill, I would be a wanted woman.

With his freshly ironed shirt, a professional haircut, and un-painted fingernails, I know exactly how he's going to react. I could hiss at him, and he would run off with his tail between his legs just as quickly as he had appeared.

"Whoa," he says at the sight of me, recoiling like he's touched a hot burner.

This is not an endearing *whoa*, rather the type of *whoa* you hear after trauma-dumping your life's story to a stranger you just met on the bus.

It's the reaction I was hoping for.

"Excuse me," I say, snapping at him, still trying to get past my annoying roadblock.

His mouth is slightly agape as he stares me down. Maybe the impact has left him incapable of stringing together a coherent sentence, or maybe he's always this dumbfounded. I don't care to stick around and find out.

"Nice hit," he says, followed by something so muffled by the loud bass that I don't catch it.

Before I get a chance to have the last word, a guy as broad as a door frame drags him back into the crowd. A sight that only irritates me more because I never got to officially tell him to fuck off for knocking my drinks out of my hands and getting my shirt wet.

"Lucy!"

I hear Cooper call out for me and make a run for it before any other giants can stand in my way. I'm not looking to get kicked out of Club Purple Haze tonight for causing trouble and miss Cooper's half-birthday celebration. It's a ridiculous tradition but fitting for an over-the-top guy like him.

I spot my friends Cooper and Maya at the back of the club waiting for me. Cooper waves me down, though he's hard to miss in his bright pink button-up shirt and white sash that says Birthday Bitch; apparently, the party supply shop was fresh out of Half Birthday Bitch sashes.

"We got shots!" Cooper says, slurring his words a bit. He stands up from the small booth tucked in the back corner of the club, but stumbles over a chair. Although he plays it off as intentional, it's obvious that he is well on his way to posting regrettable Instagram stories.

Judging by the empty glasses littering the tabletop, I am very late to the party. While I have earned a reputation of being late, half birthdays only happen once a year, and I feel bad that I have already missed so much of the celebration.

A look of concern replaces his toothy smile as he looks my wet shirt up and down. "Is it raining?"

"Just another thing making me even later to the party. I'm sorry. Please don't hate me." I squeeze into the booth.

"Let me guess, the dictator boss strikes again?" Maya scoots over so I can cram into the booth beside her.

I nod. "Sam kept me super late at the shop, and then there was this whole thing with Kit. I've got to stop getting involved with women named after American Girl dolls," I say as I greet them both with hugs and kisses on their cheeks.

I am desperate to break into the tattoo scene in Seattle. So desperate, in fact, that I work a job I hate as the shop assistant for the world's most ruthless tattoo artist—one who still times my bathroom breaks and makes me cover the tip on her daily lunch orders. I'm hopeful that if I continue to pay my dues (and her gratuities), Sam will offer me a tattoo apprenticeship. Until then, I'm stuck answering the phone, replying to emails, and taking out the trash.

Just as I settle into my seat, I get a text. The sweat on my brow from deep cleaning the shop hasn't even dried and I'm already getting a text from my boss.

SAM:

> I expect my coffee waiting for me tomorrow morning when I get to the shop.

I give her a digital thumbs-up and tuck my phone away, wishing I could also temporarily tuck all my problems away for the night along with it. Surviving her unruly tyranny is a small price to pay on the journey of achieving my dream job.

"Oh no," Cooper whines. "I like Kit. She always lets me into the museum for free."

"Yeah, well, her boyfriend really likes her too." Kit was a promising partner until I found out on our six-month anniversary that she was celebrating her third anniversary with her boyfriend. At the very least I expect to be made aware when I'm the side chick. Chivalry is as dead as our relationship. She came by the shop at the end of my shift tonight to pick up her stuff, making me even later to this party.

"Again?" Maya says.

"Enough about my cursed love life. You guys look great!" I lean back to admire my stunning friends.

Cooper is glowing, gleaming ear to ear with a wide smile. His high cheekbones shimmer when the strobe lights catch his face. Gone is the responsible demeanor of a business owner, and in its place is the Cooper I met freshman year of college who convinced me to pierce my conch with a sewing needle. He is wild and free and half a year older.

Maya looks comfortable in her white flowy maxi skirt and worn vintage T-shirt. Her voluminous coiled curls add a couple of inches to her already poised stature. A collage of social justice movement pins she's collected from work decorate the tote tucked by her side.

I didn't have time to stop at my apartment and change my outfit before getting to the club. My skirt has ink stains on the front and my baby tee—which was chosen for comfort earlier today—is now practically transparent. I look like I lost a wet T-shirt contest.

Unfortunately, it's not that kind of event. Every twenty-something-year-old in Seattle is packed into this club to see some DJ I've never heard of. The crowd is a real mixed bag. I haven't seen the gays and the straights this united since "Call Me Maybe" by Carly Rae Jepsen dropped. I don't care much for the music or the venue, but I do love my friends.

"Here, catch up. Cooper's lit and has been very active on Grindr," Maya says, handing me a tiny glass of something.

I bring it up to my face and take a whiff—tequila. I toss it back and hope it makes my migraine disappear, or at least loosens me up enough to brave the mass of people for some requisite dancing. I will need at least two more shots before I am stress-free enough to wave my arms overhead as I sway my hips off beat to the rhythm. If I'm really lucky, Cooper will find a far cuter dance partner and I will be off the hook altogether.

"What else have I missed?" I ask, sucking on a lime to ease the burn.

"We've already seen like a hundred of your exes here tonight," Cooper shouts across the table.

"I swear I can't go anywhere in this city without bumping into an ex-partner." I survey the room. For a big city, it really starts to narrow in on you as your twenties pass by.

"I spotted Nina, but don't worry, she's gone now." Maya grimaces.

Nina is an ex-girlfriend Maya and I share in common. Horrible girlfriend, but excellent taste in women. When we broke up, Nina took my favorite sweater, pots and pans, and crystal collection with her when she left, and left me more commitment issues and Maya. In the end, I think I made out better than Nina did.

"Glad I came late then." I shudder, taking another sip of Maya's beer, which I have stealthily stolen.

Cooper's phone buzzes against the tabletop, illuminating his home screen of the three of us from his real birthday party six months ago. "Speaking of exes, looks like my future ex just walked in," he says giddily.

It should take this new guy a good fifteen minutes to wiggle his way through the crowd and steal Cooper away from our group.

As Cooper taps away at his phone feverishly, Maya waves across the club into the throng. "She came," she says, her eyes growing wide. "You guys remember Arlo, right?" Maya waves her over.

"The girl who lives in her car?" I squint, trying to get a better view of her face.

"She lives in a van-dwelling," Maya says defensively.

"I guess in elementary school when everyone used to tease me for being trailer trash, I should have told them we were living the carefree nomad lifestyle," I half-heartedly joke. I search through the crowd hoping to spot my latest mistake, but I can't get a good view of the potential suitors in attendance tonight.

"I'm going to go get us another round of shots." I excuse myself from the booth before Maya's new girlfriend and Cooper's fling can join us. I owe them that much for being so late, but selfishly I am also trying to give myself some air; I don't want to be a fifth wheel. I tried that once and I am way too selfish a lover.

"Tequila!" Cooper says.

"Water for you," I shout back to him. He rolls his eyes and swats me away.

# TWO

## Jaylen

In hockey, they say you should always keep your head on a swivel. Drop your head at the wrong time and someone will come by and knock you clean off your feet. It's a guaranteed way to wind up in concussion protocol for a few games. I might not have seen her coming, but now that she's in my view, I can't look away.

I know I'm staring because my eyes are getting dry. It's like when you look into a burning firepit and suddenly you don't remember how to blink. The way the purple strobe light shines down on her stoic face makes me wonder if she's real or a hologram. How could I not notice her? How could I not stare? She looks terrifying.

As a professional hockey player, I know a solid check when I see one—or take one. I'm not usually so easily knocked around out on the ice. Luckily, my bruised ego makes a full recovery once I see how intimidating she looks.

She's got the glare of a fourth-liner fighting to avoid a demotion to the minors—scary stuff to come up against. Strap some skates on her and put her out on the ice.

Maybe she's what the Seattle Rainiers are looking for, since they clearly have no interest in signing a skilled player like me.

I haven't taken my eyes off her since we collided. I can't decide if I want to go apologize or ask for bodychecking advice.

"Let it go, JJ," Wells says. "The last thing you need tonight is to get your ass kicked." He pulls me back into the roped-off VIP section.

Wells is shorter than me but as sturdy as a tree trunk, which makes it hard to resist his pull. His face and hands are covered in tiny silver scars he's earned as collateral for the eight minutes of ice time he clocks each night. His career PIMs outnumber his career points, but he's just as respected in the league as any top scorer. Those guys never get a statue, but they're the brawn that mixes the metal.

"I wasn't going to fight a girl." I might be having a rough night, but I'm not that far gone. "It wouldn't even be the most embarrassing part of today if she did."

Wells fishes around in a bucket of melted ice, pulling out a sweaty beer bottle. "You okay?"

We're slumped over the railing together, perched up high in the VIP section overlooking the rest of the club. I pop the top of the bottle using the railing and nod. I've got a few drinks in me now and I'm not sure I can lie to him, so I keep my mouth shut.

Evan Caldwell was my teammate in New York my rookie year with the Skyliners. Wells, as everyone calls him, because hockey players are notorious for giving each other nicknames. Most are just a variation of a last name with an *ie* or *er* sound slapped onto the end. Even if the guy has a real simple last name, hockey players will find a way to complicate it.

Wells had already clocked a few years on the Skyliners' roster before I was drafted. Our dynamic was simple: I scored, and he beat the wheels off anyone who tried to touch me. Back then, I was young, arrogant, and thought I was invincible. Wells took me under his wing and showed me the ropes.

When I signed my entry-level contract and collected my fat signing bonus, I thought the struggle was over; I thought I had arrived. I was naive to the business and wouldn't have lasted a season without his guidance. There's no handbook for surviving in the NHL, just a few vets who don't want to see you make the same mistakes they did. Even though I don't currently have an NHL contract, he's still looking out for me.

I pull out my phone and, despite my better judgment, I scroll through my social media feeds. The news that the once-highly-touted draft pick was released from his PTO—a player tryout contract—is trending, much to the satisfaction of my hungry haters. Everyone is chiming in to proclaim what they've been saying for the last few years: Jaylen Jones is the league's biggest draft bust in history. To the rest of the world, the crash from first overall pick in the NHL draft to being unemployed seemed to happen in the blink of an eye, but to me it was a grueling six-year free fall.

"Put that shit away." Wells snatches my phone and turns it off before handing it back over.

"They're right." I shove my phone in my pocket.

I'm the only Black player to ever go first overall. As if that isn't pressure enough, I'm still the highest drafted player of color in NHL history. I felt the weight of everyone's expectations, and for a while I carried it on my shoulders, amassing over sixty points my rookie season and almost taking home the Calder Memorial Trophy for the NHL's best rookie. Eventually, the load got too heavy and the metaphorical ice beneath my feet began to crack.

I never wanted to be a role model; I wanted to play hockey. When I couldn't even do that right, I found myself turning into the villain overnight. Thinly veiled racism disguised as critique eventually shattered what was left of my confidence. I know I should stay off social media and ignore the haters, but I've never been good at that.

"What's that saying? Those who can't do, talk shit on the internet or something." Wells's smile resembles that of his six-year-old daughter's—gummy and proud. A black hole where a front tooth once sat will remain void until retirement. He digs his shoulder into my arm, trying to elicit a smile from my thinly drawn lips.

"What the hell am I going to do next?" I slump over the railing.

"You're going to go buy that girl another drink. She's not snarling anymore, and you owe it to her." Wells points toward the bar, where the goon from earlier is unsuccessfully trying to get the bartender's attention. It wasn't what I meant when I asked, but maybe it's the answer I needed to hear.

I gladly abandon the VIP section, where the entire team is hidden away to celebrate surviving the Rainiers' training camp with bottle service. I was released this afternoon from my PTO and have little to celebrate, but when the guys found out that my flight home doesn't leave until the morning, they dragged me out with them. Now, while everyone parties, I quietly wallow.

I would have preferred to stay back in my hotel bed racking up a room service bill that would rival Kevin McCallister's, but this girl looks like a fun distraction, and I could use one of those tonight. I'm willing to face the mob of crowded bodies for a chance to get another glance at the five-foot-nothing bruiser who sent me flying into the boards. I need to know her name. Something like Punisher sure fits her demeanor.

I wiggle in next to her, waiting for the right moment to lean down and talk. I'm more apprehensive in my approach than usual because my confidence already took a huge hit today when I was cut from the team, and I'm not sure how much more of a beating I can endure.

I lean over the bar top, and as if the bartender was expecting me, she gleefully greets me with her best customer service smile. She practically bounces over to me like a little bunny. Not only can twenty-some guys show up to a club last-minute, flash their NHL cards, and get a VIP table immediately, but they also rarely have to wait around for someone to serve them. It's one of the many perks of being a professional athlete that I will miss. I mean, that and all the free hockey tape; you would be surprised what a good roll of hockey tape can fix.

I lean into the mysterious tattooed girl and say, "What are you trying to order?" I do my best to shoot her a disarming smile. Judging by her stone-cold scowl, it might be coming across as creepy.

Right when I think she's going to tell me to fuck off, she says, "I'm good." She slumps against the bar with her chin falling into her hand in a defeated exhale.

"You've been standing here waiting forever. Tell me your order."

She glances at me out of the corner of her eyes. They narrow. "You're not hitting on me, right?"

"Technically," I say, leaning in, my mouth curving into a slanted smile, "you hit me first."

"Fine, but only because you owe me for spilling all my beer earlier. Five shots of tequila," she says dryly.

"Damn!" My head snaps back. She drinks more than any goon I've ever met too. At this point, I really want to ask her if she can skate. I turn to the bartender, who is patiently awaiting my instruction. "Six tequila shots, please."

The bartender sets up six glasses and fills them each with top-shelf tequila. As I'm pulling my credit card out of my wallet, someone squeezes by and knocks my card out of my hand and onto the ground. Having retrieved it from the floor, I hand it over to the bartender and turn to formally introduce myself. "I'm Jaylen. What's your name?" I say as I grab my shot off the bar top and turn to clink glasses with my new friend. Only she's already disappeared back into the crowd, and I've just used my best pickup line on a couple of men wrapped up tightly in each other's embrace.

"Oh," I say, locking eyes with them.

"She's gone," one man says.

"Sorry, babes," the other adds with a sympathetic pout.

# THREE

## Lucy

I couldn't dip soon enough. I'm not trying to end up with another drink spilled all over my shirt, or worse, wait around and listen to that guy talk about his fantasy football team—he totally looks like the type of guy who can't shut up about his fantasy football team.

As I make my way back to my friends, I find them both deep in conversation. Maya is chatting with that girl who illegally parks her home in national parks across the country, and Cooper is laughing at something his digital match said. They both look happy as they lean into their potential love interests like magnets drawn together by an invisible force—though the invisible force tonight is likely the tequila.

I set the drinks on the tabletop, but they hardly notice me. I down one of the shots before I can start feeling sorry for myself and when I slam the empty glass down, Maya finally looks my way.

"Thanks, Lucy," she says, picking up a shot in each hand. She hands one to Arlo and they lock eyes and toss them back. Maya wipes a dribble of tequila off Van Girl's chin, and I officially start sulking.

"Thank me by helping me pick out someone to dance with

tonight," I say, desperate for a distraction. Things with Kit went sour tonight when I forgot to bring her copy of Clairo's *Charm* on vinyl and I said we could call it even because she forgot to tell me she had a boyfriend. Not to mention I'd like to forget how much I hate my job for the next ten hours.

"You hate dancing," Maya says, with her perfect eyebrow raised.

"Yeah, and I think you've dated or hooked up with everyone in here already, which is impressive considering literally everyone is in your dating pool," Cooper says.

"He's cute." I wave at a guy standing near the bathrooms. He reciprocates with a dirty look.

"That's Joey the bouncer, and you've dated him," Cooper reminds me, though I can't remember.

"Looks like I might have ghosted him too. Well, things are over with Kit and much like the era from which that American Girl doll's backstory originated, I too am in a great depression." I slump into my hand. I hoped the shot would put me in a party mood, but instead it's making me sleepy.

"Lucy Lee Ross," Maya snaps. "Do you hear yourself? You're constantly complaining to us about being stuck replying to emails and unclogging toilets at work. You say you want a tattoo apprenticeship, but instead of focusing on your drawings or creating a portfolio, you go from one relationship to the next." Maya sets her glass down on the table.

*Damn, my full government name.* I was not anticipating a scolding tonight. If I was, I would have made that guy buy me more shots.

"Harsh much?" I cross my arms over my chest. She's not wrong, but couldn't this type of conversation wait until tomorrow morning? I look back at the bouncer but he's still avoiding eye contact.

"We love you, Lucy, but Maya is right. A bit of a bitch with her delivery, but the bitch is right," Cooper says.

Maya wraps her arm around my shoulder and pulls me in close. "I want you to succeed. You're so talented," she says.

I groan and wiggle out from underneath her embrace. "You guys are being dramatic. I haven't dated everyone."

"That girl over there." Cooper points across the room. "She lasted three months. And that guy over there, two weeks. And them over there, one date." Cooper is pointing in every direction so quickly that it's making my head spin.

"Enough! I get it, you're right. I need to swear off men." I pinch the bridge of my nose; my headache is intensifying with every tempo switch the DJ is making.

"And women," Cooper adds firmly.

My hand drops. "Well, let's not be dramatic," I say.

Dating in the digital age is complicated, but dating in your twenties is near futile. I am what you would call a serial dater. A relationship slut, if you will. I love the thrill of a budding connection but hate the seriousness that often follows after a few months. Most of my relationships tend to fizzle out before the goodbye becomes too painful.

My friends seem to believe that I use relationships to distract myself from feeling shitty about where I'm at in my life, or to procrastinate where I want to be in my career. Have they even considered that I would still feel shitty about my life regardless?

"Try to lay off the distractions for a bit and see what happens." Maya softens her approach, but it's too late—I'm mid-existential crisis and there's no stopping the spiral.

Cooper leans across the table, pressing his fingers into the sticky wooden top. "Lucy, this is a textbook midtwenties crisis. You have two choices: get a cat or make a pledge to focus on yourself and get that promotion. The answer is obvious."

"Another cat!" I shake my balled-up fists by my face and squeal with joy.

"No!" Maya gives me a shove.

"Fine. I need to focus on my portfolio and put together a

book of work so good Sam has no choice but to offer me an apprenticeship."

Years ago, I messed up my one opportunity to secure my dream career. I shudder at the memory; I can't blow this opportunity too. I have to land an apprenticeship.

"That's the spirit," Maya says, patting my back.

"The only true spirit is the one we manifest by feeding our seven chakras through the holistic journey of life," Arlo says in a singsong voice.

Cooper and I share an unspoken look of concern.

"Spirit the horse was my gay awakening," Cooper's friend says, pursing his lips.

The song changes to something that evokes a loud shriek from Cooper's friend. The beat is good enough to get the half-birthday boy out of his seat, and they disappear onto the dance floor together. As the club ignites in cheers and fist pumps, I feel a twinge of guilt for being out when I haven't sketched all week.

They're right—not the out-of-pocket thing Arlo said, but the part about needing to be hyperfocused on my goal instead of constantly inviting new distractions to interfere with my career. While everyone dances and sings, I'm quiet, thinking about how much further ahead I should be, like my friends who both have successful careers.

"You okay?" Maya asks discreetly.

I shake the mopey look from my face and replace it with a less-concerning scowl. "Yeah, I'm fine. It's been a long day." Fidgeting with the tab on the seltzer can in front of me is not the soothing stim I hoped it to be.

"Are you sure?" She gives me a soft nudge.

"I should be sketching right now," I say. The tab pops off the can and I plop it inside the opening.

"If you feel inspired, you should follow the feeling. Text me when you get home safe," Maya says. I give her a kiss on the cheek before slipping out of the booth and back through the dance floor.

★ ★ ★

The cold air smacks me awake as I step outside the club. I stand alone on the curb outside, underneath the streetlight, as I rummage through my purse for my phone. As I search, a guy looking too disheveled to be trying out pickup lines stumbles my way and shouts, "Nice tattoos. What's that one mean?" He slurs his words as he tries to point at a tattoo on my arm. He wobbles around like a Mighty Bean waiting for my response.

"It's a metaphor for daddy issues," I snap back sarcastically. I don't know which tattoo he is referring to; my arms, like the rest of my body, are covered in ink. I finally retrieve my phone from the bottom of my purse, and I open up the Uber app.

"Cool. I've been thinking of getting a big lion and like a clock or roses or some trees," he drunkenly mumbles.

I ignore him and continue looking down at my phone, trying to request a ride home. "No cars." I sigh under my breath.

"No, I don't want a car tattoo. Are you even listening to me?" He takes a couple off-balance steps toward me.

"Back up, Ted Bundy." I put my hand up, ready to catch him, because he looks like he could topple over on top of me at any moment. I brace myself for the impact.

"You're a bitch!"

Ahh, there it is; my Myers-Briggs Type diagnosis: BITCH. The words wrap me up like a warm blanket. If I don't hear it at some point during a night out drinking, I worry I've done something wrong.

"Hey, leave her alone!" someone says from behind him. It's that familiar deep voice from inside, Tequila Guy.

Ted Bundy stumbles on his way, likely to puke down some alley or start a fight with someone else.

"You're right on cue. Have you been watching me all night or something?" I ask without glancing up from my phone.

He fumbles over his words, with a disarming amount of awkward charm. "No. Yes. Sort of. I was watching you struggle to get a drink at the bar, but this is a coincidence."

"Thanks, but I don't need you to defend me from the local drunks or get me drinks. I'm fine." I only peer up from my phone long enough to notice that he is relatively sober compared to the motley crew of drunken club-goers stumbling out of the exit behind him.

"I respect that, but if you don't mind, I'm now the last person seen with you and want to make sure you get in an Uber safely." He leans against the club's brick exterior with a forced casualness.

*What is this guy's deal?* He's hovering closer to me than a Sephora employee making sure I don't steal anything. He's not my type at all: too polite, too pretty, too clean. He's wearing an ironed T-shirt to a bar for fuck's sake. I glance up quickly and remember that he's also huge. If he wants to wait around and make sure no one pukes on my shoes, then he can be my guest.

"Whatever, but you'll be waiting awhile. There are hardly any cars and the ones available are surcharged more than the drinks they're selling inside." As I'm scrolling the app looking for rides, my phone dies. I pound the power button a few times hoping for a miracle, but there's no pulse. "Great," I say, dropping my arm.

"I can order you one."

"Don't worry about it. You already got me and my friends all those shots, so we're even." I stash my phone in my purse and start walking away.

Slight change of plans. I head up the street to a local dive bar where the owner sometimes lets me request a song or two. The bartender can call me a taxicab—those still exist, don't they? Hopefully, because I'm not trying to get on a city scooter after tequila.

The air is crisp but mild for early October. Just as I begin to enjoy the solitude that comes with a late-night walk, footsteps thump along behind me. Suddenly, he's by my side. I continue on, without making eye contact. Men are like bears: if you hold eye contact with them for too long, they think it's a challenge they can't back away from.

"I'm not heading home, so if you plan on following me and figuring out where I live, you should give up now."

Most guys would have called me a bitch or given up their pursuit, but he stays buzzing by my side no matter how hard I swat. This guy wouldn't know a hint if it ditched him at the bar with the tab for six shots.

"That place back there sucked, didn't it? Can you believe the name? Purple Haze. More like Purple Lame. Are you going somewhere better?" he asks with entirely too much confidence for someone who has been shot down at least three times in the last five minutes.

I stop walking. I'm not sure if I'm annoyed or bewildered. He continues on for a couple of paces before noticing, at which point he turns to face me. He stands there staring at me like a dog waiting for a ball to be thrown. We've stopped underneath a streetlight and for the first time, I have enough patience to get a good look at him.

He's tall, but I know better than to ask him his height and give him the satisfaction of telling me it's over six feet. His exterior is hard and bulky, his face is sharp and angular, but his dark brown eyes are soft and kind. His skin is a creamy warm amber, and his black hair is just long enough that it's starting to curl into tight ringlets on the top of his head.

His clothes are nice but simple and yet he still looks incredibly stylish. Like an off-duty model. I'm not entirely sure what to make of this guy, and that feels like reason enough to keep looking at him.

"You're really persistent, aren't you," I say, having made the decision to engage.

"Some would say relentless." He beams like someone placed a medal around his neck.

"I doubt they mean it as a compliment."

"Lots of people mean it as a compliment."

"Lots of people?" I raise an eyebrow.

"I guess none you know." He shrugs and sticks his hands in his pockets.

I start walking again. He follows. I'm only a block away from the bar and I have to decide if I want to keep him around longer. He smiles down at me with the most perfect and disarming grin—contagious, like a yawn—and despite myself, I smile back at him.

The excitement of a new connection warms my cheeks, and my face contorts in agony as I feel myself considering the possibility of engaging with this man flirtatiously. Still, I am determined to stick to my new resolution; my sketchbook is calling my name. As I draw a deep breath and open my mouth to start screaming and scare him away, he speaks up.

"Your phone is dead, isn't it? I have a charger pack. You can use it if you want." He pulls a compact square charger out of his back pocket and tugs a tab, revealing an attached charging cord. He offers it to me, and I contemplate it like a chess move until finally, I abandon my old strategy and snatch it out of his hand. New plan: I'll charge my phone so I can get an Uber, then I can get home and start sketching.

"I'm going to Trolls Bridge. You're welcome to come as long as you promise not to ask me about my tattoos." I pick up my pace, continuing to trek down the street.

"Not even the tiny wishbone on your shoulder?" He is quickly by my side, poking at my flesh.

"Especially that one," I say without expression, increasing the distance between us.

"I never understood the luck behind breaking a bone," he says, not discouraged in the slightest by my increasing shortness with him.

"No one's ever told you to break a leg?" I point to the bar, so he doesn't walk right by it.

"More like threatened to break my leg." He holds the large wooden door open for me, and I walk inside with every intention of leaving as soon as my phone's charged enough to get me home.

He might be cute and persistent, but he's no tattoo apprenticeship.

# FOUR

## Jaylen

Once you've seen one dive bar, you've seen them all. Trolls Bridge is no different: better left dimly lit and best enjoyed slightly buzzed.

"This is Trolls Bridge, huh?" I say, taking in my new surroundings and the questionable smells. My shoes stick in a mystery spill under the wibbly round table.

The bar is poorly lit by glowing neon signs, most of which are beer branded, except for the green troll that glows behind the bartender. We're tucked behind a broken jukebox covered in a thick layer of dust. "I thought we were going on some hero's journey, like to Mordor or something," I add, trying to at least crack the ice. Someone breaks a rack on the pool table nearby, and I startle.

"Those were hobbits," she says without much laughter, wasting no time plugging her phone into my portable charger.

At least she got the reference. I didn't break the ice, but there's a small surface crack on top. By now most professional hockey players would have mentioned the fact that they're an athlete, finding some excuse to humbly brag about how cool their job is, but I can't use my usual lines anymore. I doubt they would even work on someone like her. I quickly have to remember what it is like to be a person, and not a professional hockey player. Without an NHL contract at the moment, I'm just a guy who can skate.

Of course, now I'm in my head worrying about what I'm going to do with my life now that I'm out of the NHL. Go play in Russia? Get a job in real estate? Start a podcast? I shudder at the thought and block it out of my mind.

"Right. So, if I ask for your name, are you going to hit me?" I shift around in my seat trying to find a comfortable position.

"Lucy." She sounds very inconvenienced.

There was no pause before her response, so either she's telling me the truth or it's her go-to fake name. Regardless, it doesn't leave much room for some cutesy nickname. What would she do if I called her Lulu? I know better than to try.

"Hi, Lucy. I'm Jaylen, but most people call me JJ," I say. I almost reach across the table and shake her hand, but thankfully I catch myself and grab my beer instead. I take a sip.

I intentionally omit my last name from my introduction in case she watches hockey. I used to wear the Jones patch across my back with pride, but it's since become a target for hate. Fans used to chant my name from the stands, but eventually all I could hear were their boos. I'm fine with just being Jaylen tonight.

"I thought they called you relentless." Lucy takes a drink of her beer, a two-for-seven-dollars special she reluctantly let me buy her.

"Funny. You come to this place often?"

Now that she's finally willing to look at me I can see that she has the coolest eyes I've ever seen. They're hazel, and not the type of hazel that people with brown eyes claim to have, a real mixture of greens and browns. I know I'm staring at her again, but it's so hard to look away when there is so much of her to look at.

"Sometimes." She folds her arms across her chest and slouches back into her chair.

"Seems like a cool place to meet people," I say, trying to be nice.

Lucy seems like the type of person who needs a minute or two to warm up to new people. She tried to fight me when we first met; now she's telling me her name. That's great progress.

"No one comes to Trolls Bridge to meet someone new; they come here to be left alone." She peers down to check her phone's battery life. "This place doesn't see a lot of tourists like you," she says, calling me out.

"What makes you assume I'm not a local?" I do my best to hide the fact that her assumption offends me. Even this stranger I just met knows I don't belong in this city, on this hockey team. I'm out of place sitting across from her, just like I was out of place at that NHL training camp.

"You're wearing nice shoes in a city known for rain and you're way too polite. You have Midwest suburbia written all over you." Lucy adjusts her crossed arms, tightening their lock around her chest.

"A suburb outside of Chicago," I say. Lucy's chin tilts toward the ceiling and she cracks the slightest smile as she's proven right. "What about you? You from around here?"

It's a strategic question that usually weeds out the hockey fans. If they're from the Midwest, they likely know my name. If they're from the East Coast, they know the team that drafted me. And if they're from Canada, they know my name, team, stats, and blood type.

Shifting in her seat, Lucy draws a long inhale. "Listen, Jaylen. I'm not going to call you JJ—it feels like a nickname you give a small child and not something you call a grown man. We don't have to do this, pretend to get to know each other. You ask me about my family, and I ask you about work, and we leave here having presented the best version of ourselves, waiting to see if the other is going to call us back. And for what? To find out months later that Noah, the guy always texting you when we were together, was never really your brother, but your boyfriend the entire time."

"Who's Noah?"

"Exactly." Lucy slaps her palm down on the table. She isn't derailed in the slightest by my confusion as her passionate spiel continues. "Let's save each other a couple of wasted months. I simply don't have the energy tonight. And if I'm being frank, I'm not looking for any type of relationship right now." An ease falls over Lucy's body for the first time tonight.

In that moment, I realize she has no clue who I am and for whatever reason, it puts me at ease too. "Okay. Should we get straight to the point and present the worst version of ourselves?" I suggest jokingly.

Now I'm getting a bit of a rise out of the anonymity between us; I knew she looked like fun when I first saw her. Lucy might be incredibly hot and wildly intimidating, but she is also totally clueless about who I am, and I like it.

"Maybe." She brings her finger to her chin. She looks me up and down, like she's sizing up her competition. "You go first," she says.

"Hmm. Let me think. Um, sometimes I talk in my sleep." I'm caught off guard by her willingness to engage, and struggle to think of anything good off the top of my head.

"Wow! Red flag! Get away! Automatically blocked!" she says with so much emotion that there is no denying it's sarcasm. Lucy quickly drops the pretend outrage and adds, "Seriously, that's the worst you got?"

I think about playing it safe again and telling her that I put hot sauce on my eggs, but I don't want to disappoint her. Plus, I love a challenge. "Fine. My life is a complete mess right now. I've never had a serious relationship because work has always come first. I pretty much put work above everything. I'm really hard on myself, to a fault, and it makes it hard to let anyone in. I'm also allergic to peanuts, which is deadly, but mostly embarrassing. I don't enjoy the fact that I can be taken out by a tiny nut."

It's more honest than I've been with myself in a long time. My life is a complete mess, but the mess didn't happen this afternoon when I got cut from the Rainiers. I made that mess back in my second year in the league when I did something so shameful, I don't think I could ever admit it out loud, no matter how cute the woman in front of me is.

It was January, almost five years ago. I still don't remember anything from that game. What I do remember is the fact that I missed my best friend Cameron's funeral to play in it. He must still be pissed at me, because I swear ever since that game I've been cursed.

It's fine; I don't forgive myself either. So I tell Lucy my life's a complete mess because it's the truth, and because I don't think she would keep talking to me if she knew the whole truth.

"Now we're talking. Okay, let me try." She rubs her hands together in excitement. "I'm a serial dater, with a long track record of crappy partners and imploding relationships. In fact, I've sworn off dating altogether for the foreseeable future. I'm focusing on work right now. Oh, and I've been told I can be a bit cold or hard to read or whatever."

A loud laugh escapes from my mouth, and she shoots me a death glare. "Sorry." I bite my lip trying to rein in my grin. Her self-awareness is sexy.

"Tell me more horrible things about you," Lucy coos mockingly as she leans in toward me.

I'm almost too distracted by her slightly parted glossy lips to answer, but my eyes narrow as I get my head back in the game. "I'm bad with names. I forget everyone's name the minute they say it. I end up having to call them Boss or Big Dog so they don't notice that I don't know their actual name. It's a great life hack because they end up thinking we're so tight that I've given them a fun little nickname. But don't worry, I'll always remember yours, *Lacy*." I lean back, pleased with myself at that last joke.

"I'm an impulsive shoplifter of trivial objects," she says.

Lucy reaches into her purse and pulls out a handful of mints, two shot glasses branded with the Club Purple Haze logo, and a stack of Trolls Bridge bar-branded cardboard coasters. I can't help but laugh as she scoops everything back into her bag.

"I piss the bed when I drink too much." I try to one-up her.

"Most men do," she says.

"I pee in the shower."

"Most people do." She dismisses me again, this time with a fake yawn.

"I don't remember birthdays," I say, but Lucy shakes her head. It's not good enough. I need something better. "Oh, this one's good. I'm a crier."

"Like after sex?" she asks.

I shake my head. "Think sports movies, Super Bowl commercials, regular commercials, sometimes those commercials that pop up before your YouTube video plays. Wow, I guess capitalism really makes me weepy." I'm really enjoying the banter; like it's a game and I stand a chance of winning this one.

"If you send me the link to a funny video, nine times out of ten, I'm not watching it. I will just reply 'lol.'"

"I think the *Shrek* cinematic universe is overrated," I say gleefully, getting caught up in our back-and-forth. Lucy gasps. I straighten up and sit taller in my seat.

"Well, I chew with my mouth open." Lucy bares her teeth at me.

"I listen to my music loudly without headphones in public spaces." I lean in toward her.

"I clap at the end of movies." Lucy leans in too.

"When someone is running toward the elevator, I act like

I'm hitting the door-open button, but I'm really hitting Door Close." I don't hide the beaming smile on my face; I'm proud of that one.

"I'm always late. I'll say I'm on my way, but I'm not. I'm still in my bed." Lucy juts out her bottom lip a bit and gives a cute shrug of her shoulders. I don't for one second believe she feels bad about that one.

"I lie to my dentist about my flossing habits." It's a confession I would never make to a cute girl I was hoping to kiss, but I'm too wrapped up in the banter to care. I want to outdo her. I want to make her smile, make her laugh. I'm breaking the damn ice tonight.

"I should be grossed out, but if anything, I'm impressed by your dedication," she says through visible discomfort.

Right when I think she's conceding, she settles into an ominous smirk. "One time I told a girl I was seeing that we had to break up because my beloved cat had passed away and I wasn't going to be emotionally available to her as I grieved. It was a lie—Sailor was fine. About a month later we ran into each other on the street outside my vet's office. I was bringing Sailor in for her annual checkup," she says.

I pull away, leaning back in my seat. "That's really bad." I don't have any pets because my hockey schedule was always so chaotic and demanding, yet I realize a confession about a beloved pet is likely something someone would take to their grave.

"Thank you. Sailor's died like five times already, but I figure cats have nine lives so it's fine."

I admire the way her round nose scrunches every time she thinks she's won. If I was a smart man, I would sit back and enjoy the cute face she's making at me. But I'm not smart; I'm a winner.

"All right," I say, and I sit up straight. I interlock my fingers and rest my arms on the table. I'm ready to take one last shot at it. Before I speak, Lucy runs her hand through her hair, and I see it. She has the number thirteen surrounded by a heart tattooed on the inside of her wrist. It hadn't caught my eye earlier; with all the ink covering her body, it would take me days to notice them all.

While thirteen is a common favorite number, I can't help but find it funny that she already has my jersey number tattooed on her body. Maybe the hockey gods are trying to tell me something—maybe they haven't completely forgotten about me. In both love and hockey, a little luck goes a long way.

"One time while visiting Seattle," I say in a low voice, "I saw this really hot girl at the bar. I couldn't get a read on her, but there was something about her. I couldn't get her out of my mind, so I kept trying to talk to her—"

"Because you're so relentless," she interrupts me.

"Because I'm so relentless I made an effort to pursue her even though I know I'll be gone in the morning, and we'll probably never meet again."

Lucy's head tilts and the faintest smile creeps across her face. It seems I have survived her twisted version of small talk, and unlike elevator doors, I am holding her interest.

"Maybe I'm okay with one anonymous fun night together." She bites her lip and my body tingles.

With my legs angled to the exit, I'm already practically jumping out of my seat as I say, "Let's get out of here."

She grabs her phone off the table and slips it into her purse as we abandon our empty beer bottles.

# FIVE

## Jaylen

Lucy follows me into the night, practically jogging to keep up. I'm not sure why anyone would insist on wearing such clunky boots; they look like they weigh about ten pounds each.

"Usually when someone says 'Let's get out of here,' they mean 'Let's go back to my place' or 'Let's get a hotel room.' They don't mean 'Let's run a 5k in the middle of the night.' My feet hurt," she whines as she thumps along beside me.

We've hardly walked three blocks from Trolls Bridge. I might be from the Midwest, but I've lived in New York for the last six hockey seasons; everything is a short walk away if you have the right attitude. Even my hotel room. At least I think it is. It's possible I made a wrong turn. I also wasn't entirely expecting Lucy to follow me and the longer we walk the more nervous I get at the thought of inviting her up to my room.

After falling a few paces behind me, Lucy succumbs to her fatigue and slumps down on the dirty curb.

"No, get up. We're so close. I think..." My protest lacks the necessary confidence to persuade her. She pouts at me, and I reluctantly sit down beside her for a rest. I do my best to repress the thought of the million microgerms currently attaching themselves to my pants.

As my attention shifts from what I'm sitting on to what I'm sitting across from, my mouth falls open. "Look at that sign over there," I blurt out. I point across the deserted street like a kid spotting cows on a long road trip. She follows my finger to Lucky Thirteen Tattoo. Dangling from the awning is a colorful stained-glass number thirteen about the size of a sheet of paper.

Turning, she snaps, "I said I wasn't going to talk about my tattoos."

"I'm not asking you about your tattoos. I'm asking you to look at the dangling sign."

"The stained-glass thirteen? What about it?" Her eyes narrow.

"We're going to steal that sign," I say with conviction. It's as serious as I've been all night. After meeting Lucy tonight, a beautiful, mysterious woman with a thirteen tattoo on her wrist, I see it as a sign. Well, obviously, but not just a sign, a metaphorical one too. Plus, if I can't have the jersey number thirteen anymore, then they can't either.

I'm not usually this reckless, but somewhere among the beers and Lucy's heavenly hazel eyes, I'm wrapped up in the moment. It's been years since I've felt this free from myself, so I'm going with it.

She laughs at my absurd request, only I'm not laughing with her. "You can't be serious. Who do you think you are, Nic Cage in *National Treasure*?"

"You were bragging about being an accomplished thief back at the hobbit bar. This should be an easy lift." I tread a fine line between persuasion and peer pressure.

"It's way too high for me to reach," she says.

I scope out the area. The sign dangles at least ten feet in the air, well above both our heads. Difficult, but not impossible. A bit like Lucy, and man, do I love a challenge.

"I'll put you on my shoulders," I try to assure her.

"There are security cameras. You might be gone tomorrow, but I live here."

"The cameras don't point at the sign." I'll have an answer for any excuse. And I'm right; the store sits at the corner of the street, but the sign hangs to the far side of the building, well beyond the store's front door and any other nearby security cameras.

"Why do you even want it?" Lucy asks, delaying us.

"Thirteen is my favorite number." I furrow my brow at her like what I said justifies petty theft. I thought she would be immediately on board with this plan. After all, she's the one with the number thirteen inked into her skin forever. I desperately wish I could bring up her tattoo, as a point of leverage or at least justification, but I promised to not mention them. So far, I'm going to respect that wish.

"What is this, Little League? Who still has a favorite number?" Lucy laughs at me.

"Forget it." I'm getting nowhere with her. At this rate, it would be faster to try to scale the wall and get it down myself. I didn't want to have to do this to her, but she's left me no choice.

I discreetly push up the sleeves of my T-shirt and I lean back on my arms. My muscles flex under the weight of my torso. I turn to her and flash a smile, showing off the results of three years of orthodontics when I was in middle school. I am shamelessly peacocking for her. I might as well rip off my shirt and start flexing in front of her like Michael B. Jordan in every single one of his movies. I figure I won't have this body much longer; I might as well put it to use tonight while I've still got it. And I know I've still got it, because she rolls her eyes and groans.

"Fine. I've made far worse decisions for far uglier people. Let's go."

I jump up with a jolt of energy and turn to extend a hand to help her off the curb. My hand engulfs hers entirely, and I pull her to her feet with ease. I don't want to let go of her, but she drops my hand before darting across the street.

"But if we go down for this, I'm giving them your name," she turns to shout back at me.

I chase after her, yelling, "How do you know I gave you a real one?"

I kneel on the sidewalk low enough for Lucy to jump on my back. I can't help but giggle as we almost topple over. With her thighs wrapped around the back of my neck, I try my best to forget that she's wearing a skirt. I pop up from my squatted position with ease, gripping on to her legs to make sure she doesn't fly off the back of my shoulders. I hope she isn't afraid of heights.

"You ready?" I call up to her as I paw the ground like a bull ready to charge.

I have to keep things silly or else I'll be too tempted to turn my head and ask to kiss her inner thigh. Her legs are soft and smell like sugar, and I do my best to ignore how far up her tattoos reach.

"Just walk to the sign," she says, annoyed with my theatrics.

I don't walk—I run. She almost flies off the back of my neck. Lucy clings to my head like she's reading a crystal ball. This is not what I had envisioned when I thought of her running her fingers through my hair, but I'll take it.

Right as we pass underneath, she reaches up and with a swift tug, she brings the sign down. With Lucy gripping my head for dear life, I continue to run up the street for another block as she giggles uncontrollably.

"Okay, okay, put me down," she says, having gotten a hold of herself.

Lucy hands over the stolen property and I cradle it gently like *my precious*. "What a thrill. I get why you do it."

"Don't let it become a habit. I'd hate to be a bad influence on you."

My grin cracks into a full smile. She bites down on her bottom lip to stop herself from smiling as widely as I am, but she can't hide her red cheeks so easily.

"Isn't that what tonight's all about—being our worst selves?" I remind her.

"Then you're welcome."

I laugh at Lucy's casual cockiness. Confidence comes so naturally to her.

The side street is silent; it's just us, two strangers standing under the moonlight with a stolen sign. We are all alone, and yet I want even more privacy. I tuck my hands in my pockets, partially for the warmth, but also because this next part of the evening is a bit awkward.

Picking up women in random cities for one night of fun isn't a foreign concept to me, but it's also not something I ever made a habit of doing regularly. Hockey is so physically demanding that by the time the opportunity ever presented itself I didn't have much game left to contribute to my off-ice extracurriculars. Maybe in my first year in the league, when I was playing well, but not lately.

When everyone thinks you're the worst hockey player in the world, you start to feel like the worst person too. No one wanted to meet me; they wanted to meet the kid who was drafted first overall. Lucy doesn't know Jaylen the top prospect; she knows Jaylen the guy who's wearing the wrong shoes. The clock is running out on tonight and I have one shot left.

"Good news for your sore feet, we're really close to my hotel. Do you want to come up? Or I could get you that Uber you wanted. It's your call." I take my hand out of my pocket and rub the back of my neck while staring down at my feet. It's cold, but I'm less caught up on the fact that Lucy is braless and more focused on the fact that her nose isn't the only place she has pierced. I brace myself to be turned down and sent packing, again.

There's an unignorable knot in my stomach that's almost never there. It was the same knot I felt during the NHL draft, the same knot I felt before taking my rookie lap in my first NHL game, and the same knot I felt before I met my baby nephew for the first time. It takes a lot to make me nervous, but since the moment I met Lucy, I've felt it.

"If they start to hurt too much, I'll make you carry me again," she says, slipping her hand into mine.

# SIX

## Lucy

Jaylen leads me through the lobby of the nicest hotel I have ever stepped foot in. Clearly the room was not purchased through some discount travel site, but likely reserved on a thick credit card with no spending limit. Jaylen gives a friendly nod to the receptionist at the front desk as we pass by on our way to the elevator.

"Did you say you were here for work?" I ask, unable to ignore the nagging questions forming in my mind. The luxury hotel is really setting off my curiosity.

"I didn't say, and I thought we were keeping it casual." He squeezes my hand tightly as we step into the elevator.

"Hold the door!" someone shouts from the lobby. I quickly pound the door-close button. Jaylen laughs as the elevator slides shut.

The inside of Jaylen's hotel room is tidy and clean, with a suitcase mostly packed and ready to go near the door. He gently places his new sign on the armchair near the window before squatting down in front of the minifridge.

"Can I get you a drink? Vodka or whiskey? Not a whole lot of options here," he says.

The bed is tightly made up with a chocolate resting on the

pillow, which I discreetly slip into my purse while Jaylen's not looking. As he searches through the fridge, I scan the room in hopes of learning more about my new friend. I spot a stylish dark green suit resting across his open suitcase, but I can't think of a single job that requires a suit, besides an investment banker or the Riddler.

"Lucy?" he interrupts my visual snoop.

"Jack and Coke or something like it is fine. Thanks," I say, kicking my shoes off.

Jaylen gets up and mixes two drinks on the top of the dresser. As he hands me one, his finger grazes the inside of my wrist. I have so many tattoos that it's impossible for me to keep track of each one. Jaylen's touch reminds me of its existence, and I find the delighted smile that spreads across his face worrisome. I pull my hand back and bring the glass to my mouth, taking a sip.

"Don't read too much into it. I got it during a Friday-the-thirteenth flash deal." I hope my warning keeps his expectations realistic. This is one night of fun for me, followed by months of hyperfocus on my dream. There's no budding relationship waiting for us in the morning, no phone number exchange as we say our see-you-laters.

"I noticed your tattoo at the bar," Jaylen says, despite my warning.

My phone vibrates against my hip, startling me and breaking our intense eye contact. I discreetly pull it out and check the notification. It's a text.

MAYA:

> Don't tell me you fell asleep watching true crime docs without texting me to let me know you're home safe. Tonight was a wild night. Let's meet up at the café for a kiki tomorrow!

LUCY:

sounds good...change of plans tn

MAYA:

Did inspiration strike?

LUCY:

you could say that

I omit the part about stealing from a local tattoo shop because my defense for jeopardizing my career is suspect at best. *He's so hot I could bark* won't hold up in a court of Maya.

I set my phone down on the nightstand and join Jaylen on the foot of the bed. Something about sitting on a bed with him feels incredibly intimate despite the arm's-reach distance between us.

"I would normally say something like 'I never do things like this,' but since I'm being my worst self you should know that I have," I say, gently kicking my dangling feet back and forth, attempting to distract myself from the smell of his warm musk cologne and whatever coconut curl cream coats his tight curls.

"What, commit a misdemeanor with a stranger and follow them back to their hotel room for casual sex, only to never hear from them again?" Jaylen says with a slight giggle.

"Honestly, it happens more frequently than it should." I gulp down the rest of my drink and place it on the floor by my feet. Jaylen does the same.

"This is weird foreplay, isn't it?"

"It's been a weird night." I bat my eyelashes a bit and lean back on the bed. My skirt rides up my legs as I lounge comfortably on the oversize plush mattress. Jaylen does the same, leaning back on his elbows as gravity pulls us together.

"Can I tell you something?" he asks softly. At some point in our conversation, he moved closer to me—or maybe I've been inching toward him.

I tousle my bangs so I can get a better view of him, and nod. I'm worried if I open my mouth a sexual demand will come blurting out and I'll frighten him off.

"I don't want to ruin the moment or blow my shot at a night with you, but I like you. I like the worst parts of you. You're…" He pauses to think, like he's choosing his words carefully.

"Please don't say I'm not like other girls," I whisper, my voice breathier than I would like. I stare at him wide-eyed and unblinking, practically begging him not to ruin the moment.

"I wasn't going to. If anything, you're like all the coolest ones I've ever met. I was going to say you're fun to be around."

"You don't have to say things like that. We're never going to see each other again," I say, staring at his perfect mouth.

"Because we're never going to see each other again, I wanted you to know."

Caught up in the moment between the handsome stranger and the fancy hotel, I kiss him. The relentless good guy only in town for one night of anonymous fun. The no-good thief. And apparently, the excellent kisser. He cups my cheek gently in his big palm and kisses me back softly. The taste of whiskey lingers on his tongue as I drink him up. His hand slowly drops from my cheek and runs down to the small of my back. We melt into each other in an instant. I draw a long breath and his tongue sinks deep into my mouth.

I am done being delicate. I grab Jaylen by the back of his neck and pull him in closer, pressing my whole body against his. Our hands are all over each other as we rush to undress one another. His body is firm, but his skin is soft and hot against my chilled limbs.

He pulls away from my mouth to catch his breath. Slowing our pace, I lay my head on the pillow as Jaylen kisses down my neck. His lips graze down the middle of my sternum and he continues to taste my body well past my stomach. I squirm on my back in anticipation as he kisses my body like he's missed it.

His tongue traces along the insides of my thighs until I let out a nervous giggle; it tickles in the best way possible. I remember the thrill of being on his shoulders, and the friction of his neck on the insides of my upper thighs. He stops to stare up at me as I lie out before him naked with my legs spread.

"Is everything okay?" I prop myself up on my elbows, wondering what's the holdup. I don't think I can endure any more anticipation.

"You look so good. I only get one night with you, and I want to remember every inch," he says before disappearing between my legs.

His mouth is hot against my delicate skin, and the friction makes me call out his name; despite only learning it a few hours ago, it comes to me naturally. His tongue presses against my clit and right when I think the pleasure is too much, there's a bit of suction and my legs start to tremble. I lace my fingers through his hair and pull him in closer to me, but we can never get close enough. He slides two fingers inside me, and I come in seconds.

Our movements are familiar, but the pleasure is exhilarating—almost dangerous. He enjoys my body with such euphoria that I'm jealous of the connection he has with it. I pull his face back up to my mouth—tasting myself. As he hovers over me, I wrap my legs around his hips.

"Fuck me," I whisper, looking at Jaylen with pleading eyes. It's like I've never needed anything more.

Jaylen reaches across the bed for his pants. From his wallet, he pulls out a tiny gold package and makes quick work rolling the condom over himself. Much like the rest of his body, his dick is impressive. As I size him up, I realize why he was so confident in his pursuit.

He plants a firm kiss on my lips before he grabs his hard cock and guides it inside me, slowly but forcefully. The pressure makes him gasp for air. I bite my bottom lip to prevent myself from letting out an embarrassing primal scream.

Jaylen wraps his arm around my lower back and lifts me up so I'm tilted closer to him. He grits his teeth as we grind against each other. His muscles flex under the strain as he props both of us up. I can't help but watch the veins in his forearms pool with blood. His movement gets deeper and harder as he tentatively watches my moans get faster and louder. We move in unison as I scream out in pleasure, and a few thrusts later he allows himself to reach the apex deep inside me.

After he finishes, he wraps his arms around me. I nestle into him as we both gather our composure and pant, catching our breath.

"Again?" he asks with a devilish grin.

# SEVEN

## Lucy

I awake the next morning in a strange dark room to the sound of muffled vibrations. It takes me a few seconds to remember where I fell asleep. The thick blackout curtains leave the hotel room just as dark as it had been when we finally went to bed. The long vibrating buzz continues to echo off the wooden desk, until I regain full consciousness. I feel around the nightstand for a light, but by the time I find the switch the buzzing stops.

I roll over to face the other side of the bed. Jaylen is gone. The alarm clock on the nightstand reads 9:30 a.m., and I yawn in the face of a morning that came too soon. I have exactly thirty more minutes to pretend I can afford a room in a hotel as nice as this one.

I look around the room, but Jaylen's bag is gone and so is the stolen sign. Some empties are lying on top of the dresser, and next to them Jaylen has left a couple of twenty-dollar bills for the hotel cleaning staff. I roll my eyes at him one last time even if he's not around to see it. He might really be the only genuinely good guy I have ever met. I sit there completely naked underneath the white sheets with a thread count higher than my credit score and contemplate my next move. As soon as I snuggle my face against the plush down pillow, the loud vibration echoes against the nightstand again.

Conceding to its summoning, I reach for my phone to see what's so urgent. I have three missed calls from Sam, and another incoming. I clear my throat and sit up straight. "Hey, Sam, I'm right around the corner." I try to produce a highly professional tone, but it sounds like I've been up all night smoking Marlboro reds.

"I told you to keep your ringer on loud at all times. I need you here early today, so haul ass," Sam shouts, and hangs up on me before I can reply.

I sink back into my pillow and pull the covers over my head. *What the hell happened last night?* Judging by the pain between my legs, the beginning of another UTI. I can't believe I already let myself get so distracted that I'm about to be late for work this morning. Even if my night with Jaylen was worth being a bit late, it wasn't worth jeopardizing the opportunity to apprentice for Sam.

I slip into last night's clothes and head into the bathroom to touch up last night's makeup. I fill my bag with all the tiny bottles of free hygiene products that I can fit. I saunter out of the bathroom and throw open the heavy curtains. The sky is Seattle's signature shade of gray with a misty rainfall washing away the city's sins of last night.

I briefly take in the beautiful view of the pier and the Seattle Great Wheel. I haven't been on that thing since I was a kid, but I still remember feeling so high up in the sky that I was overcome by terror. I wanted to scream but couldn't find the air to make a sound. When I was little, things that were supposed to be fun always felt dangerous.

*Why can't I just enjoy a nice view?* I close the curtains.

As I'm bent down zipping up my boots to leave, I notice the end of a black tie peeking out from under the bed. Jaylen must have forgotten to pack it this morning in the dark. I pull it out and slip it around my neck; it's soft and silky against my fingertips. Closing my eyes, I remember how it felt to rub them down Jaylen's chest. It even smells of his warm musk. Like Jaylen, it feels expensive, so I slip it into my purse to keep as a memento or to sell on eBay. It feels like real silk. I bet I could get $20 for it.

I strut confidently out of that hotel like the high-class escort I feel. I am unapologetic, I am fierce, and I am a bit hungover.

I rush into Come As You Are Ink seconds before my designated ten-o'clock start. Without a minute to spare this morning, I'm still wearing yesterday's outfit. No one around here pays much attention to me unless they're barking demands, so I'm optimistic that it will go unnoticed.

Sam is already working on a client's stencil, which means I'm late to open up shop. I toss my bag behind the front desk and waste no time setting up for the day.

"When you said you were right around the corner, I thought you meant the corner outside the shop." Sam begins to shave her client's arm. Hyperfocused on her task at hand, she avoids looking at me.

"Honest mistake." I hold my breath as I await her orders for the day.

Whenever I'm late for open, Sam assigns me the dreadful task of cleaning and restocking the bathrooms. Before she opens her mouth, I'm already grabbing the disinfectant spray and rubber gloves from under the counter and making my way to the back of the shop.

"You can do the bathrooms tomorrow. I have something else for you today."

*Great.* I drop the cleaning supplies and head over to her station to learn what diabolical thing could be worse than deep cleaning dirty toilets.

"What's up?" I ask, leaning over Sam's shoulder to get a closer look as she places the stencil on her client's arm with precision. It's a beautiful design, but I can't help noticing areas where I would have changed the layout to better fit the composition of his bicep. I bite my tongue.

"You smell like the deli counter at Safeway." Sam grimaces, taking a step back.

I pull the collar of my shirt up to my nose, but I can't smell it. "I had some street meat last night after the bar." *And then seconds and then thirds.*

"Well, pull yourself together. You're filling in for me on a mural commission. You double-booked me today by accepting this arm sleeve tattoo when I had the day blocked off. I don't bail on my clients, so you're stuck with the mural." Sam fills a row of tiny cups with black ink while the client goes to check out the stencil's positioning in the mirror.

Despite Sam's extreme unprofessionalism in front of the client, I, the meager shopgirl, must remain calm, cool, and collected. Luckily, these extreme work conditions are nothing new to me and I've come to expect the worst—which is usually mopping up a faint client's vomit, not a mural assignment.

I'd take the vomit any day.

"Oh, I can't," I say, searching for an excuse that would violate the Washington State Department of Labor's workers' rights, but I can't think of one good enough for Sam to feel sympathetic. Eyeing the front door, I wonder how hard I would have to slam it shut on my hands to break them. Or perhaps more effectively I could hack them off with the scissors on Sam's workbench.

"Oh, yes, you can. I know you paint," Sam says. The client resettles themselves into the chair and Sam's gun buzzes with the flick of a switch. The sound breaks my thousand-yard stare at the nearest exit.

"I *used* to paint." I haven't picked up a brush since my senior year of college and vowed to never touch one again. It's the whole reason I'm here, rushing to work for my unruly boss, cleaning bathrooms at a tattoo shop.

There was a time in my life when I thought I could make it as a painter. When I was naive enough to believe I could trust my dad to be there for me just once in my life. I'm not sure which dream was more idiotic.

On the night of my senior art showcase, I was supposed to meet with an influential art handler and a museum director. Unfortunately, I never got an opportunity to speak with them because I missed the whole thing dealing with my drunk dad. He was supposed to be my ride to the venue, but never showed up to pick me up from campus. The city bus made me very late to the event. When I finally got there, he was inside being asked to leave by security for causing a scene. The whole thing was so embarrassing that I decided to leave the showcase without saying hi to anyone, let alone formally meet the art handler and museum director. I haven't seen my dad since.

After that, I realized I missed my opportunity to be a painter, and with bills and student loans to pay off, I couldn't waste any time trying to make a living off it. I tried a few jobs in the service industry, but after spending so many hours in a tattoo chair as a client, it seemed like the perfect job for me. My dad hates tattoos, so I know he'll never find me here.

Giving up painting was like throwing out all the color in my life. It was a dark time for me. Thanks to tattooing, I've finally started to find those colors again. I want to continue moving forward. I want to tattoo. Painting would be taking a step back into the darkness.

"Then it looks like today is the day you start painting again," Sam says dryly.

"Are you sure you don't want the bathrooms cleaned? Can't one of the other artists do the mural?" I practically beg, but I know if I drop to my knees Sam will relish the sight, and I'll have no chance of getting out of this assignment.

Sam sets her gun down on the metal tray to her left. "I thought you were interested in tattooing. You have to pay your dues before you get offered an apprenticeship. I need to know you're serious about this. I want to see you show up to work on time, and not in yesterday's outfit. Prove to me that you can see a project through, from start to finish. These are the dues, Picasso."

I have to remind myself of my goals. If I want to build a career for myself, then I need to be willing to make sacrifices. I thought the only sacrifice would be letting go of the cute distractions, but it looks like I am also going to have to face old wounds. What's left of my soured enthusiasm drains as I accept that the only way out of this assignment is through.

"What's the address?" I ask, and without having to say the words, I agree to paint.

"It's written down on the piece of paper next to the computer. There's money on the counter for supplies—I want to see receipts for every purchase. Anna is expecting you soon for the consultation today, so get going. There's a city scooter parked out front. Hopefully the breeze will air you out a bit," Sam says, pointing her tattoo gun aggressively in my direction.

Before I head out, I dab some stolen hotel essential oils all over my body and leave smelling like a tub of Vicks VapoRub.

# EIGHT

## Jaylen

The word *Delayed* flashes beside my flight number. My boarding time is pushed back two hours. The last thing I want right now is to be stuck in this city any longer than I have to be. I want to get home to my house in Chicago, crawl into bed, and host a pity party for one while I figure out my next move.

My phone vibrates in my pocket—an incoming call from my agent, Lamar. I silence it. I'm not ready to talk to him yet. He wants to discuss European hockey league options, and I'm in no mood to hear the offers. I don't want to know how low my value has dropped since being released from my PTO with the Rainiers.

I slouch lower in the stiff airport seating, hoping to find a spot comfortable enough to doze off for a bit before boarding. Closing my eyes, I think about sneaking out of the hotel this morning. I picture Lucy out cold, snoring like someone struggling with sleep apnea. I feel a pit of guilt sink into my stomach—and not because she never got her adenoids removed as a child—because sneaking out on her without an awkward goodbye feels scuzzy, even for a hockey player. I hope she got the forty dollars I left on the dresser for her ride home this morning.

I remember the way she giggled uncontrollably while I carried her on my shoulders last night as we ran down the block. I quickly realize I'm struggling to get the visual out of my mind because I don't want to leave her quite yet.

Not in a love-at-first-sight type of way. Not even in a potential fuck-buddy type of arrangement. I just like her. She's cool. What type of music would she recommend? What viral videos does she find funny? What did she think of the *House of the Dragon* finale? Does she even watch *House of the Dragon*? At least I'm leaving Seattle with one decent memory.

Seattle kicked my ass this month. It took away the only constant I've ever known in life. It took away my last shot at saving my NHL career. It took away the only thing I've ever loved.

A man settles in on the chair beside me with a loud sigh. The commotion disrupts my failed attempt at a nap. "Were you visiting Seattle for work or pleasure?" He points to my Chicago Bulls hat. The man's attempt at small talk taunts me.

I can't believe I got fired before I even got the job—that's what it feels like when you're released from a PTO. I was so desperate for a job that I took an audition. I still remember my draft year, when teams were salivating over themselves at the thought of drafting me in the first round. Agents, general managers, coaches, everyone was blowing up my phone trying to get a piece of Jaylen Jones. Now no one would even take a league minimum flier out on me. I might have been in town for work, but I am leaving unemployed.

"I guess pleasure." I sink deeper into my seat.

Speaking of agents blowing up my phone, mine is calling me again. I chatted with Lamar yesterday after my meeting with the general manager, but I assured him I would call as soon as I landed in Chicago to meet up and discuss what's next. I send his call to voicemail.

My head is throbbing from lack of sleep and electrolytes. I don't have the energy to deal with my agent or the chatty stranger next to me. Not wanting to stick around long enough for him to recognize me, I excuse myself and head for the coffee line—maybe some caffeine will help me survive this delay.

On my walk to the coffee kiosk, I find a company gift card on the floor. I'm not above checking to see if there's a free coffee on it—especially since I'm newly unemployed. Lucky break, there's ten bucks loaded on the gift card. As I begin to transfer the money to my app, I get another incoming call—Lamar again. I ignore the call and finish the transfer. Another notification comes through, this time a text message.

LAMAR:

> Jaylen Anthony Jones, you better pick up your damn phone, boy!

I can't even read it without hearing Lamar's bellowing voice cuss me out. I do as I am told, and quickly call him back.

"JJ!" He answers on the first ring.

"Hey, Lamar, sorry I missed your calls. I'm at the airport right now waiting for my flight. Let's talk about my next move when I'm back in Chicago." I keep my voice low as I stand in line for my free coffee.

"You're not flying anywhere today," he says.

"Why? Was I delayed again? Is there bad weather in Chicago?" I peer past the couple behind me, trying to get a look outside at the weather in Seattle. It's rainy, but nothing you can't fly through.

"No, Jaylen, the only place you're going today is practice. I've been trying to call you all morning because the Rainiers have changed their mind. They're offering you a one-year, league-minimum, prove-yourself contract," he says.

The loud buzzing background noise of the public airport goes mute, and everything blurs around me. I almost drop to my knees in the middle of the coffee line and sob into my hands. I can't believe what I am hearing from Lamar. It's far from the multiyear, hundred-million-dollar, league-record deal I once envisioned myself signing, but it's one more shot in a game I thought already ended in a loss.

"Hello? You still there?" Lamar asks.

"I'm here." I step out of the line, excusing myself as I weave around people and head for the exit.

"I got the call from the GM earlier this morning. I guess last night one of the players took a drunken joyride on an electric scooter and tore both his ACLs. He's out for the season. They're going to send over the paperwork so we can get it in before they submit their final twenty-three-man roster to the league. It's crazy how a bit of luck can really change everything," Lamar says giddily.

"The term *luck* feels a bit inappropriate." I make my way down a flight of stairs, but the line for Ubers is longer than the coffee line I just left. There's a rental car desk to my right with no line.

"Call it whatever you want, just don't be late for practice today. Oh, and Jaylen," Lamar says.

"What?"

"Welcome back to the goddamn National Hockey League."

# NINE

## Lucy

When I arrive at my destination, I triple-check the piece of paper with the address scribbled on it to make sure I'm at the right place. It's not a restaurant, or a bar, or even someone's house—it's an arena. The same one where some of my favorite bands have come to play a show.

I hope I get to see inside the green room. Maybe I'll even get some free concert tickets out of this miserable job. I push the call-box button and huddle under the awning to stay dry as the rain picks up again. It doesn't take Anna long to come get me.

"You must be Sam. I'm Anna, marketing manager for the Rainiers," she says, greeting me at the door. "Come in." She ushers me through a lobby with photos of musicians, sports teams, and special events hung on the walls. The receptionist welcomes me with a cheery hello.

"Actually, I'm Sam's shop assistant, Lucy. She had something come up, so she assigned the project to me." I run my fingers through my hair trying to tame the bird's nest of knots at my nape, but it's useless and I decide to accept the added volume.

The overhead fluorescent lights reflect off Anna's shiny black hair, which is clearly her natural color judging by the health of her ends. She looks like a personable daytime talk show host in her fashionable oversize two-piece suit and white leather sneakers. I almost want to get on a couch with her and confess my deeply buried emotions and pent-up anxiety surrounding painting, but I bite my tongue.

As I take in my new surroundings, I notice I can't stop itching my neck and hands. It must be a symptom of my hangover, which is officially kicking into full gear. I am an unrelenting combination of hunger, dehydration, and exhaustion. It's not a pleasant blend with my existing anxiety—still I soldier on. I interlock my hands behind my back to restrain myself from scratching, but my body is still flush.

"Hmm, can you paint?" Anna holds a large metal door open for me and we head into the building's office space.

"Yes, better than Sam. Don't tell her I said that." I follow Anna to a large open lunchroom. I almost pocket a snack or drink as we pass by, but I figure the first day on the job is a poor time to start stealing things.

"Good. As long as you don't fuck this up, I don't really give a shit. Things around here have been a literal dumpster fire, and I don't have the energy to deal with any more last-minute problems," she says, her bluntness catching me off guard.

Anna looks like a sweet young woman, like the type of friend who tells you when you have something stuck in your teeth and remembers your middle name. I didn't peg her for the type to curse at work, but who am I to judge what is or isn't workplace appropriate when I pulled up here with a terrible case of sex hair.

"Do not fuck up. Got it?"

Anna is starting to sound like my boss.

"Got it." Before I have a chance to ask her any follow-up questions, she's cutting me off.

"Good, because I literally just found out that I have HPV and that my dog needs to get his teeth removed. All of them. Did you know it costs two thousand dollars for a dog tooth extraction?" Anna asks without pausing long enough for me to offer up a response. "And then I'm supposed to come into work and forget about my issues and deal with the fact that some overpaid baby who can't be bothered to call an Uber drunkenly fell off a scooter. The guy could hardly skate backward—what gave him the impression he could operate a scooter?" Anna vents, and the pace at which she speaks increases along with her steps; I'm speed-walking to keep up.

I want to tell her that everyone gets HPV, but it sounds like that's not even her biggest issue this week. "I'll do a good job. I'll make you look good, I promise," I say instead.

I immediately regret the words as soon as they come out of my mouth. I was planning on half-assing this mural to get it over with as quickly as possible, but instead I've agreed to give it my all. I'm not sure I'm even capable of painting at a high caliber anymore.

Anna leads me through the arena's main concourse, down an elevator, and through more halls and doors until there's no way I will ever find my way back out of the building. It isn't until we stop at locked double doors with a sign overhead that says Restricted Area: Rainiers Personnel Only that I remember Seattle has an NHL team. This must be where they play.

Anna pulls out the badge attached to her hip to unlock the doors. This time we wander down a hall padded with rubber floors, until we stop down a quiet narrow corridor.

"Here it is. This is your canvas." Anna points to a large beige cement wall anticlimactically.

"It's a wall all right," I say, because what else am I supposed to say about a beige wall?

"The players come through this tunnel on their way out to the ice. We would like them to pass something more inspirational than this." She motions again to the canvas.

"That shouldn't be hard." I would have thought the millions of dollars a year in salary would have been inspiration enough, but what do I know?

"Here." Anna dumps a thick file folder into my arms. I briefly flip through the first few pages and find action photos of hockey players who I assume make up the Rainiers' hockey squad.

"Feel free to use whatever photo works best for the art piece, but be sure to include everyone. There are more details in there, like our specific team colors and the team's logo," she explains.

"Cool." I set the folder down and pull out my tablet. I notice my forearms are covered with red splotches coloring all of my ink with a pinkish tint. Sometimes they get like this when I'm feeling stressed out or anxious, both of which I'm feeling right now. I ignore my nerves and begin taking photos of the wall for my initial sketch.

In the distance I hear echoing whistles and loud thuds. Clapping noises sound like bang-snaps and then someone shouts, "Nice shot!"

"You'll find contact information and your schedule in the folder as well. And girl to girl, avoid the players, if you know what I mean," Anna warns, staring down the hall.

"I'm not really into athletes. I prefer my men with an iron deficiency and at least three phobias," I say, distracted as I calculate what type of paint and supplies I'll need for this job.

"No, I mean like get the hell out of their way when they're passing through the halls. We can't have someone tripping over a paintbrush and ending up on the IR."

*Does she mean ER?* Hopefully there's a glossary of hockey terms at the back of the folder she gave me. "Understood. Overpaid babies who should be Bubble Wrapped," I say, trying to win her over.

"Exactly. If you need anything—don't. Please, don't need me. It's officially hockey season and I have way too much to do. You've got this, Sam!"

Anna is already gone before I can assure her that I've got this mural handled or remind her of my name.

With my headphones on and music blaring, I immediately get in my creative zone. I enjoy this step of the process. The planning, the mapping, the sketching. This part of the mural feels like I'm still creating designs for tattoos, but I know eventually I will need to paint.

I reach out and touch my canvas and like hearing an old familiar song, I remember how it felt to be heartbroken. What is a father if not the first man to break your heart?

When I was a kid, I would lose myself in the canvas, painting homes from which I wish I came. Homes with wraparound decks and lush gardens. Ones with a fat cat sunbathing lazily in a windowsill.

I would fantasize a new life for myself inside each home, always calling dibs on the top-floor bedroom. I thought if I could just get the lighting right, I could make it realistic enough to make it believable. I never figured it out. I guess I never figured any of it out because my dad never cared much for my art—or me.

My dad bailed on Mom and me when I was too young to remember him leaving, and yet I still felt the loneliness. He used to show up sporadically throughout my childhood and whisk me away for an afternoon at his convenience. We would go to the movies, or some local tourist attraction. It would always start off fun. He would buy me a treat and take an interest in my life, but as the afternoon crept on our time together usually ended with a fight. Often a lopsided one where he would find something about me to pick apart. I would do something wrong—like drop my ice cream, or fall asleep during the movie, or get too scared at the top of the Seattle Great Wheel—and ruin the afternoon. I never did any of those things on purpose, but it didn't matter how much I apologized. He would drop me off at home and I wouldn't hear from him again for months. It felt stupid to cling to the idea that he could change, so I gave up ever having a relationship with him years ago.

The only reason I invited him to my senior art showcase was because he directly asked me to. He showed up on campus weeks before with persistency and a handwritten letter about being sorry for my childhood. He was turning his life around, he said. It was an uncharacteristic period in our relationship where he was calling with no expectations and showing up when he said he would. It obviously didn't last long and instead culminated in an epic drunken binge. The further away he stays, the safer I am.

For this mural, I've been instructed to include the words "We win when we all show up," but besides that I have free rein to figure out where to put twenty-three players on the wall. As I settle into my work, sketching an outline on my tablet, I get increasingly hotter until my lower back breaks out in beads of sweat. I feel like peeling off a layer of clothing, but I'm already embarrassingly underdressed as it is.

I set my tablet down and slip off my headphones so I can gather my composure. Even in silence, I am beyond overstimulated. I try to settle my mind by repressing the thoughts of my dad and my senior art showcase. I feel a bit faint, and a lot hungover.

*Am I having a visceral reaction to painting again?* My nose begins to sweat across the bridge. Disoriented, I wander down the long tunnel, following the light and sounds. My mouth is dry and chalky; there has to be a water fountain nearby. I begin to feel lightheaded, and I start to really regret not making time to stop for breakfast this morning.

The hallway suddenly opens up into a large ice rink. A chill slaps me in the face and the overhead lights blind me as I try to shield my eyes with my hand. As my vision begins to pinhole, I spot a water bottle on the bench and make my move for it. Before I can get within arm's reach, I hear someone call out, "JJ!"

I look up to see Jaylen—Jaylen from last night, Jaylen who is only in town for *one* night—skating up the ice. He looks me dead in the eyes and his mouth drops. His pace slows, but his movements do not stop. He's about to skate right past me. Close enough to reach out and touch—or better yet, punch.

In the blink of an eye, the player skating alongside Jaylen passes him the puck, but he's not paying attention to the drill anymore because he's staring at me. The puck deflects off Jaylen's stick and comes hurtling toward my head. Before I have time to react, everything goes black.

# TEN

## Jaylen

This is bad. This is very bad. I rush over to Lucy, who is out cold, toppled over the team's bench. She's bleeding from her head, and I'm responsible. When I find her pulse, I let out a long sigh of relief. I softly call out her name and tap her on the shoulder, trying to wake her up.

What is she doing here anyway? This is not an ideal situation for my first practice on the team. I'm trying to stay under the radar, play well enough that Coach Pete keeps me with the squad and doesn't demote me to the minors. Instead, I'm standing over my one-night stand, hoping I didn't kill her.

Immediately I assume everything she told me last night was a lie and she's an overzealous fan who must have been stalking me for months—why else would she be rinkside right now? How long has she been following me around? Was her hard-to-get attitude last night a cover? Worst-case scenario, she's not a fan, but a hater who's trying to sabotage my second chance.

Lucy looks like she did this morning when I sneaked out of the hotel room. Her cheeks are rosy and her eyelids are a smudged smoky gray. Blood trickles down her head, and I remind myself not to jump to conclusions before she regains full consciousness.

Before the athletic trainer can get over to us, she starts moving her limbs and slowly blinks her eyes open. *Thank god.*

"Motherfucker!" she shouts into the echoey empty arena. Her words carry all the way up into the nosebleed seats. She grabs her head but drops her hand away when she realizes she's bleeding. She turns to me and gives me a look similar to the one players give when they're trying to fight you.

"I'm so sorry, Lucy," I say, helping her up into a seated position.

Coach calls an end to practice and all the guys shuffle off the ice and back to the locker room. I stay with Lucy and help her to her feet. She doesn't say much while the team trainer and I assist her down the hall to be seen by the team doctor, Dr. Sara Baker. Lucy moans and groans loudly as we make our way to the treatment room. The trainer applies pressure on the wound with gauze and as the once-white cotton soaks bloodred, I feel absolutely terrible for what I've done.

"Thanks, JJ. Why don't you go hit the showers while she gets stitched up," our trainer suggests.

Judging by Lucy's glare, it's probably best that I get out of the way.

When I come back, her forehead is bandaged up and she's sipping on an electrolyte drink. Her skin is ghostly pale, even for her. The blood dripping down her face might be gone, but her menacing glare is still on full display.

"So, what's the prognosis, Doc? Is she going to live?" I say, hoping a joke will lighten the mood. It does not. I swear Lucy just snarled at me.

"She has a minor concussion, but she still has all her teeth." Dr. Baker hands Lucy an ice pack to hold against her head. "Take it easy today. Ice and get lots of rest. I'll see you back in five days to get those stitches out. Sound good?" Lucy nods and Dr. Baker begins cleaning up her supplies.

Lucy's eyes hit mine like laser beams. "Do you always have

to lie to girls to get them to fuck you?" she says to me without stuttering.

My jaw drops. *Damn.* She got right to the point.

"I'll give you two some space," Dr. Baker says, reading the room. She leaves the mess and quickly makes an exit.

"You took a puck to the head. Your memory might not be the most reliable right now." She was fine omitting personal details last night. It's hard to believe hitting her in the face with a puck is the second-worst thing I've done to her.

"You said you were only in town for one night. Let me guess—you have a girlfriend?" Lucy points her drink at me like a pirate with a sword. If I get any closer, she'll likely bonk me on the head with it.

"I don't have a girlfriend." I hold my hands up in the air as I defend my innocence, while she forces me to walk the plank.

"That's *exactly* what someone hiding a girlfriend would say." Lucy scratches at the back of her neck.

Her right eye twitches and her nostrils flare. I didn't want to go into the whole embarrassing story, but I guess I have no choice. I think if I told her to google me, she would toss the bottle at my head.

"I was supposed to be on a flight home this morning, but things changed," I say, slowly inching closer, careful not to scare her away. "When I ran into you last night, I had just found out that I was cut from the team. I was trying to take my mind off the fact that I didn't have a job, and you were fun. I got a call this morning from my agent while I was at the airport telling me that a last-minute roster spot opened up. So, here I am."

"Happy to have been a distraction," she says, lowering the bottle. "Seems I'm really good at that." She gestures to her forehead. Then she opens up a granola bar—one I recognize from our players' lounge—and begins to aggressively chomp her way through it.

*Give me a break. I didn't mean to say it like that.* Pressing the pads of my fingertips into my forehead, I squeeze my eyes shut and try to hide, but the guilt finds me like a flare in the night. I can't keep doing this to myself; this is what got me cut from this team in the first place. I can't let my emotions distract me from securing a multiyear deal at the end of this season. Lucy was a welcome distraction last night, but I can't have her rink-side throwing off my game.

"Hold on," I say, dropping my hand. "What are *you* doing here? I play for the Rainiers—don't you have some feminist punk band to front?" My suspicion of her grows. I can't have her lurking around here trying to mess up my opportunity. I feel terrible for hitting her in the head with a puck, but who stands rinkside without keeping their head on a swivel looking out for rogue deflections?

"Tattoo shop, but good guess. I'm painting a mural outside your locker room," she says with a mouth full of granola.

I pull another bar out of my pocket and offer it up. She snatches it out of my hand without a thank-you, like a tiny feral animal.

"Great, so you'll be around the rink a lot." I pace around the room, silently plotting a strategy to avoid the hallway. I'll have to walk around the rink and enter from the visiting team's bench. An inconvenience no doubt, but a potentially necessary step.

"This is not great. What about me right now is screaming *great* to you?" Her tone is so threatening it's unmistakably rhetorical.

I know she's trying to prove a point, but I forgot how cute she looks when she's angry. She's making that face she made when we first ran into each other, all squinty eyes, scrunchy noise, and jutted jaw. I cover a smirk by running my hand over my mouth.

Lucy lets out a long sigh. "I think I'm just having a bad 1,461 days," she says, dropping her interrogation in favor of self-pity and scratching—a lot of scratching. She claws at her arms and legs like she's trying to escape her body.

I inch closer to her and that's when I smell it, but I take another bigger inhale to be sure. "Why do you smell like Icy Hot?" She smells like a candy cane, and a bit like my hockey gloves.

"Because I smelled like booze, premarital sex, and sin this morning," she says in a low voice, through her teeth. "I rubbed some essential oils on my skin and now I can't stop itching myself. Maybe I'm allergic to assholes." Her voice is shrill as she claws at her neck.

The closer I get, the more visible the red welts on her blotchy skin appear. I head over to a cupboard and grab the antihistamine medication. I'm no stranger to anaphylactic shock; I once rubbed up against a PB&J on a flight home from a coast-to-coast road trip and thought we were going to have to pull an emergency landing in Kansas.

I want to remind her that she was moaning my praises into the early morning, but I'm not trying to make an enemy, so instead I say, "To me, that sounds like a lovely evening."

Lucy doesn't have to like me, but if I'm going to see her around the rink, I hope we can at least be cordial. I don't need her sabotaging anything for me in the name of revenge. I'm still trying to crack the team's opening-night lineup.

"It was fine." Lucy tosses the pills into her mouth and takes a swig of her drink. She hops off the table and presses her ice pack against her forehead as she walks past me.

I follow. "Where are you parked?"

"I rode a scooter here."

"Those things are so dangerous. I have a rental car out back—I'm giving you a lift." I need to get verbal confirmation that she isn't going to spike my water bottle with laxatives.

"I'm not getting in a car with you—you just tried to kill me." She stomps out of the room and down the hall, headed to her disheveled heap of belongings.

"It was an accident. You're not supposed to wander around practice anyway. You distracted me." My voice is louder than I would like, but she is so good at baiting me, and honestly, I like it when she does. I take a deep breath and reel in my emotions. My adrenaline is still hot from practice.

"You shot the puck at my head," she snaps back. Her face is flared and she squeezes the gel ice pack so tightly it might pop. As guys are leaving the locker room, they walk briskly past us to avoid interrupting our heated debate.

"That's not my shot. My shot is at least ninety-eight miles per hour. That was a deflection." Now we're face-to-face, arguing over a technicality, when I should be begging her not to sue me.

"You're awfully good at deflecting. You can't seem to stop," she says with a smirk. Her color is back. Her cheeks are pink, and the red splotches on her neck and wrists have faded significantly. We both take a step back. I unclench my jaw and her posture relaxes.

"You're right. I'm sorry. For everything. Obviously, for hitting you in the head with a puck. But I'm sorry if you thought I was lying or only using you as a distraction. I had a fun night, and I meant that."

"Me too." She drops the ice pack to her side, so I can see her full face.

She's so hot, it's distracting. I can't even think straight when I look at her, which is bad because if I can't think straight, how am I going to skate or shoot straight? I need to end whatever this is right here, right now.

"Look, you should know that I'm not at a place in my life right now where I'm looking for a relationship." I start to give her my typical line about how I can't get into anything serious, how hockey is my main focus, blah-blah-blah, but she cuts me off.

She tosses her head back and starts laughing hysterically, like the villain in a cartoon. I think she might be severely concussed, and I consider running to grab the doctor to take another look at her.

"Fuck you. I have eight stitches in my head, a colossal UTI brewing between my legs, and my boss so far up my ass that she can see that disgusting, sorry excuse for a granola bar I just ate. Look at me. I am still in last night's outfit. Spare me the line— I *know* the line, and if anyone gets to say it right now, it's me."

Lucy pivots away from me and speed walks toward the laundry room, which she mistakes as the way out. I discreetly point her to the correct exit, and she rolls her eyes and leaves without saying another word. I think about running after her, but I've already caused enough of a scene for one day.

A heavy hand drops on my shoulder. "I see you've still got square wheels when it comes to the ladies," Wells says, chirping me.

"I don't know what the hell just happened. I have had the weirdest twenty-four hours of my life." When I stepped on the ice this afternoon, determined to make a lasting impression on my first day back in the NHL, this was definitely not what I had in mind.

"Maybe you need a little weird in your life."

# ELEVEN

## Jaylen

I took my time getting to the rink this afternoon. After the extra morning workout and with the one I'll have to do tonight during the game, I'm dragging my feet. While my team is gearing up to play in the home opener, I'm a healthy scratch—again.

I still remember the first time it happened in my career. Coach called me into his office to tell me I wasn't dressing for the game, and it felt like the walls were closing in on me. I can't lie; it hasn't gotten any easier over the years. It still hurts to watch my team play while I'm sitting in my suit up in the press box snacking on popcorn.

We're back from a winless road trip, looking to collect our first two points at the home opener. I'll be watching this one from the small TV in our gym at the rink, getting in another workout with the rest of the extra guys not playing tonight.

With an iced coffee in hand, I beeline down the hall to our locker room. I don't want the social media admin getting any good photos of me to post tonight; I don't need people online commenting that I've yet to clock any ice time as a Rainier.

As I round the corner, I come crashing into Lucy. I was not expecting her to be here this late in the afternoon or I would have rappelled down from a helicopter directly into the locker room, or at the very least, dug an elaborate tunnel from the parking lot in—anything to avoid this distraction. My iced coffee crushes into her chest and spills all down the front of her top.

"Oops," I say as the rest of the coffee spills on the floor. At least it was iced and I don't need to involve the team doctor this time.

"Again? You've got to be kidding me." She brushes the pooling coffee off her top and examines the damage. It missed her shoes but soaked her shirt.

"I'm sorry. Give me a sec." I dart into the locker room and come back with a clean Seattle Rainiers shirt. I hand it over to her, and she promptly begins using it to clean up the mess. She wipes herself off and then uses it like a rag to clean the coffee off the floor.

"Thanks." She hands back the soiled T-shirt.

"Oh." I'm too stunned to say much else. I figured she would have worn it, but maybe blue isn't her color. My gaze lands on her healing wound. "Your face looks terrible." The words spill out before I can filter my thoughts. The gash on her forehead is healing, but now a purple-and-blue bruise is spreading across the top of her head.

Lucy quickly adjusts her bangs to hide the injury. "Thanks, Jaylen. That's what every girl wants to hear." She turns away from me and continues sketching on the wall with a pencil. It looks like she's working on Wells's outline.

"I didn't mean it like that." It's like I can never say the right thing around her. When I'm not causing an injury, I'm saying something stupid. Talking to her was a lot easier when I knew we would never see each other again. I've got to start avoiding her altogether.

"It's fine. Now, if you don't mind, I've got a job to do." She climbs her step stool and continues to work on the mural.

"I thought you quit. I haven't seen you around in a couple of days," I say, lingering despite my better judgment.

Lucy wasn't at practice the day after the puck incident. Then we hit the road for a while. I'm relieved to see I didn't scare her out of a job, and besides her gory forehead, she looks as good as ever.

"I did ask if I could quit. More like begged, but my boss wouldn't let me. Because of the whole head-injury thing, they let me stay home for a bit while I sketched out the design."

Lucy's complete focus is on her work. Her mouth parts as she draws the outline of Wells's crooked nose; after five breaks, it hooks to the right. I'm anxious to see what she does with me. She'll probably make me look ugly on purpose as a mild form of payback for the whole puck thing.

"Good. It's good to see you." I try saying the right thing for a change. I start to head into the locker room when she calls out to me.

"Hey, Jaylen?"

"Yeah?" I say, far too eagerly.

"Hope you break both your legs out there." A wide, threatening smile spreads across her face.

"Thanks. I think…" I say with grave concern. She isn't listening to me. Lucy's headphones are once again over her ears and her back is already turned to me.

I walk into the room with all eyes on me. For a moment I think I've been demoted to the minors and I'm the last to know. Wells tips his head toward the whiteboard at the back of the room where Coach Pete is putting the finishing touches on a last-minute lineup change. As he sets the marker down and steps out of the way, I see my name slotted on the third line. Without a word, Coach Pete disappears into the coaches' room.

I play it cool, like it's business as usual, but on the inside my stomach is doing somersaults. A cocktail of emotion swirls around inside me, leaving my body jittery. Excitement, nervousness, determination, and anxiety all battle it out for control.

When we leave the locker room for warm-ups, Lucy is gone.

I'm not sure why I'm looking for her when I have the most important game of my career to think about. It's for the best that she's already left for the night. I probably would have accidentally walked over her foot in my skates and cut off her toes or something horrific like that.

Warms-ups are a blur and before I know it, the MC is announcing my name at the start of the game. I rush out on the ice to face the fans; the crowd doesn't know how to respond. They're split, half optimistic and half expecting me to catch an edge and fall on my face as I take a quick lap around our end of the rink.

When Coach Pete gives me and my line the go-ahead to take the opening face-off, I almost yack up my pregame pasta all over myself. I remember what Lucy said to me: "break both your legs." She must think I really suck at hockey—maybe she's right—but I'm about to take the opening face-off in a game I never thought I would play again. All I have to do is win it back to my defense. One play at a time—that's how I'm going to get my game back.

I lean in, hovering over center ice, watching the referee dangle the puck between me and my opponent like two lions about to face off for the last piece of meat. The puck drops and I win the draw.

I finish the game with two assists, five hits, and a plus-three rating. It's not the best game of my career, but it is my best game in years. And more importantly, we win. I haven't felt this good on the ice since my rookie season. I don't know what came over me out there, but I don't feel trapped in my mind. My heart doesn't feel like it is going to explode out of my chest. I actually had fun out there and I haven't had fun on the ice in years.

My performance was good enough to earn me the locker room hustler of the game, which explains the oversize novelty chain around my neck. That honor, paired with the encouraging remarks Coach Pete shares in the tunnel after the game, releases the pressure I put on myself enough to allow me to relax a bit.

I sit back in my locker cubby, half-undressed but still rocking the prized goofy chain with dangling compass pendant proudly, and take a moment to soak it in. I didn't break any legs, but I might have broken my curse of bad puck luck. Since the team had such a great game, Coach Pete canceled our practice scheduled for tomorrow morning, which is basically his way of telling us to enjoy the night we've earned.

"You coming out tonight, JJ? We won't take no for an answer," Felix Lambert, one of the young defensemen on the Rainiers, shouts at me. He tosses a roll of black stick tape at my torso in an attempt to get my full attention. Lamber, as he's better known, is a young guy from Quebec City. So young, in fact, that he still has a thick French accent and broken English, or Franglais as he calls it. He's a good skater and plays with a lot of heart, but his most impressive talent is how fast he can run his mouth.

I catch the tape and sit up to chuck it back at him. "Sounds like I don't have much of a choice."

"Or else you pony up money for the fine fund, bro," Kirill Sokolov, another young guy, pipes up. Soko is sure to talk loudly and slowly so everyone can understand him despite his Russian accent. His English is good, although as soon as the media comes around there is suddenly a huge language barrier, conveniently excusing him from doing press.

Over the years hockey players have created various loopholes for collecting money for team parties. There are fines for being late, for walking on the team's logo in the middle of the dressing room, for not wearing the proper airplane attire. Tonight, I had to participate in something called "money on the board." Players put up money on the team's whiteboard for different reasons, like playing their first NHL game, playing a game in their hometown, or when they celebrate milestones like engagements, weddings, or the birth of a child. The money is always used for team outings, like the one these rookies are clearly trying to organize. Tonight, I put a band on the board for my first game as a Rainier and another for recording my first point with the team. By the sound of it these guys are already looking to spend it.

"I'm out of cash, boys—I put it all in the pool tonight. But I'll tell you what, if you can get Wells out to the bar, I'll buy the first round," I say, shooting a menacing look across the locker room in my friend's direction.

"Get that black card ready, JJ. Hannah already told me she'll do school drop-off tomorrow morning with the girls." Wells beams and rubs his hands together in anticipation.

"Boomer's coming out on a school night?" Lamber pipes in to the delight of Soko.

"What's with this nickname 'Boomer'? Why do you two keep calling me that? Everyone has always called me Wells. What am I missing?" Wells throws his hands up, looking around the room for a clue.

Soko and Lamber giggle into the collars of their shirts. I, on the other hand, can't hold back. I'm laughing at Wells's expense so hard that I choke on my words. "They're calling you a boomer because you're so old," I say.

Wells's face drops and the rookies know they better run.

I hang several paces behind my teammates, dragging my feet on the walk to the club. When you travel for work as much as I do, you're always lost—homesick for a place you haven't called home since you were a preteen. Seattle is chilly and wet, and while I don't know what street I'm on, nostalgia hits me like a breeze—I recognize the area. Before I have time to take out my phone and confirm my suspicion, I recognize a neon glow leaking out onto the sidewalk.

I pause outside of Trolls Bridge, long enough to laugh to myself at the idea of Lucy stealing troll coasters while the bartender and I weren't looking. My teammates are almost out of eyesight as they cross the street and make their way to the front of a long line wrapped outside the club. I stand outside the dive bar, tempted to dip inside for a quick peek.

"JJ, what's the holdup?" Wells shouts down the street.

"Coming!" I yell back, remembering I need to focus on my hockey career. I dart across the street to catch up with the rest of the group.

"Don't bail on me already. I need someone to help keep these rookies in line. Last time we all went out Lamber went viral for his performance of Celine Dion's 'The Power of Love' on the bar top," Wells says, pulling me into the front of a long line next to him.

Normally I would have some quick-witted comeback about how Wells was never one to shy away from the karaoke mike back in New York, but I'm still looking back at Trolls Bridge. I know I need to stay away from Lucy and anything else that's going to throw me off my game, but I keep staring, hoping to catch a glimpse of her.

"Right." I nod, pretending to listen.

"You good, man?" Wells asks.

I finally snap out of it, pulling my stare away from the bar. "Yeah, of course." I shake off some of the rain that's collected atop my thick curly hair.

One of the guys at the front of the group is talking to the manager, trying to get a last-minute VIP table, which shouldn't be an issue for the city's winning team. Soko and Lamber round the corner and come strolling up to the group. The entire team greets them by giving them a hard time for their tardiness. They wave it off and join Wells and me in line.

"Soko, what the fuck are you wearing?" Wells wastes no time on pleasantries.

Soko—in head-to-toe designer garb—proudly models his outfit. He sports Gucci-branded shoes, a Gucci-branded track-suit set, and a flashy Gucci hat. All of the G emblems are en-crusted with multicolor Swarovski crystals, shining under the streetlight like a bedazzled hockey WAG's playoff jacket. His signing bonus must have just hit his bank account.

"What? It's Gucci," Soko says, doing a spin. He sticks out among our team, the lot of which are decked out in our nicest Lululemon like we're about to hit the golf course.

"No shit—it says Gucci a thousand times all over you." I'm all for personal style, but Soko looks like he raided Gucci Mane's closet.

"Is this a new sponsorship deal you signed?" Wells says sar-castically.

Soko's face lights up naively—even more than his outfit. "You think Gucci would do a sponsorship with a hockey player?"

Ignoring Soko's question, Wells turns to Lamber. "You let him leave the condo looking like this?" Wells motions at the outfit. Lamber shrugs.

Soko snarls. Turning up his nose, he says, "You Americans don't know anything about fashion."

While we bicker on the curb, a hostess arrives to take us in. Wells shoves the two rookies through the door and wraps a heavy arm around my shoulder as we step inside.

The club is loud, dark, and crowded. I'm already counting down the minutes until I can convince Wells it's time for us old guys to head home. We follow a bartender toward the back of the club, where she escorts our group to a roped-off private VIP section. Everyone finds a seat while I place an order for bottles and hand the bartender my card. Wells and I settle into our seats while Soko and Lamber are at the edge of theirs scop-ing out the room for prospects.

"Pace yourself, boys. We just got here," Wells says.

The two rookies are pointing to people in the crowd and

whispering among themselves. "Speak for yourself, Boomer," Lamber says. "Not all of us need to stretch before, during, and after a game. I'm surprised you didn't bring your foam roller to the club with you." Lamber discreetly slips Soko a high five.

He seems to have an infinite supply of old-man jokes, most of which don't seem to rile Wells up too much. Most professional hockey players don't make it past five NHL seasons. I almost didn't. Wells has clocked ten NHL seasons and counting. Lamber and Soko will eventually find out the hard way that the dream doesn't last forever. If they thought making it here was hard, just wait until they realize how hard it is to hold on to a roster spot.

"I can't wait to watch you come up short, just like you did defending that two-on-one tonight. Always take the pass away and force a bad-angled shot, bud," Wells chirps back.

Once the drinks arrive, Lamber pours himself one and darts off into the crowd with Soko close behind him. Soko's outfit is so bright and tacky that he's clearly visible even as they wiggle themselves deeper into the crowd of people.

"Are you going to tell me what's wrong now, or do I have to wait until you've had a few of these?" Wells lifts his glass of Jack and Coke and shakes the ice cubes, clanging them against the glass melodically.

"I think I'm just tired. I'm not used to clocking that many minutes," I say with a cocky smirk. I'm not lying either—I'm exhausted. Tonight's game was emotionally and physically draining. I lean back on the couch, settling into my spot for the night.

"Come on, spill. Or else I'll get Dumb and Dumber to come back here and I'll tell them about the incident with the mechanical bull at Howey's your rookie year. I'm sure they'll have some cute new nickname for you too." He leans in, making the threat more menacing.

I pause for a second, contemplating how much I should confess to my old friend. There's a lot on my mind and heavy on my heart. I'm happy I played well tonight, but I already feel the debilitating pressure to perform even better in my next game.

I'm also thinking of Cam, because I feel guilty that good things are happening in my life again.

I wish I could talk to Wells about this stuff, but I can't risk losing another friend. If all that wasn't enough to worry about, I'm still thinking about Lucy. No matter how hard I try to force her out of my mind, I can't.

"It's the girl with the tattoos, isn't it? The weird one that you hit with the puck." Wells is as good at reading my mind as he is at reading plays on the ice.

"She's not weird. At least not in a bad way. Wait, how did you know?" I ask, shocked to discover that my buddy still has killer instincts even though it's been years since we were teammates.

"It's always a girl, or guy. You know I'm not one to judge." Wells takes a sip of his drink.

"Very Gen Z of you," I say jokingly, still dodging the original question.

"I don't need the whole Boomer nickname gaining traction. Now quit stalling. Talk."

"There's nothing to say. We hooked up one time when I thought I was on my way out of town, and now she's outside our locker room painting a mural like this is the Renaissance. Why can't they hang a picture up on the wall or something?" I'm on a stress-powered vent and I don't know how to stop myself.

I don't know how to articulate what is going on with Lucy. It was a one-time hookup, except now I have to see her all the time, and I think she hates me.

"Wow, you've got it bad," Wells says matter-of-factly.

"I do not," I snap. Just because I don't understand what's going on between us doesn't mean I've got it bad for her. I have a bad case of wanting to make sure the girl I hit in the head with a puck doesn't hate me enough to ruin my career. That's a totally normal reaction after giving someone a head injury.

Plus, Wells doesn't know what he's talking about. He met his wife in high school and is one of the few professional hockey players who has always put his relationship before anything, including hockey. Wells and Hannah's relationship is part of the reason why I've always kept things casual with women. If being in a successful, lasting relationship requires putting it before hockey, then I'm not capable of having one. I do not have it bad, for anyone, ever.

"Sure." Wells giggles into his cup as he takes another sip.

"I can't have any distractions this season. I need to get my game back." I bounce my glass on my knee, causing the ice to shake. I can't let anyone—no matter how hot or cool they are—distract me from what I'm here to achieve. With Lucy looming around our locker room for the foreseeable future, I need to have my head down, focused on what really matters— saving my career.

"Looks like you found it tonight. Did you do anything differently? I'm trying to stick around a few more seasons, and could use pointers," Wells says.

"No, just spilled my coffee all over Lucy on my way in." I hear the words as I say them out loud and it hits me. "I spilled my coffee on Lucy, and she told me to break a leg. Technically she told me to break both of them, but she doesn't strike me as sporty." I cup my chin.

"So you're going to cut caffeine out of your diet?" Wells's face scrunches up as he tries to follow along.

"Never. It's an essential part of my pregame routine. What I'm trying to say is, what if I've been looking at this all wrong? I thought I needed to avoid her because she was distracting. What if she's...lucky?" The possibility fills me with a jolt of energy, and I jump out of my seat.

I'm not really the type of guy to experience an epiphany; I

think this might be my first. Things have really started look-ing up for me since I met her. Immediately after our one night together, I get a call saying there's suddenly room for me on the roster. Then I bump into her again right before my game and I play well. This can't be a coincidence.

"Please don't do this whole superstitious thing, JJ. Next thing you know you need to eat the same meal every day, wear the same tie, and never wash your gitch. You'll be talking to the goalposts and avoiding the red line by Thanksgiving." Wells tries to pull me back down into my seat.

I slip loose from his grip. "Easy. I'm not that unhinged—I'm not a goalie." I pace around the VIP section, rubbing my chin. "I don't think I need to spill my coffee on her before every game, but I need to talk to her. I'm desperate to play consis-tently and get a long-term contract."

"Then it sounds like it's worth a shot. Next time you see her ask if she'll yell at you before every game—you seem to really like when she does that."

"Shut up. It's not like that. I'm not looking for a relation-ship." I finish my drink in a few big gulps.

"Then go join Thing One and Thing Two out there and let yourself have some fun. You shouldn't have any trouble find-ing them. Soko's outfit is flashing like a damn disco ball under the lights," Wells says encouragingly.

I ditch my glass on the table and grab a couple of beers out of a bucket of ice before heading out into the crowd. Instead of sticking around longer, I hand the drinks to Soko and Lam-ber before saying bye to some of the other guys on the team.

I need to head home and figure out how I'm going to con-vince Lucy to be my good-luck charm.

# TWELVE

## Lucy

Cooper is hosting an open mic at his coffee shop, Brewed This Way, a Lady Gaga–themed café by day and event venue by night. I arrive a bit behind schedule but make it before any of the performers hit the stage. Maya is already helping Cooper behind the counter serving guests coffee and tea while I quickly weave through the crowd to help them.

"Look who finally showed up," Cooper says, maneuvering past me with a hot coffee in hand.

"I know, I'm sorry. I've been MIA so much these past couple of weeks between this stupid mural and the tattoo shop." I have yet to tell my friends about the night I spent with Jaylen or the bad luck that ensued, and I'm hoping my full-coverage foundation keeps the secret I'm hiding under my bangs.

"It's all good. We were beginning to worry you ran off with someone and joined a cult after you left the club on Cooper's half birthday," Maya says as she refills cups and lids on the counter beside the espresso machine. She's so busy that she hasn't looked over at me yet.

"Give me a bit of credit. I would never do that again." I take someone's espresso order and head over to the machine to make it.

"What happened to your forehead, Lucy?" Maya gasps. My cover is blown. She reaches for my bangs, but I narrowly dodge her hand.

"Ohhh," I say, bringing my fingertips to my fresh scar as if I forgot it was there. "It's really nothing. I was taking Sailor to the vet last week and she scratched me slightly while I was putting her into the travel carrier." I hand the waiting customer their drink.

"Are you okay? It looks really bad." Maya pushes my hair aside and gets a close look. Cooper stops by to check out the gash too. It's healing nicely. I got the stitches out a few days ago, and the bruise is mostly only yellow now.

"It looks bruised. Why is it bruised?" Cooper says, leaning in close to my face.

*Guess I need to invest in a better full-coverage foundation.* "Back up, Dr. Grey," I say, turning into the espresso machine to hide.

"What's going on? You aren't trying to start another fight club again, are you?" Maya spins me around.

"Roller derby team! I was trying to form a roller derby team. And no—if you must know, I got hit in the head with a hockey puck at work," I say.

"A puck? Weird things happen in tattoo studios." Cooper shakes his head.

"The mural I'm painting is for the Rainiers. I got hit by a rogue puck my first day on the job."

Cooper shrieks, his interest in my injury piqued. Maya gives him a dirty look, and a few guests turn to stare. "That's amazing! I love hockey."

"Since when?" Maya asks in disbelief.

"Since I grew up in upstate New York and was obsessed with the captain of my high school's hockey team. We sat beside each other in English, and I needed an excuse to talk to him. I could tell you anything you'd want to know about the 2017–2018 Buffalo Bisons," he brags.

"What happened?" Maya asks.

"Not much, really. Horrible season for the Bisons." Cooper pouts sympathetically.

"No, not the hockey team. With you and the captain?" she asks.

Maya and Cooper continue to banter with each other, but I have little motivation to get them back on track. The less they know about my night with Jaylen the better. Even though the whole thing was very casual, and there are no lingering feelings between us, I know how it looks. It looks like I'm distracted again, so distracted that I took a puck to the head.

Cooper sweeps nonexistent hair behind his ear bashfully. "Unlike the 2017–2018 Buffalo Bisons, I knew how to score," he says proudly.

"Nice." Maya scoffs before she excuses herself to introduce the band while Cooper and I hang back behind the counter.

Maya works in the nonprofit sector for Seattle Pride and is responsible for hosting these charity artist showcases once a month at the café. This place looks like a MUNA fan club meeting, which makes sense considering Maya knows just about every lesbian in town. It's the lesbian three degrees of separation; behind every well-functioning society is a well-connected chain of lesbians getting shit done.

"These women make all their own instruments out of ethically sourced wood. The violinist collected her own hair for years to string her bow," Maya says in a whisper as she leans back against the counter next to us. The band begins their set.

"What the fuck is ethically sourced wood?" I lean over and whisper in Cooper's ear.

"When I ride my bike over to a hookup's house rather than drive," Cooper says with a smirk.

As the band settles into their set, the door chimes open and standing in the doorway is none other than Jaylen fucking Jones. He quickly realizes he's walked into the middle of a concert and creeps awkwardly toward the counter. I practically flinch at the sight of him.

Cooper goes rigid. Jaylen is now standing in front of him, but Cooper isn't even blinking. I worry he's having a stroke, but then suddenly he starts talking. "Oh my god." His voice trembles.

I step forward to intervene. "What do you want?" I ask, already annoyed.

"Lucy, be nice to my customers. Do you know who this is?" Cooper pushes me back behind him.

I walk around the counter and drag Jaylen outside by the wrist. "What are you doing here?" I ask once we have a bit of privacy. The last thing I need is him turning up when I'm around my friends. I don't need another lecture from Maya, especially when I don't deserve it.

"I was walking home from the club and I saw you in the window. I live up the street. Is that okay? Should I move?" he asks.

I presume he's being sarcastic, but he's so well-mannered that it might be a real offer. His hands are buried in his pockets as he looks down at me. Even in his own neighborhood Jaylen has this permanently lost look on his face.

"You just so happened to see me in the window?" Seems made-up considering I'm at a café while a band named Bedrock Butch plays environmental folk for a bunch of queer people. I look like every other bitch here tonight.

"Fine. You posted about this event on your social media. You should really be more careful giving out your location like that. Someone creepy could see it and show up unannounced."

"You hear yourself, right?" I lean back to look through the front window and check to see what Maya and Cooper are doing. They both watch us from a distance whispering, but when they see me look their way, they immediately avert their eyes and pretend to make drinks.

"My friends don't know that we hooked up. They think I've dedicated myself to shifting my focus from relationships to work, so I can't have you showing up here unannounced and potentially saying something stupid to convince them otherwise," I add.

Jaylen doesn't flinch let alone dissuade. He seems as optimistic as ever when he says, "Lucy, I need you to be my good-luck charm this season."

"Like that!" I snap. "That is exactly what I was worried about. Absolutely not. It was a one-and-done situation."

"Come on, good things happen to me when you're around," he pleads.

"And I get hit in the head with pucks and soaked with nasty chain-store coffee. Shove a horseshoe up your ass and call it a day. I'm not interested in dating right now. We had this talk already." I cock my head over my shoulder to peer through the window again, knowing my friends are growing suspicious. They're helping a customer, but Maya periodically peers up at me.

"It was one puck. And it's not dating—I'm not interested in dating either. I'm interested in winning hockey games and securing a multiyear contract at the end of this season with the Rainiers."

His rationale feels like a bit of a stretch. I've been called a lot of things by men, but *lucky* is a new one. I don't fully trust that he isn't a bit interested in rekindling our bedroom connection from the first night we met. And if I'm being honest with myself, I'm a bit offended if he isn't.

I don't give him an answer; I don't even say anything. This isn't a good idea. The closer Jaylen gets to me, the harder it is to resist him. It's easy to hate him from a distance as I stare at the fresh scar on my forehead every morning in the mirror. But when we're face-to-face, I think about asking him to kiss it better. It's a feeling I need to repress. I don't need to get involved with some big-shot hockey player when all Jaylen does is distract me from work.

"Think about it. I can give you a ride to work, or get you tickets to a game. All I'm asking is that I get to see you for a minute on game days. Or at least a good-luck text." He smiles a sleazy-car-salesman grin. His face strains to maintain his optimistic attitude while I give him nothing but an expressionless glare in return. "Maybe a FaceTime on road games," he adds, pushing his luck.

I groan.

"We'll start with home games," he says. He grabs me by both shoulders and squeezes my arms in his big hands. "Will you at least think about it? The whole city will be thanking you by the end of the season."

I groan a bit louder, and longer. "This is a really weird ask. And I've had a guy ask me to step on his balls before."

"Well, I definitely don't want you to do that. But I'm happy to hear you'll think about it. I'll be seeing you at the rink very soon." He pats me on the shoulder and takes off up the street. I'm just thankful he doesn't try to hug me goodbye, which seems like an invasive Midwestern thing he would do.

When I return inside the café, both my friends greet me with crossed arms, popped hips, and tapping toes.

Maya is the first to speak. "Seemed like a pretty passionate conversation."

Cooper gasps as if he's heard someone say Lady Gaga's *Chromatica* was a flop. "That night, when you disappeared from my party. The next morning you sent me a text saying you slept with someone with abs like Batman's batsuit."

"I knew it!" Maya shouts.

A few people turn and shush us, scolding us like loud schoolchildren in a library. Cooper drags us each by the hand into the back storage room. I'm trapped, surrounded by napkins and coffee beans and two friends who want an explanation.

"Cooper, I told you that in confidence and under the influence of a minor concussion. I didn't know he was a hockey player. I thought his incredible physique was the result of a very disturbed obsession with CrossFit. It wasn't my finest moment, but he told me he was only in town for one night, and now he's everywhere I look—even this café." I slump down onto a stacked box and hang my head between my knees. Suddenly I have a throbbing headache.

"I can't believe the biggest bust in NHL history busted inside my bestie." I've never heard Cooper so proud of me before.

"Technically he also busted on me," I say from my toppled-over position on the box. I run my hands through my hair and take a deep breath. I pull myself together and get up off the floor, ready to continue defending myself against dating accusations.

Cooper picks up his phone and hastily taps away at the screen. "His Wikipedia doesn't report any racist, homophobic, or sexual assault incidents. That's great, right?"

"The bar is literally in hell for men," Maya says. Maya peers over Cooper's shoulder at his phone. "Check his Instagram followers. I bet it's all hot Instagram models wearing some trendy fast fashion company."

"Look at this post." Cooper shoves his phone in my face. It's a photo of Jaylen holding two muscular arms full of kittens at an animal shelter. The caption reads: "They might have nine lives, but they're waiting for you to give them a shot at one good one."

I let out a loud, agonized groan and collapse back down on the box.

"What a slutty post. What a whore," Maya says. She isn't wrong; as far as male thirst traps go, volunteering at an animal shelter is about as straight to the point as they come.

"The comments are desperate. 'Can I take you home?' 'I wish my kitty was in your hands.' 'Ruin my life, Jaylen.'" Cooper is taking great pleasure in conducting this digital background check. Even more so than the time I matched with a disgraced YouTuber on a dating app. I did not subscribe.

"Guys, it's not like that at all—I'm not interested in him. It was a one-night thing. I'm so focused on work and this mural because once I pull this off, I'm going to ask Sam for an apprenticeship," I say, hoping to speak it into existence. "Plus, Jaylen's not looking to date either. He's mentioned it almost every time we've talked."

"If he's not interested in you, then why did he show up here? I highly doubt he's into environmental lesbian folk music," Maya says, crossing her arms.

"He could be. He carries a metal reusable water bottle around the rink with him," I say.

Maya gives me that look, the one where she's silently screaming *reallllly* through a closed mouth, and I cave. "He wants me to be his good-luck charm," I blurt out to get it over with. It sounds even more ridiculous coming out of my mouth than it did out of Jaylen's.

"Is that a sex thing?" Cooper says, peering up from his phone.

"I didn't ask. I just told him no." The pins and needles itching the bottom of my feet tell me it's time to get a grip and pick myself up off the floor.

Cooper and Maya speak at the same time.

"Good," Maya says, finally unlinking her arms.

"You should do it," Cooper encourages.

Their words tug me in opposite directions like an angel and devil on each shoulder.

"Athletes take their superstitions very seriously, but I can think of a lot worse things than being a hot hockey player's muse."

I wave Cooper off. "I'm not indulging Jaylen's neurotic behavior. I don't have the capacity to worry about his career when mine needs all the attention it can get."

"Come on, the next act is up soon." Maya wraps an arm

around me—and much like my special friend in high school did—she drags me out of the closet.

"Please don't be another song about preserving farmlands," Cooper whines, dragging his feet behind us.

# THIRTEEN

## Lucy

On Wednesday, Jaylen brought me a Brewed This Way coffee to pregame skate and scored his first goal as a Rainier. On Friday, he brought me a muffin and recorded an assist and had what he called a few memorable hits. On Sunday, he brought me a coffee *and* a muffin and was promoted to the second line.

None of these interactions have been consensual, and they've all added to his delusion that I am somehow responsible for his improving luck simply by being at the arena.

Thanks to Cooper, Jaylen has unfortunately learned my favorite coffee order and cornered me into choosing to accept or waste them. As long as he's not spilling them down the front of my shirt, I'm not going to complain to HR. I'm almost done this mural, and soon all of this will be behind me.

Not just Jaylen's shenanigans, but painting is wreaking emotional distress on my creative spirit every day. I can feel myself slipping further and further away from my goal of a tattoo apprenticeship with each day I waste painting this hockey mural.

I stand back and snap a progress photo of my art and send it to Sam as an update and a reminder that I am over here going above and beyond to prove myself to her. I don't want her forgetting about me or my talents while I'm out of the shop painting.

SAM:

> Looks good so far. Make sure they're happy with it because it's my reputation on the line. Don't screw it up and I'll take a look at your portfolio soon.

LUCY:

> Great I've been practicing realism cuz I know how much you love that style. Want to see a raven I just finished?

SAM:

> Not now.

> Shop needs more paper towels. Get some and drop them off once you're done painting for the day.

I set my phone down and get to work finishing up the mural. The promise of Sam looking at my portfolio soon gives me the hit of dopamine I need to get my ass in gear and get this thing done as soon as possible. With my paint tray loaded with varying shades of yellows and creams, I get to work finishing off the last of the Swedish players' flowy blond locks.

"Happy to see you're alive." Anna's sneakers squeak against the rubber flooring. She parks herself at the bottom of my ladder, craning her neck up toward the top corner of the mural where I'm adding some highlights with my trusty spotter brush.

"Thanks. My face is healing up nicely." I pull my bangs up to show off my fading scar.

"I meant for legal reasons. It would have been a lot of paper-work if you died."

"Right," I say, making my descent down the ladder.

"Taking a puck to the head is never fun, but you haven't really worked for a hockey team until you've taken some rubber off the dome at some point." Anna's phone chimes and her gaze drops to the screen. As she taps away, I set my painting supplies down.

"Does everything in hockey sound like an innuendo?"

Anna reflects for a beat, cupping her chin. Her freshly mani-cured nails are the same blue as the Rainiers' logo. "When you're a pervert, yes." She gives me a cheeky grin. I can't tell if Anna hates me or if this is normal workplace camaraderie.

"Hey, Anna!" Jaylen comes out of the dressing room in full hockey gear. His wide smile is as bright and eager as always. Anna is average height, but next to Jaylen on skates we both look like kids watching airplanes fly overhead.

"Great, he's talking to me." Anna smiles like someone sup-pressing a sneeze.

"I've been thinking…" Jaylen says, leaning into his hockey stick for support like it's a walking stick.

"Aw, cute," she says softly.

It doesn't deter Jaylen from interrupting our conversation. He gestures toward the mural. "Since this is our rink, don't you think we should be in our blue home jerseys?"

"Don't you think you should get out on the ice?" I snap back. I know what he's doing. I can tell by the way he's leaning into her and smiling wide enough that it reaches his eyes. He's try-ing to get his way. He's trying to make this god-awful com-mission last forever.

"You don't like how the white jersey stands out against the blue backdrop?" Anna asks, entertaining him. She's only human; Jaylen's charm is hard to resist, and it doesn't help that she is contractually obligated to make sure the players are happy.

Jaylen wobbles over to the mural and uses his stick to point out areas of improvement. "I do, but what if it was reversed? Blue jerseys and a light background. Right now, it kind of looks like we're all drowning in water. What if we were skating on ice?"

Jaylen's gold chain peeks out of his shoulder pads and catches the light, and I know it's over for me. There is just enough bare chest and chain necklace showing for him to get his way. I'm going to be stuck here forever, painting this mural and telling him to break various appendages.

"I do like that better. Great suggestion, JJ," Anna says with more positivity than I thought she was capable of faking.

"Yeah, great suggestion," I say through my teeth.

Jaylen mouths the word *sorry* to me sympathetically.

"It will take me at least a week to change the colors." I bend down and start riffling through my supplies, making sure I've got enough paint left. I'll need to pick up some more Super White from the paint shop, but I've got enough wash brushes left over to make the changes.

"Should we get you a helmet?" Anna's sudden charisma has run dry, and I'm left with the stinging realization that there's nothing I can say to convince her to leave the mural as is.

"I'm never going near the ice again." And once I'm done with this mural, I'm never going near a paintbrush again either.

Anna leaves without a goodbye, but Jaylen loiters.

"If you were actually serious about creating good luck for yourself, you would start with a new number," I say, motioning to the thirteen stitched on his shoulder sleeve.

"Thirteen? I already told you, it's my favorite number. My childhood best friend picked it out for me when we played mites together." He relaxes into an over-the-head arm stretch. "Even if I wanted to, it's a pain in the ass to change your number during season. Promotional material and merch is already made. I'm not trying to be a dick and inconvenience anyone."

"Except me," I mumble, turning my focus and energy back to the mural.

"Say yes to being my good-luck charm and I won't have to."

A group of players pop out of the locker room and Jaylen is swept up down the hall. With Jaylen off my back for the time being, I get back to work completely revamping everything I've already completed. I know art is supposed to be a labor of love, but I remember the love hitting me a little harder than this.

I'm not as good as I used to be; my creative instincts aren't nearly as sharp. I should have known blue jerseys on an icy white background was more aesthetically pleasing. If I really had a knack for this, I wouldn't need Jaylen to point that out. I guess not painting for four years dulled all my edges.

It's no wonder I quit chasing this dream—the second-guessing is exhausting.

As I stretch my neck after hours of repainting, a large rolling laundry bin slowly wheels out of the locker room and into my peripheral vision, creeping up the hall toward me like a robot vacuum.

"Hello?" I call out.

There's no response. As the laundry bin continues to creak down the hall, I notice someone covered in towels hunched over behind the bin. They pick up speed as they go to pass me. I step out to stop them, but they don't slow and instead run right over my foot. I yelp in pain, hopping on my good foot while the other throbs. Figures, the one day I don't wear my combat boots I sustain a foot injury.

"Sorry!" Jaylen jumps up from behind the bin, sending the towels that once concealed him to the floor. "Are you okay?" he asks as he frantically picks up the towels and shoves them into the bin.

I bend down and examine my foot. "I'm fine. You weren't going to kidnap me by shoving me into that laundry bin, were you?" I slowly ease more weight on my injured foot. I'll live.

"Of course not. Why, would that have worked?" He leans

against the rolling laundry bin in a cocky cool-guy pose, but quickly stumbles as the bin starts to roll back.

I watch in slow motion as it rolls its way directly toward my sketchbook and paint supplies. It's loose like a rogue shopping cart in the wind as it slams into open paint bottles, knocking them over like a bowling strike. I limp over and assess the damage. He's tie-dyed my black-and-white sketch of a raven—it looks like a parrot. *Great.*

"Here, take a towel." Jaylen is at my side offering up a damp towel from god knows which hockey player's wet butt cheeks.

"It's fine." I brush him off. While the raven sketch is now a mixed-media piece, none of the other work is damaged, and the mess is minimal. Jaylen is quick to mop up the spilled paint with his towel before tossing it back into the bin.

Getting back up to our feet, I notice he's in costume. He looks like a samurai with the red jumpsuit base, long brown vest on top, and yellow tie around his waist. But the red makeup carefully caked around his right eye like a bruise lets me know he's dressed as Zuko from *Avatar: The Last Airbender.* Another player soon follows out from the locker room, slipping into a fur-trim blue jacket—another *Avatar* costume.

"Halloween was last week," I say, screwing on the lids to my paint and proactively avoiding another spill.

"I was hoping you wouldn't still be here when we finished practice. I was trying to avoid the ridicule from you by sneaking out of the locker room. We're going to Comic Con this afternoon." Jaylen wiggles his fingers, motioning me to lay it on him, like a wrestler provoking their opponent. "Come on, hit me with your best chirp. I deserve it after what I pulled with Anna."

"I think you guys look great." Their costumes look custom; I'm impressed.

"I've got Jaylen to thank for introducing my daughter to *Avatar.* Harper is convinced she's the real Princess Yue," Wells says, reminding us of his presence.

"Lucy, this is Wells." Jaylen quickly jumps in to accommodate a formal introduction.

"It's Chief Arnook today." Wells shakes my hand.

"It's sweet that you guys are doing this for Harper. She's going to have a blast today," I say.

"I'm doing this for myself. I love Zuko," Jaylen says proudly. "Check this out." He reaches behind his back and pulls out two large prop swords. "I had them custom-made to look exactly like they do in the show." He waves them around in slow motion. Wells takes a step back, dodging one of Jaylen's swings.

"That's amazing." I lean in to get a closer look. I didn't think I would ever discover common ground with Jaylen, but his appreciation for one of the more nerdier subcultures is rather refreshing.

He quickly pulls them away from me, and while sliding them into the scabbard strapped to his back, he says, "You don't need to mock me. I already know it's nerdy."

"Talk some sense into him, Lucy. No one needs a sword that costs more than a hockey stick—never mind two of them," Wells says.

"They're actually dual swords. Two halves of one single weapon," I say.

Jaylen's jaw drops and the corners of his mouth slowly creep into a smile. "You know Zuko?" His voice is slow and gravelly, like that night we met. He almost sounds sexy now that he's not begging me to wish him good luck.

Looking into his eyes right now is dangerous. Jaylen has teen-heartthrob eyes—shiny, wide, and hopeful, the type you would see in some coming-of-age movie where the senior high schooler is played by a hot thirty-year-old actor. It's getting increasingly difficult for me to continue being so short with him the longer he stares me down. I'm worried if he doesn't look away, I might start begging Jaylen to take me to senior prom. I can't let him distract me like this.

"You're not the only one who likes anime. You're not that

interesting," I say, bending down to grab my work tote and sling it over my shoulder.

"*Avatar* isn't technically anime," he argues.

"Are we really doing this? Are we really going to have that debate now, because I thought you had somewhere to be." I push up my sleeves, ready to get into one of Reddit's most heated debates.

"I'll meet you in the car, JJ. Don't let her near that sword— she might cut you," Wells says, patting Jaylen on the shoulder as he steps by. We watch him disappear around the corner.

"Come with us and we can fight about it all afternoon. I'm sure I could fashion you a Mai costume quick with hockey tape and what you're already wearing." Jaylen's eyes travel up and down my body and suddenly I wish they were his hands.

I cross my arms. "I'm clearly more of a Katara."

"Not a chance," he scoffs dismissively, and I know we could be at this all day and enjoy it.

The concept of Jaylen is easily dismissible. The vapid jock archetype looking to distract me from personal growth for the sake of his own selfish needs is uninspired. But he doesn't feel so trite standing in front of me now in full cosplay, leaving to take his friend's daughter to Comic Con. He might actually be interesting; not nice or pleasant or pleasing, but actually interesting.

I pull myself back, physically and emotionally. "I can't today anyway. Not only would I be embarrassingly underdressed next to you guys, but I've got to run an errand for work." *And I should probably redo my raven sketch.* Although thanks to the chiseled model standing in front of me right now, I find myself a bit more inspired by the human body than a bird.

"Too bad," he says, lingering in the hall.

"Have fun without me."

"I'll try."

# FOURTEEN

## Jaylen

I find myself excited to come to the rink every day—a complete flip in optimism from years past when I would pull up to the parking lot as late as possible without risking retribution. My good fortune continues as I find excuses to linger in the hall with Lucy anytime I run into her.

Today, I come bearing a poster from Comic Con. Before I round the corner, I pause in front of a trash bin, second-guessing myself. *Is this too thoughtful?* It's an important day, because I am going to ask Lucy to dinner. She's almost done with the painting and has yet to agree to be my good-luck charm. Once she's done with the commission, she won't be hanging around the rink anymore and I can't let my luck run as dry as her paint. Having her around has clearly helped my game, but having Lucy agree to fully support me all season would give me the edge I need to secure my role on this team.

I think if I can persuade her to come to dinner with me and hear me out, then I can convince her to become part of my game-day routine. I don't want to give her the wrong impression about us with this poster, but I need her in a good enough mood to agree to dinner. My season comes first; she knows that. I pick up my head and continue down the hall.

Lucy is locked into her art, adding beads of sweat to one of the guy's temples. My color swap suggestion hardly slowed her down and she's nearing the end of her project. The mural is beautiful. Everyone looks so realistic, I can't believe it's a painting. Lucy has one person left to paint, and it's the one I'm most anxious to see.

"Hey, Lucy!" I shout as I approach. I hope to get her attention without startling her off the ladder. I'd like to make it through one interaction without a workplace accident. As long as my clumsiness doesn't carry out onto the ice, I'm not overthinking my embarrassing fumbles too much.

She notices me and slips off her headphones. "I think I liked you better in cosplay," she says, climbing down her stepladder slowly. She sets her paint tray on the ground and wipes her hands on the butt of her paint-covered denim.

"I've still got the costume at home."

"I bet you've got a few others too."

I hand her the rolled poster. "I got you this from Comic Con."

She slips the elastic off and unrolls it in front of me. I got it signed by the *Avatar* voice actors for her. Judging by her smile, she likes it.

"Wow, thank you. This is really cool, but I'm still not going to be your good-luck charm." She bends over to roll it back up.

Lucy's shirt is low-cut and the tattoo on her sternum is playing peekaboo with me. I'm worried if my eyes linger on her too long, they will inevitably fall between her breasts. I quickly reposition myself. Resting my hands on my hips, I look up at the mural, admiring her work.

"Looks like you finally have to do me," I say.

"Excuse me?" she bites.

I point to the empty space up in the top corner. Everyone on the team has a completed portrait on the mural—everyone but me.

"Right. I've been putting it off," she says, eyeing the empty space like it's causing her as much pain as I am.

"I'm not that ugly, am I?" I'm obviously shamelessly fishing for a compliment and can't help myself.

"You know you're not ugly. It's always been harder for me to paint things, or people, I know personally. It's hard to separate the emotion from the art." Lucy moves to her supply station. She tucks the poster into her bag and begins pulling some browns and creams from her pile of paint. She shakes the bottles vigorously.

"That's probably what makes you such a great painter." I watch her, like I have the past couple of weeks. She's really good at what she does, even though she's complained through the entire process.

"I'm *not* a painter, remember?" She grabs the chosen paints and starts filling up the tiny divot in her paint tray.

"You keep saying that, but if you work at a tattoo shop, what are you doing here painting this mural?" The first time I tried to ask Lucy about her job, she told me to mind my own business. The last time I asked, she told me she was working her way up to becoming a tattoo artist. I'm still a bit confused because I didn't know there was a whole process to becoming a tattoo artist; I just thought you did a few shitty tattoos until they started getting better.

"That's a good question. My boss seems to think part of paying my dues includes murals." Lucy squats down and fishes through a cup of paintbrushes on the ground, pulling a few out and sticking them in her back pocket.

"Kind of like how I had to wear a diaper and a bib and walk around in the freezing cold in juniors for rookie initiation." The memory sends a shiver up my spine.

"No, because that sounds like something you would actually enjoy." Lucy has a laugh at my expense.

She's not wrong; the bib did come in handy. It's hard to eat on a moving bus without getting any sauce on your dress shirt.

"I, on the other hand, hate this. I haven't painted since… It's been a long time, but I really want my boss to offer me a tattoo apprenticeship, so I'm trying to show her that I can reliably finish a project."

"Looks like you won't be hanging around here much longer since you're almost finished." My stomach starts to knot.

I knew my time with Lucy was running out, but I had hoped she would have agreed to be my good-luck charm before the mural was complete. We're down to one last face, and I'm not sure I'm going to be able to convince her to indulge me.

"You're not going to make any more suggestions to Anna, are you?" Lucy rolls her eyes at me and climbs back up the ladder to get started on my portrait.

"Again, I'm sorry about that. I needed to buy myself more time with you."

"I can't lie—I'm not looking forward to buying my own coffee again."

"If I had your number, I could continue bringing you coffee," I say as harmlessly as I can. I've been casually trying to give Lucy my number all week, and every time she laughs at me like it's the punch line to a joke I didn't make.

"You're really not going to drop this whole lucky-charm thing, are you?" Lucy uses a larger brush to mix the brown colors on her tray.

"I need you, Lucy. To wish me good luck, of course." I sound so desperate that I physically cringe at myself. "Let me take you out to dinner this week." I'm practically begging her to hang out with me, but I don't ever want to go back to the way I was before. For years I felt so weak and hopeless that it was frustrating and impossible to play through. I felt so guilty over what happened in my second year that I could never consistently play good hockey. Now that I am, I'm going to do whatever it takes to keep it going.

"That sounds like a date." Lucy raises an eyebrow, peering down at me over her shoulder.

This girl must have some really shitty exes because she will not let up on reminding me of the fact that she's not looking for a relationship. Luckily, I'm not proposing anything serious. A casual text here and there, maybe a friendly in-person hello when convenient.

"It's not. It's a business dinner. An expensive one. I promise."

"Wait a minute," Lucy says as she stares down the long hall toward the ice and then back at me. "There's no practice today. Why are you here?"

"I forgot something in my locker yesterday and I came to grab it." I didn't, but I also didn't want to tell Lucy that the only reason I showed up today was to see her and give her the poster. This could be my last chance to convince her to hear me out, and with another big game coming up this week, I can't risk messing up my hot streak.

"If you've got nowhere to be, get over here." She descends quickly down her ladder and waves me over. She squares my shoulders up to hers and stares at me inquisitively, then the paint palette, then the mural, then back at me again.

"What are you doing?" I swivel my head around, checking to see if anyone is around the rink today.

"Hold still." She mixes a drop of yellow into her creamy brown paint, creating my exact hue. "Perfect," she says under her breath.

I don't care about how my portrait turns out anymore; I'm focused on her and her heart-shaped mouth. She smells so good, and I bet she tastes even better. "Yeah," I whisper back.

Being this close to her knocks all the air out of my lungs. When did my legs cement themselves to the floor? I need to back off before I scare Lucy away. She looks at me, staring into my eyes with a focus so intense I wonder what she's noticing. It doesn't matter. Getting her to agree to be my good-luck charm is the only thing that matters right now.

"I should grab that…thing," I say, stumbling back. My brain is able to get my legs to stumble off into the locker room, safe from Lucy's seductive pull.

Alone in the room, I collapse like a runner crossing the finish line, catching my breath.

"Jaylen!" Lucy calls out to me. I stand up straight, forcing myself into a casual stance. "I need to get your eye color right…" She falls silent once she gets inside the locker room. She looks around in amazement. "I've never been inside one of these before," she says, wandering in.

Lucy is headed toward the center of the locker room and is about to step on the team crest woven into the carpeted floor.

"Watch out!" I launch my body at her, shoving her out of the way, but I land on our logo in the process.

"Oh no," I say, jumping back. "It's bad luck to walk on the team crest."

"Then why put it on the floor? That's dumb."

Lucy finds my name on the locker nameplates and begins digging through my cubby. She pulls out my jockstrap and holds it up in both hands, laughing to herself. I don't usually let people touch my equipment because it's bad luck, but she's been known to have a lucky touch, so I let it slide.

"Didn't know you guys were strapped like that," she says, peering through the straps with a judgmental gaze.

"You think a puck to the head hurts, try blocking one with your dick."

"I'm sure you'd be fine. You'd probably hurt the puck."

*What does that mean? Is that sexual or an insult?* I can never tell with her.

Lucy hooks my jock back up and starts snooping through my toiletry bag: tape, mouth guards, wax, some candy. It's mostly a hockey junk drawer.

"What's this?" She pulls out a tiny white package, no bigger than a to-go salt packet from a restaurant.

I reach for her, shouting a dramatic and lengthy "Don't!" But I'm not quick enough. She brings it up to her nose and gives it a generous sniff.

Her head snaps back and her eyes shoot open. "Woo!" she says like she's possessed.

My warning comes seconds too late. "It's smelling salts."

"Everything is tingling! God, I feel so awake! Wooo!" Her whole body gyrates like an invisible Hula-Hoop is looping around her hips.

"You good?" I ask, apprehensively. She looks like she's just been brought back to life with a defibrillator.

"Woo! I'm great!"

"Are you sure? You keep doing that Ric Flair thing. And your eyes look particularly crazed, even for you."

"I've never been better." She discreetly smells it a second time, tossing her head back after a long sniff. As she breaks out into a coughing fit, I wrestle it out of her hands and toss it in the trash.

"We should get out of here before you accidentally break a mirror or something," I say, slipping between her and my locker belongings.

"Fine, but only because I've just been hit with newfound motivation to finish my work and I'm worried if I stop moving my heart will explode."

On her way out of the room, Lucy stops by the team crest again, lifting her foot and watching me panic for a moment before she playfully hops right over it. She laughs to herself, power walking out of the locker room and back to her workstation. I struggle to keep up with her new pace.

"That dinner, does it come with dessert?" she asks, picking up her paintbrush.

"Of course."

I will buy her the whole menu if it means playing well.

There's so much pressure in professional hockey to never miss a game—even if it means personal sacrifice.

I've played through broken bones, sprains, and cuts, but the death of Cam was a wound I should have properly treated before returning to the ice. I was still young and had too much to prove to willingly remove myself from the game and travel back home for the funeral service.

Cam and I grew up playing youth hockey together, and I still think of him every time I step on the ice. We drifted apart after high school when our lives went in completely opposite directions. I was drafted by the New York Skyliners and became a professional hockey player getting to live out my childhood dream every night, while he got involved with the wrong people and into some really bad things. We kept in touch a bit throughout my first year, but I didn't make much of an effort to stay close. I still have a bunch of unreplied texts from Cam sitting on my phone. Sometimes I think about sending a message back, but someone else probably has that number now.

I was still riding the high of my breakout rookie season, looking to follow it up with a career second year in the league and avoid the sophomore slump, but instead got a call from my mom telling me Cam died. Overdose. And I couldn't make the funeral service because I had a game that night. So, while everyone back home mourned the death of Cam, I hammed it up for twenty thousand screaming fans. Signed autographs on my way out of the building like I was somebody.

I tried to justify what I did by making up for it on the ice, but my game kept getting worse and worse until I could feel my career slipping through my fingers. I've finally got a grip on it again, and I'm not letting go this time.

"I'll go, but I'm coming with my list of demands," she says. Her voice shakes me back to reality, and her reply is so unexpected that it takes me a second to process.

"So, you've already thought about it," I say with too much excitement in my voice.

"Maybe. Now if you don't mind, I should really finish doing your face."

She's facing the wall, but from my angle, I can see her slight smirk.

# FIFTEEN

## Lucy

"Lots of nice things to steal in here," I say, hoping to cut through some of the awkward silence that lingers between us. My body is so tense that my shoulders are practically touching my ears. I tug at my vintage tank top, willing it to cover more of my midriff. Had I known Jaylen was taking me to a restaurant of this caliber, I would have worn a shirt that covered my belly button—or at least put on a bra.

I discreetly brush at my pants under the table, shooing off the last of the stubborn cat hair my lint roller missed. I feel the judgmental eyes of rich elderly guests on my marked body; they must be wondering to themselves why one of the line cooks is eating out front among the paying customers.

"Please don't. It's a nice restaurant, and they sort of know who I am," Jaylen says, looking around to see if anyone heard my joke. "All the guys told me this was the best spot in town." He fidgets with the silverware.

When Jaylen said he was taking me somewhere nice, I thought he meant the type of place that makes you wait to be seated, or the type with a bathroom that doesn't require a code to unlock the door. I wasn't expecting the nicest place in town. The view alone is staggering: we're seated next to large windows that overlook the water and mountains. And I guess the view across the table isn't bad either.

I dismiss Jaylen's inability to take a joke and open up the menu, reminding myself not to audibly gasp when I see the prices. To my surprise, the prices aren't listed, which is far more frightening. I'm going to ask the server for the most expensive thing on this damn menu. If Jaylen wants me to play along with his superstition, then he is going to pay for it.

I drop the menu when I spot the server approaching with a basket of bread. I intercept the warm, freshly baked rolls before he gets a chance to set the basket down on the table. I ask the server for their finest bottle of red and bite into a roll.

Jaylen leans across the table. "That's a four-hundred-dollar bottle of wine. You're not going to make this easy on me, are you?"

"Excuse me," I start, wiping breadcrumbs off my fingers. "My good luck has you the talk of the rink and if I'm not mistaken, the first player of the game too."

Jaylen nods. "First star of the game. And you're right. Thanks for agreeing to come tonight. You know I still feel really bad about your face."

"You've got to stop saying it like that," I say through a mouth full of food. I swallow my bite. "Look, you've been really nice to me these past few weeks, but I only agreed to this dinner because I was all hopped-up on smelling salts."

"You sure you're not here for the free bread? Your eyes really lit up when he brought that basket out to the table. I'll buy you a loaf from the corner store right after this if you want. I'll buy you whatever—just hear me out." His voice is low but pleading.

I pretend to ignore him as I slather another bun in butter and plop it in my mouth.

Our server returns to present us with our bottle of wine. He fills both glasses and takes our orders. Jaylen is polite the entire time, with many pleases and thank-yous. I bet if someone bumped into him, he would apologize. I can't picture him hitting or fighting someone on the ice; he's probably quietly whispering "sorry" in their ear the entire time he throws punches at their face. He probably sends a condolence card to every team he beats.

Jaylen moves his glass aside. "Name your price," he says, dropping the pleasantries. He sits up straight in his chair, his hands anchored on the tabletop. Jaylen is ready to cut a deal.

"This is crazy. I'm not a rabbit's foot."

"All the greats have their thing. In warm-ups, Wayne Gretzky would purposely miss his first shot on net wide right. Superstition and luck are the foundation of any good hockey player. Playoff beards, stick-taping rituals, lucky ties, not touching trophies. And if I start talking about goalies, we will be here all night. It's only a good-luck agreement, and I wouldn't be asking if I wasn't desperate." Jaylen's pitch sounds rehearsed.

"This is really important to you, isn't it?" I push my bread aside, not wanting to spoil dinner.

"Hockey is the only thing I know how to do. I lost it once, and I'm not going to let that happen again." His head hangs in a way that makes me actually feel sorry for him. He looks up at me with the same convincing look he gave me right before we stole the thirteen sign, and I know telling him no is going to be impossible. "Help me with my career and I'll help you with yours," he says.

"How can you help me? Do you own a tattoo shop I don't know about?" I look over his bare arms—unmarked, virgin skin. He looks like he's never even stepped foot in a tattoo shop before.

"I don't know. Lots of guys on the team have tattoos. I'm sure someone knows somebody."

My eyes get wide. "Jaylen, you're a genius."

"Oh. Thank you." He scoots up taller in his seat.

I palm my glass and swirl my wine. "I'll tattoo you for my portfolio," I say menacingly.

He throws both his hands up as if a truck was heading into him and blurts out, "Absolutely not!" A few heads turn and he quickly lowers his voice and says with a forced calmness, "How about one of my teammates instead? Soko has a rubber ducky tattooed on his ass. I'm sure he'll be down."

While I'm immediately insulted by his reaction, I choose to take it out on him with my demands. "Fine. I'll give you my phone number and text you before every game, but I'm not tattooing anyone's ass cheek—only waist or higher. And I want Rainiers tickets for me and my friends."

"Done!" Jaylen practically jumps out of his chair like his team scored a big goal.

"That's not all," I say, motioning him back into his chair. "My friend Maya is having a big charity event next month and you have to come. I already checked the team's schedule and you're free that afternoon. I hear professional athletes are a big attraction in this city, and it could help her raise money for a good cause." The tattoo is for me, the Rainiers tickets are for Cooper, and the Jaylen Jones appearance is for Maya. After all, I owe them at least that. Thanks to their motivational pep talk, I was able to put together a portfolio to show Sam.

Not to mention the mural I painted exceeded my own expectations. It took a bit of time, but eventually I worked past the uncomfortable fear that I was creating something terrible. Even Sam was impressed with my art; I think she might be coming around to the idea of giving me an apprenticeship. Tonight, before I left the shop, she told me to leave my portfolio behind for her to look through. My fate is finally in her hands and now a professional hockey player will be my first tattoo client.

"Deal, but only if you let me drive you home after the game. I don't like you whipping around on those electric scooters so late at night." Jaylen lifts his glass across the table to cheers me.

"I'm fine," I say, annoyed by his protective nature. I stare his wineglass down, contemplating if it's really worth it.

"It's not you I'm worried about—it's the people walking on the sidewalk." Jaylen extends his hand even farther toward me, practically shoving the glass in my face.

"You have a deal," I say, and the delicate clinking of our glasses makes it official.

"An arrangement." He lifts the glass to his lips.

"Don't be weird." I guzzle about half my glass with four big gulps.

He holds out his phone so I can add myself as a contact. As I grab the phone out of his hand, my fingers touch his. I forgot how big they were; I almost quiver. He texts me immediately so I have his number too. I play it cool, but on some level I'm happy to have it.

If it wasn't for Jaylen lurking around me every day as I painted, I'm not sure I would have been able to finish the mural. He was an annoying distraction, but a distraction nonetheless. Painting was a more emotional process than I anticipated. It brought back memories of my childhood, my absent father, and the life I gave up when I blew my opportunity to become a credible painter.

Jaylen said he loved my portrait of him. I couldn't tell him how much that meant to me, but it really felt good to hear him say it. It made me realize that if I can find a way to paint again, then I am capable of landing a tattoo apprenticeship.

"This is great, can I call you my Lucy Charm?" He laughs.

"No," I say, deadpan.

"You're right, that was pushing it."

With business out of the way, I settle into my seat and try to enjoy a fancy dinner. "So, how's work?" I ask. Not because I'm trying to give him a hard time, but because I'm genuinely interested in talking to him. Usually when I see Jaylen, he's surrounded by teammates or team staff and I'm doing my best to hold it together emotionally while I paint.

"Are you engaging in small talk? Is that the type of question you ask on a date?" he teases, smiling behind his glass of wine.

"This isn't a date," I say defensively, dropping my glass to the table with enough force that wine splashes up the sides.

"Right. I know that. Work is good. The guys here are great, don't get me wrong, but Coach Pete is a bit of a hard read sometimes. He won't put me on the PP, but he's got no problem sticking me on the PK. It's not that I'm not willing to grind a bit, prove myself to him and the boys, but I'm not trying to eat pucks all night. I'm playing well. I think I've earned PP time. Plus, we want to be a playoff contender this season. I can help, but not when I'm clocking so many shorthanded minutes. I don't get why we're playing timid," he rambles passionately.

I briefly think Jaylen is speaking another language before I realize he's talking hockey. Once, in middle school, I saw the second half of *The Mighty Ducks* on cable TV. I do my best to remember anything from the movie, and miraculously something comes to me. "Right. It's not worth winning if you can't win big!" I hope it is the right thing to say.

"Exactly, you get it." He swirls his tall-stemmed wineglass. "I know it's petty of me, but I really hate being treated like a pigeon." Jaylen continues to vent about work while speaking in tongues.

"I'm sorry, pigeon?" I struggle to keep up with the metaphors.

"Yeah, like a scrub."

"Pigeons are really smart," I say, hoping it cheers him up about his potential role on the team as a pigeon. I'm also unsure if we're talking about real pigeons, or if it is all some big confusing hockey metaphor.

"They're the rats of the sky," he says in a defensive tone.

"Rats are really smart too."

Thankfully the arrival of our appetizers interrupts our conversation; I only know the one *Mighty Ducks* quote and I'm all out of pigeon facts.

He scoops calamari onto his plate. "Since when did you become so optimistic?" Jaylen calls me out—and I like it. Usually, he lets my argumentative ways go unchecked, but not tonight. Am I finally getting a glimpse of the Jaylen I met at Purple Haze?

I stab my fork into a fried piece of squid and eat it directly off the serving tray. "Since when are you so hard on yourself?"

"You clearly don't know me. I'm the biggest draft bust in NHL history. I almost didn't have a job this year. Usually when I meet someone really hot, I'm not focused on begging them to be my good-luck charm so I can keep playing well enough to stay in the lineup." Jaylen chomps the bite off his fork and leans back in his chair to chew.

I think there's a compliment in there, but I try to not let it distract me from all the self-deprecation he's serving up. I've been around the rink a lot lately, and while it looked like I was painting a mural with my headphones on, sometimes I forgot to charge them. I've eavesdropped enough to know they're all talking about how the "old JJ" is back.

"Obviously, I don't know anything about hockey. But sometimes when you've got nothing left to lose, you can see what it is that you really want." I stuff my face with a few more pieces of squid before all the circle shapes are gone.

"Is that why you're so focused on getting this tattoo apprenticeship?" He calls me out again, and I choke my bite down.

"Maybe," I say, pausing to gulp down a mouthful of water. "Or maybe I want to pursue the arts and tattooing feels like the best way to do that and still have a secure job."

"Only you would call tattooing a safe bet."

The server comes out with our main dishes before I can tell Jaylen there's no such thing as safe bets when it comes to art.

Somewhere between the main course and dessert we order another bottle of wine and get into a playfully heated debate over anime including manga canon versus anime canon and our ranking of the big top three. The only thing we agree on is that *Hunter x Hunter* is our favorite, and that's common ground enough to keep our banter friendly.

I came here tonight knowing I would be tempted to fall for Jaylen again, and I could blame the wine for my weakening resistance to him, but the truth is that I was already warming up to him before the wine. I don't want a relationship—I stand by that—but I like being around him.

As Jaylen hands the server his credit card tucked inside the billfold, he accidentally knocks my wineglass in the process. The glass tips over the edge of the table and the red wine spills into my lap. I jump up, hoping to avoid a stain, but it's no use; the wine quickly seeps through my light denim pants and stains my crotch a dark maroon.

As the two men fumble over themselves to hand me a cloth napkin, they come face-to-face with my messy crotch and both back off. "Oh." They collectively sigh at my misfortune. Jaylen is babbling out about a hundred sorrys a minute, while the server runs off to fetch some club soda.

I burst into laughter. "It's fine. This happened to me all the time in high school." Suddenly, Jaylen is laughing along with me until we're both as red in the face as my stained crotch. "You've got to be the clumsiest person I've ever met." I sit back down and dab at my pants with the cloth napkin, but it's no use—they're ruined.

"I'm not normally. I get nervous around you, and it's like my brain loses connection to the rest of my body."

It's a sobering confession. We lock eyes and there's a moment of longing between us. It's a stillness like the moment before you're about to fall asleep. I think about kissing him, but he clears his throat and I'm jolted awake. I'm suddenly very aware that everyone in the restaurant is staring at us, scoffing into their plates over the loud scene we caused in the middle of the dinner rush.

"We should go before they have us kicked out," I say.

Jaylen is the first out of his seat, but before leaving, I reach back and grab the half-full bottle of wine off our table. It would be a shame to waste it.

Once we're outside of the restaurant, Jaylen asks, "What does the rest of your night look like?"

I take a swig of wine from the bottle and hand it over to him to do the same. "A new pair of pants," I say, jokingly. We laugh again. "But seriously, I've got to get back home to do some work. I've got an early morning tomorrow."

It's a lie. In reality I'm probably going to go home and do the same thing I've been doing the past couple of nights as I lay awake in bed: I'll open my phone and type Jaylen's name into every search bar imaginable. I'll analyze all fifteen of his posts on Instagram several times. And I'll continue to scour the internet for any newfound information on him.

His Google search results are mostly harmless and hardly insightful. A search of his name only brings up hockey statistics that I have no interest in and terminology better suited for a truck commercial than a human—grit, edge, horsepower. Who cares how many goals he's scored so far this season? I need to know if he engages in deranged pastimes like hiking or if he knows the difference between *there* and *their*. I need to know what his ex-girlfriends look like, because I bet they all look like they could make a six-figure salary promoting laxative teas on social media.

Not that any of these details matter, but when someone has a Wikipedia page, it's hard to not look.

"I know this wasn't a date, but I still had fun with you," he says.

I stand there nodding at him like an idiot, still trying to summon the courage to invite him back to my place. Neither of us are looking for anything serious. If I have to be his lucky charm, shouldn't I at least be getting a couple of consensual orgasms out of the deal? He scores, I score?

Jaylen slowly turns to leave and I have a realization—or rather I come to my senses and decide that when a beautiful hockey player is standing in front of you asking what you're doing for the rest of the night, you go for it.

"You know what? Fuck it. Want to come back to my place?" It's a very direct question, but it's getting late, and we know each other well enough by now that I don't have to beat around the bush. I mean, he's already done plenty more than that around mine.

Jaylen hardly lets me finish my sentence before he's nodding his head. "Yes," he says eagerly, like he's been holding it on the tip of his tongue.

# SIXTEEN

## Jaylen

Lucy forces open the front door to her apartment, displacing a pile of clunky shoes gathered near the entrance. As expected, her place is as eccentric and interesting as she is. Like trying to fit a sleeping bag back into its sack, her apartment is overflowing: too much stuff and not enough room.

I move a pile of clothes off her couch and make myself comfortable gazing around her place. Abstract colorful artwork lines her walls. The paintings look like the artwork in those *Magic Eye* books; I stare hoping to find the secret image but end up cross-eyed instead. Perched on a bookshelf across the room is a set of taxidermied mice dressed and posed as various anime characters. I don't know if I'm impressed with her collection or creeped out. Half the stuff in here looks acid trip inspired and the other half looks like cursed artifacts. Cabinets bang open and shut as Lucy gets a couple of wineglasses from her kitchen and pours us each a tall glass, finishing off the bottle from the restaurant.

"Nice place," I say, accepting the drink from her hand.

The apartment itself reminds me a bit of the first place I ever rented in New York: exposed brick, cement floors, tiny furniture. Hers is far more cluttered than anything I've ever lived in before. When you live a lifestyle like mine, you learn to consolidate; as a professional hockey player, my life involves a lot of traveling and moving around. I never found the time to fill up all the space I had, at least not the way Lucy fills up a room.

I wiggle into the couch, but I'm too big to get into a good position. I would have preferred to take her back to my place, where I have a California king bed and a fridge full of my favorite foods, but when a pretty girl invites you back to her place, you don't ask too many questions.

"Thanks. I lived with my friend Cooper for years while I waited to get into a low-income apartment. I got lucky and got into one of the nicer ones. Plus, it's close to work," Lucy explains as she dips out of sight into the next room. When she reappears, she's in her underwear, carrying a new pair of pants in her hand. "Do you like your neighborhood?"

I try to keep a straight face while she changes into sweatpants in front of me. I almost forgot about the matching snake tattoos on her hips. "I do. Most of the guys live out in the suburbs, but I prefer the city. It's an easy commute to the rink." I try to look everywhere but at her black lace underwear. I tug at the legs of my pants, discreetly adjusting myself because I'm pretty sure I'm about to get hard. Lucy will probably work herself into a fit of tears laughing at me if she notices.

"And you're close to the best coffee shop in town," she says, plugging her buddy Cooper's café like a good friend.

"Exactly. Hopefully, I'll get a multiyear deal after this season, and I can settle in and buy something. I didn't want to be tied down this year, so I rented." I take a sip of wine. I'm talking a lot—too much.

Lucy angles herself on the couch beside me. Setting my glass on the coffee table, I inch in closer to her, being as bold as to rest my arm along the back of the couch. Her lips have my full attention as she licks the wine off her supple pout. I, too, am desperate to taste its bitterness.

Neither of us are looking for anything serious right now, but that shouldn't stop us from having a bit of fun. We kept it casual before; I'm sure I can do it again. As I start to lean into her, she pulls back and jumps off of the couch.

"Oh!" she says, darting back into the bedroom. I practically fall forward in her absence.

"Is everything okay?"

I hear the frantic opening and shutting of dresser drawers in the distance. "I have something of yours to return to you…if I can find it," she shouts across the apartment.

Intrigued, I get up to walk to her but stop in the doorway of her bedroom, standing there like a vampire waiting to be invited inside. She turns to me and holds out a black silk tie.

"What's that?" I can't hide my intrigue. I'm not one to oppose a fun prop in the bedroom; there's no shame in needing an assist.

"Please don't think I'm weird or anything because I've held on to this, but you left your tie at the hotel after that night we spent together. I guess I kept it as some type of trophy. Not in like a weird serial killer way, but like a fun reminder of a crazy night. It still smells like you." Lucy brings it up to her face and takes a big inhale. She rubs the silk tie against her cheek. "It's so soft too," she coos. She hands the tie over to me, but I refuse it, pulling back instead.

"That's not mine." I burst out laughing.

"Yes, it is. I found it under *your* bed, in *your* hotel room." There is a slight panic in her tone.

"First of all, that's not mine. Second of all, I'm not even sure that's a tie. It looks like some type of bondage strap."

"What!" Lucy shrieks, dropping the mystery strap on the ground in total disgust.

I continue to chuckle at the thought of Lucy holding on to someone's sex strap thinking she was returning a lost tie. I wonder how many times she sniffed it and laugh a bit harder.

"I'm glad you find this funny," she says with a grin as she kicks it away.

"I'm sorry, I'm being mean. It's cute you held on to it." I like the way her cheeks flush with embarrassment, but I like the fact that she thought of me more.

"Really, it's cute? My misfortune is *cute* to you?" She continues to tease me, doing that pouty thing with her bottom lip. She slowly approaches, inching her body closer to me until we're face-to-face.

I nod. I'm not sure I have enough blood left in my brain to form a sentence, but I'm determined to try. "It's cute when you blush," I whisper.

I want her and I can't hold out any longer. I lean in and Lucy's wine-stained lips part. We kiss, agreeing to momentarily forget about our unwillingness to get into serious relationships, because the only thing that matters is this moment.

Lucy pulls me into her room and pushes me down on the bed. She slides on top of my lap and straddles me as we continue to make out. She runs her hands over my pecs and briefly wraps them around my neck. I let out a desperate moan. Taking her ass in my hands, I lift her and flip her onto her back. While standing over her, I pull off my shirt with one tug. Lucy shimmies her tight little shirt up over her head. Her chest is bare, and I stop to admire her from this angle. She looks so good lying there, waiting for me.

She pulls me down on top of her and wraps her legs around my waist. There's no hiding my hard dick from her anymore. I know she can feel how big I am through my pants, because her breathing is becoming more labored as I grind against her. The pressure causes a moan to escape her mouth.

She brings her hand up to quiet herself, but I quickly pin it down to the mattress. "Don't. I like that smart little mouth. I want to hear it say my name." The wine from dinner is making me cockier than normal. Despite running my mouth like

I'm in control, my body is shaking over her. Like I'm going through withdrawal, I need her now.

"Then make me." Her lips part and we continue to kiss passionately, tangled up together half naked. I run my hands down her stomach, and as I start to slide my hand down the front of her pants, I hear it.

I stop what I'm doing. "Wait, wait, wait," I say, sitting up to focus on the sound. It's a wet noise, but somehow also sounds like dry grinding. It projects through the entire room.

"Already?" Lucy sighs.

"No, don't worry," I say, with a cocky smile. "What's that noise?" I look around the dark room. The light from the table lamp beside us is just bright enough to illuminate all four corners in an ominous shadow, but I can't see anything out of the ordinary.

Lucy props herself up on her elbows and looks around with me. "Oh, it's just Sailor grooming herself," Lucy says, undisturbed. With her arms wrapped around my neck, she kisses my mouth.

I kiss back momentarily, until the noise becomes even louder, and my attention is once again disrupted. "It sounds like someone's sanding wood in here. Seriously, it's so loud. Are we on top of her?" I roll off Lucy and begin to search for her cat. I lean over the side and peer under her bed, but there's no cat in sight.

"Don't you think you're concerned with the wrong pussy?" she asks, joining in on the search.

"It sounds like an ASMR slime video in here. That can't be healthy. What if she needs medical attention?" I continue to look around her room, checking under a dresser and desk.

"She's fine. She's up there." Lucy points to the five-story cat tower looming in the corner of her bedroom.

My eyes follow the tower up to the top floor, where Sailor is perched, shamelessly cleaning her butthole at a vigorous pace.

"Wow." I jump back. This is the first time I've ever made

eye contact with an animal grooming themselves. The entire situation is made worse by my throbbing boner. "I'm not sure I can keep going with her looming over us like that. She's really going at that thing. It's physically hard to look away." I stare unwillingly. I rub my eyes to break the trance.

"Sure, twenty thousand fans is nothing, but you can't perform in front of one cat." Lucy grabs my forearm and brings me back on the bed next to her.

"I'm used to scoring under pressure. I'm not used to seeing a cat's butthole that close up."

I didn't want to be rude when Lucy suggested going back to her place, but now I'm wishing I was. I'm trying to be nice—out of fear I will be labeled a cat hater, which is most definitely a deal-breaker for her. I don't hate cats, but I would prefer they didn't watch me have sex.

"Fine." Lucy rolls her eyes before getting up to guide Sailor off the tower and across the floor. "Sailor, shoo."

We pick up where we left off, but before I can even get on top of Lucy—Sailor strikes again. Croaking replaces the momentary silence. Lucy tries to kiss me, but I can't ignore it; Sailor is definitely having a medical emergency now.

"Is she okay? The cat sounds like she's dying an actual death," I say.

"She's being dramatic. It's probably a hair ball."

Lucy starts kissing my neck, but out of the corner of my eye, I see the cat's back arch, the way I hoped Lucy's would tonight. Instantly, I know something bad is coming.

Vomit.

I can no longer hide the disgust on my face as I watch in terror. After getting it all out of her system, Sailor leaps back up her tower and curls up into a tight ball and settles to sleep.

"Really, Jaylen? I watched one of your little hockey games last week and saw a man stop a puck with his face, pick his tooth up off the ice, get ten stitches on the bench, and play the next shift. Someone had to come out with a shovel and scoop up all the bloody ice. And if that's what's happening in front of everyone, then what type of barbaric things are happening behind closed locker room doors," Lucy says shrilly, still laid out on her bed topless.

I love it when she antagonizes me, but I'm too distracted to pay attention to her this time. I take a big whiff. "Can you smell that?" It's rancid. I can't even focus on how hot Lucy looks because the room is filled with the vile smell of bile.

"You've never had a cat, have you?" Her arms are now crossed over her chest, covering herself.

"No, thank god." The words slip out of my mouth before I can filter them. "Wait," I say, hearing myself, but the damage is done. Lucy pulls herself away from me without saying anything. "That came out wrong." I try to salvage the moment.

"Don't worry about it. I get it. It was gross," she says, head hung.

I feel terrible for what I said, and even worse because now Lucy clearly feels awkward around me. I reach down, grab her shirt off the floor, and hand it to her. She snatches it from me and quickly covers herself. I rub my hands over my face. I want to scream into them, but I don't want to make her even more uncomfortable.

"Should I go?" I ask, bracing myself for her response.

"Yeah, I've got stuff to do tonight." She sits—fully dressed and cross-legged on her bed—picking at her nails.

"Text me the details for the charity event and let me know what game you want tickets to. I'll make sure you get good seats," I say, sitting on the edge of her bed, trying to give her space. I grab my shirt off the floor and pull it over my head.

"Sounds good. I'll text you good luck." Lucy still won't look up at me. "I should work on some sketches now," she adds, turning to grab some art supplies off her nightstand.

"Okay. Have a good night." I get off the bed and practically bolt for the door. I've never felt so stupid, not even the time I fumbled on a penalty shot and cost my team the win. I worked so hard to get this far with her, and now thanks to a stupid slip of the tongue, I'm right back at square one with Lucy.

# SEVENTEEN

## Lucy

JAYLEN:

Hey Lucy! Did you see it's a full moon tonight? I don't really know what that means but seems like something witchy you'd be into.

Not that you're witchy.

At least not in a bad way.

Hello?

LUCY:

JAYLEN:

My phone vibrates against my leg, as it has done periodically for the past few weeks. I ignore it and continue organizing a supply closet at the back of the tattoo shop. I feel it buzz again and decide it's time for a break. As I suspected, it's Jaylen—again.

I've been dodging his texts since that awkward night I was left cleaning cat barf off my bedroom floor alone. I've since spent most of my nights falling asleep face-first in my sketchbook with the lights on. Jaylen's been trying to strike up a conversation, but all I give him is our agreed-upon "good luck" text before games.

My initial reaction that night as I cleaned on all fours was to block his number and pretend none of it ever happened. However, my friends already know about the charity appearance and the free tickets, and unlike Jaylen in the bedroom, I don't disappoint.

I open the text and ignore the funny video he sent, as I have the last three videos from him. Instead, I fulfill my contract by telling him, "Knock dead."

It's read the moment I send it and he's typing before I can swipe out of the conversation.

JAYLEN:

> I think you mean knock them dead lol.

LUCY:

> nope

JAYLEN:

> I'm cool with a classic "good luck."

LUCY:

> i'm sure you're cool with whatever as long as it doesn't purr

JAYLEN:

IT WAS THE VOMIT THAT
FREAKED ME OUT! It's a real
thing. It's called emetophobia.

LUCY:

well good luck with that

I put my phone on Do Not Disturb and stash it in my pocket.
It briefly crosses my mind that all the funny videos he's been
sending me are a reference to our first night together—when
I confessed to him that I never watch the funny videos friends
send me—but I can't be sure that version of Jaylen still exists.

The only version of him I see is on the promotional team
photos scattered all over downtown, reminding me he's an
NHL player and our tentative friendship is contractual so he
can play well. I pass a fifty-foot Jaylen on my walk to work
every day and fight the impulse to vandalize it by sharing his
phone number. I fantasize about writing something like "For
a good time, call 555-0100" as a form of payback for what he
said about my cat.

Once I make it past the oversize Jaylen shrine, I have to walk
through a street lined with Rainiers flags. I've been trying to
get him off my mind, but the city, the team, won't let me forget.

I pick myself up off the supply closet floor with a groan. It's
weird being back in the tattoo shop full-time again. I was excited to get back to what mattered most, but I still think about
the mural. I would rather be painting at the rink than what I
did at the shop today: unclogging a toilet, buying two different
lunch entrées from two different restaurants for Sam, and replying to a backlog of emails. The only thing that keeps me moti-
vated at this job is knowing it's not going to be like this forever.

Sam's finishing up her last tattoo of the day, which gives me a bit of time before I have to start sweeping the floors and closing up shop. With a rush of determination equal parts frustration and impulse, I stop by Sam's booth and hover over her as she shades a rose on her client's ankle.

"Looks amazing," I say, announcing myself. Sam's had my portfolio for a while now and every day I show up to work eager and ready to hear her feedback. She has yet to say a word about it.

"Get me some more paper towels, will ya," she says.

I take my time ripping off fresh sheets of paper towel, slowly stacking the sheets neatly on her tray. "I drew a couple roses in my portfolio, but I love your interpretation. Speaking of which, have you had a chance to look through it yet?"

She sighs. Loud enough I can hear it over the buzzing tattoo gun and long enough for me to know I've overstepped. "Not yet. I've been busy, but don't let me stop you from taking it back and working on it some more. It's over there." She motions with her free hand toward the workbench behind her.

The binder I gave her is buried under loose sheets of scrap paper and restaurant napkins. There's a coffee stain on the front—a perfect circle, just like some of the geomatic designs I drew inside. I dig it out of the junk and clutch it to my chest. Maybe next month she'll have time to look through it, but until then, it's staying with me, where it's appreciated. I swallow my emotions. Now is not the time for a mental breakdown. I'll do that later in the safety of my bedroom with the company of a grocery store sheet cake.

Sam doesn't notice, but I slip away and head to the front desk, where I'm sure a handful of new tattoo appointment requests awaits.

While checking our latest Instagram DMs, I notice that the shop is tagged in a new post. It's a picture of a guy with shaggy brown hair and a proud wide smile on his face. The caption reads, "Can't wait to start my apprenticeship with Sam at Come

As You Are Ink next week. I guess hard work really does pay off."

My hands go slack, and the work tablet falls to the floor.

Sam pulls her attention away from her client's leg. "Careful!" she snaps at me. "If you break that, it's coming out of your pay-check."

Just once I'd like to not feel like an inconvenience to every-one. I could easily run out of the shop in tears, but instead, I clear my throat and gather my composure the best I can. "My bad." I hardly get the words out.

I'm so pissed I could cry, which is frustrating because I wish I could confront Sam and tell her off, but if I open my mouth, I know I'll begin to sob. Instead, I bite my tongue like I'm sitting across from Grandma at Thanksgiving dinner and she just called me a homophobic slur. *She'll die soon*, I remind my-self. And while Sam's life expectancy is much longer than my meemaw's, she is already officially dead to me.

"Don't forget to clean the bathrooms before you lock up to-night" is the last thing Sam says to me before leaving for the night.

As soon as the door swings shut behind her, I start googling tattoo apprenticeships. It's a deep dive into local artists and shops. I reach out to a handful of them asking if they have any employment opportunities or upcoming apprenticeships. I skip Lucky Thirteen—for obvious reasons—but keep hunting for something good.

Eventually, I find a nationwide search for a paid apprentice-ship with one of my favorite tattoo artists, Hunter Gunn. Her work has been featured in *Ink Magazine* for years, and some of her clients include celebrities and musicians. It's a long shot since I don't have tattooing experience, but I'm desperate enough to apply. The apprenticeship would take me out of state, a factor I'm not too worried about since I likely won't get the job. The deadline is approaching, and they want an impressive portfolio—

I'll have to add even more art to my existing binder of work. I forward the information to my email, clear the computer's search history, and log out for the night.

Usually, I'm the one getting fired from a job, but tonight feels like the perfect opportunity for a first. I grab some of the leftover paint from the closet and drag it out front near the entrance. With paintbrushes and a step stool in hand, I get to work expressing myself the only way I know how.

Bikini Kill blares over the sound system as I slap paint on the shop's wall. The timid approach I used for my last mural is replaced with an assertiveness that satisfies not only my creative cravings, but also my need for revenge.

My focus is so consumed by my art that I don't notice the door open. It isn't until I hear someone loudly and intentionally clear their throat that I finally turn around.

I shriek in terror as the presence of an unexpected guest shocks my body into fight or flight. My body picks flight, and I drop my wash brush. I freeze up while my brain tries to process who sneaked up on me. It's Jaylen—it's always Jaylen.

He's wearing a nice suit and a big smile. His shirt is unbuttoned two buttons deep, which I notice immediately, because it is an incredibly slutty thing to do. Forcing myself to not stare at his plunging neckline, I turn to shut off the music so I can yell at him.

"What is wrong with you?" I say, gasping for air as I bend down and grab my brush off the floor. I might need it handy to fend him off. Only a stalker would show up to someone's place of work unannounced dressed like Patrick Bateman. I thought ignoring his texts was a clear enough message, but obviously Jaylen is more brawn than brains.

"The door was unlocked. The sign says Open."

The Open sign's neon glow is visible from where I stand. I always forget to turn that sign off at night.

"We're closed now. If you're looking for a tattoo, you'll have to come back tomorrow," I say in my most authoritative voice, though it's still shaky from the fright.

Using what was left of the paint from my project for the Rainiers, I have created a beautiful yet vulgar mural articulating the words I could never say: an unfaced person slumped over with multiple knives sticking out of their hunched back.

Jaylen reads aloud, "Beware of backstabbers."

It's written in my clearest and most legible penmanship.

"Won't you get fired for this?" he asks.

"That's the point. I'm quitting." I stand proudly by my work.

"Remind me never to break up with you." His comment breaks the tension in the room, and even earns a laugh out of me.

"I know it's a bit abstract, but I think the intended audience will get the message." I made sure to outline my work with black paint so it's harder to cover up. Sam is always harping on about the importance of a solid black outline.

"It's beautiful," he says softly. "A bit unhinged, but beautiful."

"I'd love to stand here and discuss the motives behind the short brushstrokes and my use of the color red, but I was just leaving for the night." I begin to tidy up the paint, but quickly stop when I remember that it's no longer my problem.

"I get it. I won't take up too much of your time. Please hear me out. I was driving home from my game tonight and I was craving pizza. Apparently one of the best spots in town is right across the street from here. Anyway, I got you a slice." He hands me a paper bag stained with grease.

Jaylen is extending an olive branch—well, a pizza slice—and I'm hungry enough to accept it. "Thanks. It's obviously been a long day and I'm hungry."

We grab a seat together on the weathered couch near the front desk. "Cool shop, but I think I like your addition the best," he says, before sinking his teeth into his slice.

"Me too." I lean back on the couch. Revenge art is exhausting.

"Pizza isn't the only reason I'm here. I want to make sure things aren't awkward between us. Last time I saw you, things got weird." He sighs, setting his drink down on the coffee table, swallowing his pride along with a gulp of soda.

My shoulders drop and so does my guard as I release my breath. "It's fine. I probably shouldn't have invited you back to my place in the first place anyway."

The following game after the cat barf incident—for obvious reasons—I wasn't in the mood to text Jaylen good luck. Apparently, texting "gl" doesn't count as a proper good-luck message because he was "held scoreless" in his hockey game against the worst team in the league. I know this because it ended some goal streak he had going for himself. He still had a couple assists, but it really reinforced my concern that getting involved could jeopardize my good-luck mojo and the delicate balance of our agreement. I haven't missed a proper good luck since.

"Why's that?" Jaylen's body angles back. He fusses with the cuffs of his sleeves.

"You're not looking to date, remember? Plus, I really need to focus on my career. Now more than ever since I'm officially unemployed." I hear myself and panic instantly sets in. "Oh my god, I'm unemployed! I'm so fucked." I pull my knees into my chest and bury my head into my lap.

"Don't worry. Someone once told me when you have nothing left to lose, you can finally see what you want." Jaylen pats my back.

"That's horrible advice, Jaylen! I have no income. I only said that to you because I didn't know what else to say," I snap.

"You'll figure it out. You're feisty."

"Thanks, I'll be sure to put that on my résumé." I wallow for a moment, until I remember my plan. I pop my head up. "Actually, there's this apprenticeship search. It's my dream job. I think I'm going to apply. Maybe you can write me a fake recommendation letter since I don't think Sam will write me a glowing review anymore."

While I'm worrying about my future, Jaylen has rolled up the sleeves of his dress shirt, exposing his vascular, thick forearms. Sexy in a time of crisis like this? This man has no shame; he might as well whip his dick out.

"Would a tattoo help your odds of getting the apprenticeship?" Jaylen finishes what's left of his drink and tosses it across the room into the recycling bin. It's a perfect shot.

"Won't hurt. Who did you convince? Soko?" I toss my empty can but miss terribly.

"No."

"No? Jaylen, that was part of the deal." I can't hide the frustration in my voice. I was already stressed to begin with. I need all the help I can get if I'm going to send my application to Hunter Gunn.

"Let me finish," Jaylen says, rolling his eyes. "He said no—technically, he said something in Russian that sounded rather threatening, so I didn't press it. What if you do it on me?"

I'm up and out of my seat before he finishes getting the words out. I've been around the shop long enough to know that when someone makes the impulsive decision to get tattooed, you better get moving before they change their mind.

"Where are you going?" he asks as I buzz around the shop to set up.

With cling wrap in my hand, I briefly pause long enough to say, "Setting up for your tattoo."

# EIGHTEEN

## Jaylen

While Lucy gleefully sets up her station, I wipe my clammy hands against the thighs of my pants. Suddenly the pizza is sitting like a brick in the pit of my stomach. I have half a mind to run out of that tattoo shop while her back is turned. She's wearing those clunky boots again—I could easily outrun her.

Running from Lucy isn't nearly as appealing as running to her, so I stay. Soko seemed a bit more interested in getting tattooed when I told him the tattooed girl who painted the mural was doing it. I could have pressed him on it. I could call him right now and ask him to come by the shop; I bet him and Lamber have a few drinks in them and would be down to get his-and-his permanent mementos. You'd be surprised how many hockey players share secret tattoos with their teammates.

I don't move. Instead, I quietly watch her as she works. My confidence in my decision to do this for her grows with her widening smile. When I got here, she was on the verge of tears. I want to be the one who cheers her up. Best-case scenario, I redeem myself for my jackass behavior back at her place. Worst-case, I get a laser tattoo removal sponsorship deal next week.

Lucy flips open her tablet, stylus in hand, and looks to me.

"What are we thinking?" she says, taking the end of the stylus between her teeth.

I creep closer to her workstation. "Something small." My voice is soft. I grind my teeth together. The room feels like a sauna—stuffier than when I first got here.

"Location?"

"Somewhere that doesn't hurt." I gulp.

Lucy drops her tablet and pen down on the padded reclining chair. "You have no idea what you want? Something cool? Something meaningful? Something funny?"

I shake my head as I crack my knuckles. "Something easy?"

As someone who suffers from trypanophobia, this is a thought I actively avoid. I've got some friends with hockey-related tattoos, but that's so cliché and corny. I try to think of something meaningful. Something discreet that isn't too obvious. What comes to mind brings a soft smile to my tense face.

"Could I get the initials *CB*?"

She nods enthusiastically. "Lettering is one of the basics. This will be great for my portfolio." Lucy's attention drops to her tablet as she traces out a few different fonts and designs.

CB is an inside joke; it was what we called Cam. "Cheddar Bomb" was his nickname because when he was a little kid, his hair was the color of Cheetos and every now and then he would blast an absolute bomb from the point and score. It seemed like the funniest nickname at the time. That was back when we were annoying boys together—terrorizing skaters at the Ice Skating Ribbon, filling up on Costco samples after Sunday practice, and keeping hotel guests up with lively ministick games. I take a blue Sharpie to every fresh white tape job and write CB on the end of my stick before each game. I look down at his initials as the anthem ends and I touch them on the bench after every goal.

I try to play for Cam, but I haven't always been great at honoring him. I keep hoping I can play well enough to quiet the part of me that feels guilty for abandoning him. When I score, I hold myself back from pleading to the rafters rationalizing my past decision. *See! It was worth it. I had to focus on hockey so I could become who I am today—who they all needed me to be.* People don't know about that superstition. Lots of guys write things on their sticks; no one's ever asked about "CB."

Lucy shows me her designs and I impulsively pick the Old English font because it looks the coolest. While she sizes it, I worry I've picked the most intricate design.

"You should pick a place that won't interfere with any future sleeves or chest pieces." Lucy uses her best customer service voice. I've never seen such patience from her.

"I'm not too worried about that. This will be my first and last tattoo," I say. "Um, right here is fine." I point to the fleshy space on my ribs, right below my pec. Lucy gives me the nod of approval on her way to the back room. Glancing over at her workstation, I see the tattoo gun and feel faint. I grab on to the chair for support.

"Take off your shirt," she says, reemerging with a thin piece of paper rustling in her hand.

"Aren't you supposed to buy me dinner first," I say anxiously, struggling to get my buttons undone. I feel wobbly on my feet, like my first time on skates.

"We just ate. You're not nervous, are you? I thought they called you relentless." She cuts out the stencil.

I gather my composure, if only for a moment. Shirtless, I lean into her. "I've had my broken nose reset on the bench. I've been stitched up between shifts. I've been punched and hit back twice as hard. You've never met someone as relentless as me."

I don't move. Lucy's mouth parts slightly as she looks up at me from her chair. She smells so good I could kiss her, and she's close enough I could reach.

"All right, tough guy. Get in my chair." Lucy bites her lip

as she motions me to the recliner. I love it when she tells me what to do.

When I hear the buzz of the tattoo gun, all the bravado I mustered up disappears. I do my best to not faint, or worse, pull a Sailor and yack all over Lucy. I keep telling myself that it can't be worse than eating a puck. I tuck my hands under my thighs, willing myself to stop shaking. Hopefully by lying on them I won't be able to yank the tattoo gun out of her hand when it comes near me.

"Ready?" she says, bracing herself with one hand on my stomach and the other cocked and ready with the tattoo gun.

I let out a long exhale. "Yes." I press my eyes shut.

I was, in fact, not ready. As Lucy lowers her gun toward my skin, I begin screaming in agony. The piercing cry of someone being murdered—or worse, someone stubbing their pinkie toe on the coffee table—fills the room.

The loud noise startles Lucy and she jumps back. "I haven't even started." She laughs. "Are you sure about this?" Her tone is sympathetic as she rests her hand on my forearm.

"Not even a little bit, but I scored my first hat trick in four years tonight so let's get this over with."

I let out a nervous cackle as the tattoo gun buzzes again. I'm sure to keep my eyes straight ahead and white-knuckle the entire thing.

When she's done, Lucy passes me a handheld mirror so I can take a look. The tattoo is amazing. It's only two letters, but she did them perfectly. Her touch was much softer than I expected, though it is still my first and last tattoo.

"It looks great," I say, handing back the mirror.

She tilts her head to the side and gives it another wipe clean with paper towel. "Yeah, not bad for my first tattoo," she says.

"First!" I'm too lightheaded to be getting worked up like

this again. I lean back in my chair while she preps gauze and bandage tape.

"Those your mom's initials or something?" she asks. I fumble over my words trying to come up with an excuse. Spinning away from me, she adds, "Forget I asked. You're not obligated to tell your artist the deeper meaning behind your tattoos." She peels off her black gloves with a snap and tosses them into the trash.

"I don't like to talk about it, so thanks for understanding."

I feel bad lying to her, but I'm not ready to tell her about Cam—not so soon after finally getting back on her good side. She's so naturally confident; I don't want her to know how much of my confidence I have to fake.

I grab Lucy's wrist before she can pull away from me. Maybe it's the adrenaline coursing through my entire body, or her cold hand against my hot skin for the past twenty minutes—whatever it is, I need to get something off my chest and I'm not leaving until I say what I came here to say.

"I'm sorry for what I did back at your place. I was a dick to you and your cat. You've been extremely helpful and accommodating to me with all these good-luck texts, and you didn't deserve how I treated you—you both didn't deserve it." My eye contact does not waver. I don't stutter a word.

"Sailor kind of deserved it. But I appreciate that." Lucy cups my cheek with her free hand. Her cold palm feels refreshing against my flushed skin. I want to close my eyes and sink into it like the cold side of a pillowcase and fall asleep.

"Are we cool?" I ask, looking up at her.

"Yeah, we're cool." She gives me three playful smacks on my cheek, awakening me from my daydream. She grabs her phone off the desk behind her. "As long as you let me take a few pictures of your new ink for my portfolio of course."

# NINETEEN

## Jaylen

The dressing room is buzzing after practice. The team is on a hot streak, which means the mood is light. We currently sit second in the conference heading into Christmas break. If we can hold on to this lead through the rest of the year, we'll be in good shape to secure a playoff spot.

Everyone is chatty today, still riding the high of last night's win over our division rivals. We're all chirping each other as we shed our sweaty gear.

"Hey, whatever happened to that chick who was painting the mural? The one who took a puck to the face like a champ," Lamber asks. He tosses his jersey into the laundry tub parked in the middle of our locker room.

"She finished it, dummy," Soko says, throwing his jersey on top of Lamber's head. Lamber rips it off his face and throws it right back at him.

I pretend I'm not listening, but the second I hear them mention the mural, I'm eavesdropping. My palms begin to prickle beneath the damp leather of my gloves when the guys mention Lucy. I take the gloves off and shove them into the top shelf of my locker, but my hands still feel hot. I act indifferent to the conversation as I face my stall and continue taking off the rest of my hockey gear.

"I know, but did none of us get her number? She was hot," Lamber shouts across the room for everyone to hear.

There's no way Lucy would ever go for a guy like Lamber, loud and immature—or would she? I grit my teeth together and repress the jealousy I have no authority to feel.

"JJ did," Wells says. I feel his hand pat me on the back as he passes by on his way to dump his jersey into the laundry basket.

"Shut up," I say to him through my teeth. I keep my voice low because if the other guys hear me, they might think I'm trying to hide something. I just don't think it's cool to talk about her behind her back. I usually stay out of this type of locker room talk; I don't want to be in the middle of it.

"JJ's got a girl?" Lamber says with much delight. His expression is even more animated than when he gets one past the goal line.

"No way. I thought you were one of those guys who's all hockey, no fun." Now Soko is joining in on the action.

They both inch closer to me, as if there's more of the story to share. Like I'm going to tell them all the dirty details of our wild night together or hand out her phone number like a referral. I would never do that. I didn't even want to tell them that I know her, because then I would have to explain our relationship. If you would even call it that. If anything, she's like a coworker.

"Hockey *is* fun," I say, hoping they drop it.

"Yeah, when you're leading the league in points. You going to bring her around here? Get her and her hot friends some tickets?" Lamber shoots me a pervy grin. He's not letting this go. He's right beside my stall, standing inches away from me with Soko close behind him. We're all down to our gitch and should be stripping down to hit the showers, but they're blocking my way.

"Your new tattoo! Those her initials? Must be serious," Soko says, his nose scrunched from laughing.

"Is it Instagram official though? Nothing is more serious than making a relationship public on social media," Lamber says to Soko as the two discuss the varying levels of commitment.

"She's not my girl," I say in my most convincing voice.

"Right, she texts you before every game to wish you good luck because she hates you," Wells says from his stall a few spaces down from me. "Hannah used to do that for me when we first started dating. Now all I get are texts asking me to pick things up on my way home from the rink." He looks down at his phone and flips it around to flash us the screen. "Looks like we're all out of milk and Goldfish."

This is why Wells is always the last one out of the locker room; he would be quicker if he'd shut up and mind his own business.

"Really, Wells? It's a superstitious thing. She texts me good luck, and I play lights out. That's it." I only give them enough of the story to get them off my back.

"*Tabarnak*, give me her number—I could use a little luck. I bet I would score a hat trick if she sucked me off," Lamber says. He and Soko burst into a fit of laughter. Like two juvenile pre-teens, they giggle, knocking into each other like bumper cars.

I don't get the humor—I see red. Like watching my linemate get hit from behind, I don't even pause to think; I jump to her defense. I grab Lamber by the collar of his undershirt and pull him toward me. With a cocked fist and snarl, I threaten, "Say some shit like that again, Lamber, and I'll break your fucking jaw."

Lamber throws his hands up and his body goes limp. A bead of sweat drops down his temple. He stumbles over his words. His French accent is thick as he tries to remember the right English words to say. "Whoa, sorry, JJ. It was a dumb thing to say. I take it back."

"You good, bro?" Wells is quickly at my side. I see him eye-ing my fist and realize that it's still cocked.

I slowly release the tension in my knuckles. "I'm good," I say, letting Lamber go. He and Soko find their stalls and finish getting undressed without another word about Lucy.

I sit down and give myself a moment to calm my adrenaline. *What the fuck was that?* I never lose my cool, at least not off the ice. I have to stop thinking about what Lamber said about her or else I'll never get my heart rate down. I take a few breaths, but it's still racing.

I haven't felt this out of control all season. It's scary how fa-miliar it feels. This is how I used to get during hockey games when I couldn't hit the net, when I couldn't get my legs to move fast enough to keep up with the play. This is how I felt when I used to suck at hockey.

Coach Pete pops his head into the locker room, and every-one goes silent. He points to me and motions me into his of-fice. The boys make a mocking "oooh" call as if I've been summoned to the principal's office.

I pull on a hoodie and slip into my shower slides. I stall a bit while I try to calm myself down, but what Lamber said still rings in my head. I tuck my hands in the front pocket of my hoodie. *Great.* Now I'm about to get in trouble for what he started, and because I'm a good teammate I'm going to take it on the chin.

I pause before opening the door. The last time I was called into an office was when Coach Pete and the general manager told me I didn't make the team. I might be on a real rip this sea-son, but the memory remains. I take one last deep breath and hope for the best.

"Hey, Pete," I say timidly, easing into his office.

"Grab a seat." He motions toward the chair in front of his desk. "We should talk." He spins away from his laptop to face me.

"It won't happen again. I let my emotions get the best of me," I say before he has a chance to bring it up. Ever since I bailed on Cam's funeral, I've been trying to get better about taking accountability for my actions. I shouldn't have gotten physical with Lamber today and I know that.

"It better happen again. You scored the game-winning goal last night and had a monstrous hit in the first period that set the tone for the whole game." The same big smile I saw on his face after my hit last night makes an appearance.

I relax a bit. "Thanks, it was a nice hit." I take my hands out of my pockets and rest them on the chair's arms. It's been a while since a meeting with the coach has gone this well; usually, they're asking what the hell is wrong with me.

"No, thank *you*—you're making me look good out there. Which is why I called you in here today. As you know, Benny got traded last week, which means I need to appoint someone as the assistant captain. You haven't been on this team long, but the boys already really look up to you. You're relentless out there every night." Coach Pete reaches under his desk and pulls out my jersey with a newly affixed *A* on the chest. "The *A* is yours," he says, handing it over to me.

I run my fingers over the patch. "I don't know what to say." I wore the *A* briefly during my second year in New York but had it taken away when I stopped producing nightly highlight reel content. It's an added pressure to carry around on the ice, but I feel strong enough this season that I might be able to handle the weight. Plus, with my good-luck charm I can't lose.

"Don't say anything. Keep playing well. I mean it. Don't change a single thing you're doing. I know you want something long-term next season, so keep it up and you'll be getting a lot more than an *A*." Pete shakes my hand, and I get out of there so I can shower up and head home. He told me not to change a single thing, and I don't plan on it.

# TWENTY

## Lucy

JAYLEN:

This hotel has mini Kiehl's shampoos and conditioners in the bathroom.

LUCY:

steal them for me

JAYLEN:

Ok, but it's going to cost you...

LUCY:

good luck

JAYLEN:

Not sure that's good enough. There's a bodywash too.

LUCY:

best wishes? bon chance?
fingers crossed? you were
made for this?

JAYLEN:

Damn. That last one got me a
little hard.

LUCY:

lol loser

Whoever says women take too long getting ready has never met a hockey player. Jaylen's post-practice shower ran longer than anticipated and now I'm darting across busy streets to the sound of rage-induced honking with Jaylen in tow. We need to hurry up or we're going to be late for the start of Maya's charity event.

"Maya and Cooper." I slowly articulate and enunciate each syllable up to a seemingly unfazed Jaylen.

"Lucy, I got this. I'm not going to forget your best friends' names. Maya the Bee and Mini Cooper," Jaylen says.

I stop walking. Grabbing his arm, I pull him back so I can get to the bottom of whatever he thinks he's doing. "I said no nicknames." There's no way I'm going to let him give my friends some weird, impersonal nicknames that he thinks are funny.

We come to a halt as I interrogate him on the sidewalk. I continue to hold up my end of the bargain: following his hockey schedule like a season ticket holder so I can text him good luck. This is part of our agreement. He needs to be on his A-game. These aren't some professional hockey players he's facing off against today; they're my queer besties. If he thought the internet hated him for an own goal, wait until he sees Maya's reaction when he inevitably forgets her name.

"It's a trick for remembering names. Maya the Bee like the cartoon and Mini Cooper like the car," he explains.

At least he's trying. "Good idea, but it's Maya like Maya Angelou."

"You're right. That's way better. You're good at this," he says. He thinks he's complimenting my word association skills, but Maya is, in fact, named after Maya Angelou. With no time to explain, I continue to pull Jaylen toward the entrance of the event.

The streets are lined with canopies for local vendors who are getting ready to open up shop to the public. I can already smell the various food trucks parked inside. Sound check for today's live music is heard from the sidewalk. Rain-or-shine Seattleites are outdoors. Luckily today, the sun peeks through thick, rolling gray clouds. The rays shine down on the slick pavement, enhancing its glare. I use my hand to guard my eyes as I search for my friends.

The streets are already filling up, and I'm anxious to get in and get this official introduction over with. I'm more nervous than I should be, but it feels like I'm about to introduce them to a partner. Only somehow, it's even worse because we aren't dating.

The sooner we get this over with, the better. Eventually the hockey season will end and Jaylen will be nothing more than a footnote in the deep lore of my friendship with Maya and Cooper. Like the many who have come before him, someday Jaylen will be referred to as a descriptive yet mildly offensive nickname like Sandals Guy or LARP Girl.

"Love the spirit here. I gotta say you guys really know how to rep your colors," Jaylen remarks as we pass an assortment of flags and rainbow coloring proudly plastered as far as the eye can see.

It dawns on me that I haven't told Jaylen what charity this event benefits. All he knew was that he had to show up, and luckily he's here with a smile on his face. "Yes, the gays are a rather powerful fandom—just don't say anything negative about boygenius."

"Never heard of him." He laughs at himself. I can't hide my disgust at the confusion. "Kidding. I love Phoebe Bridgers. Sometimes you have to have a good cry in your car on the drive home after a big loss," he adds shamelessly.

"Lean into that and you'll do fine here." I pat him on the back and usher him across the sidewalk.

"Lucy!" Cooper shouts. He's standing with Maya under a white canopy marked Information near the entrance. Maya is talking into a handheld radio while juggling a worn clipboard in her other hand. We make our way over to them.

"I don't care if they recently broke up. I'm not moving anyone's tent. They will have to be civil for one afternoon and work side by side," Maya shouts into her walkie-talkie.

"I understand, but the vendor is saying her ex took their dog in the breakup and is no longer allowing visitations," a stressed voice broadcasts from the handheld device for everyone to hear.

Maya pauses momentarily with pursed lips and pinched eyebrows. "Move that son of a bitch next to the porta potties." She clips the walkie-talkie back on her belt loop. "Lucy!" Her mood flips as she greets me enthusiastically with a hug.

"Everything looks amazing!" I say with my head on a swivel. Maya has been working tirelessly on this Seattle Pride fundraiser for months and it shows.

Cooper loudly clears his throat as he eyes Jaylen up and down.

"Oh, right. Guys, this is Jaylen." I formally introduce Maya and Cooper, offering Jaylen a lifeline, but apparently he doesn't need it.

"Maya, it's great to officially meet you." He reaches to shake her hand. "And, Cooper, my favorite baristo," he continues, enthusiastically shaking Cooper's hand.

Cooper blushes, smitten at the fact that Jaylen remembers

his name. A reaction that triggers a hip pop and head shaking from Maya.

"Oh god, was that a pronoun joke?" I groan, annoyed by Jaylen's over-the-top display of charisma. Cooper shoots me a glare before returning to Jaylen all smiles.

"Such large hands, Jaylen. You know what they say about large hands," Cooper says, still holding Jaylen's hand hostage in his grip.

"Big gloves," Jaylen says.

Cooper laughs, but Maya is not so easily charmed.

"So, Jaylen, what time and place were you born?" Maya fishes for his signs.

"Don't answer that," I blurt out. Wikipedia already told me he's a Capricorn, and I'm trying my best to not let that dictate my feelings toward him.

"Hmm, I'm not sure. I'll have to ask my mom," he says politely.

"Lucy, you're practically glowing. Are you doing anyone? I mean, are you doing anything different to your skin?" Cooper says, with a mischievous grin.

I narrow my eyes at him. "It's sweat from the run over here," I say. Cooper is obsessed with my unique friendship with Jaylen, but I'm not going to let his innuendos trip me up today.

"Really? It's not from a recent facial? Perhaps a new serum you're using?" Cooper is not letting up, but it's better than another bust joke.

"Nope, but recently I have been dedicated to self-fulfillment. You know, tending to myself lately." While Cooper and I go back and forth, Jaylen looks confused.

"Ugh, you guys are gross," Maya interrupts. "I hate to be rude and break up this stimulating conversation, but I should go do a lap and make sure no other vendors are mid–custody battle."

"Is there anything I can help you with? I have time before my autograph booth," Jaylen politely offers to Maya.

I see Cooper out of the corner of my eye winding up to tell Jaylen he needs help with something inappropriate.

Maya slowly lowers her yellow-tinted shades down the bridge of her nose. "You want to help?" she asks in disbelief, looking him up and down.

Most people only ask to help because it's the polite thing to do, but if there's one thing I know about Jaylen, it's that he's keen to lend a helping hand. It's both his best and most obnoxious quality.

"Of course. I've always been really passionate about…" Jaylen leans to the side to read the large sign hanging above one of the nearby vendor's tents. "Lesbian farmers," he says.

"Really? You're not here to take pictures and sign autographs and feel good about yourself?" Maya presses him, but Jaylen doesn't crack. She slips her glasses back up her nose with the push of a finger and quickly skims her clipboard, in search, I'm sure, of the most humbling task to assign him.

"I'm here to help out with whatever you need. Is there anything heavy you need lifted or moved?" Jaylen immediately offers up his brawn, pushing up the sleeves of his jacket.

"No. There are a bunch of lesbian farmers here. No offense, but they could sling you into a hayloft with one hand like a minibale."

"I am not offended because I don't know what that means," Jaylen says gleefully.

"Fine. Come with me. I need help hanging vinyl promotional signage, and I could use your height." Maya pivots on the heels of her worn Blundstone boots and disappears into the sea of vendors. Jaylen quickly follows her like her dutiful student.

I watch as he disappears behind a row of vendor tents. That introduction went better than I expected. He might actually leave here having won over both my friends, a feat few men accomplish. With Maya and Jaylen gone, Cooper and I take time to roam the streets and catch up.

"How are things going with Mr. Rainier?" Cooper coos, playfully leaning into me. We dip into a tent selling fragrant honey soaps.

"I can't complain. We've got a good system going now. All I do is send him a text every now and then and he keeps my bathroom overflowing with tiny luxury hotel shampoos and conditioners that he steals for me when he's on the road traveling from hotel to hotel." I sniff a chunk of yellow soap. I purposefully omit the fact that Jaylen let me illegally tattoo him for my portfolio. I don't need Cooper reading into it—something I have actively been avoiding myself.

I can't explain what's going on between Jaylen and me because that would require my own understanding of our situation. When we're alone together there's an undeniable connection; we're not a perfect match, but rather two unique puzzle pieces that effortlessly fit together. It's familiar with him, like we're old friends reconnecting, except we're practically strangers. Jaylen's the most normal person I've ever met—just totally levelheaded. Sometimes I think he might be into me, but sometimes I think he's a nice guy to everyone.

Cooper huffs and his head tilts to the side. "You expect me to believe that the only thing going on between the two of you is a text chain? Be honest with me, because I totally ship you guys. Team Jacy all the way."

I roll my eyes as I continue to smell the various chunks of natural soap. Clearly, I'm not in the market for any soap; I have an entire sudsy apothecary in my bathroom at home. I am, however, desperate to avoid this conversation.

"The only ship happening between us is a *friend*ship. It's not physical," I say. Except for the night we met, the time Sailor cockblocked me, and when Jaylen eye-fucked the shit out of me after I tattooed him. Technically we didn't have sex after the tattoo, but the way he grabbed my wrist was more intimate than some of my actual hookups.

Texting Jaylen is easy, being around him is hard—literally, his biceps are rock-hard. A gust of wind blew Jaylen's cologne my way on our walk over here and I thought I was going to let out a loud moan. I think I'm scared what happened last time will happen to us again. If it's not my neurotic cat, then it'll be some other force of nature telling us we're wrong for each other.

"Too bad." Cooper interlocks his arm in mine and leads me out of the tent. We leave empty-handed, making our way to the food trucks for a little treat. Cooper knows me well; talking about my feelings is hard, and I do deserve something sweet.

"Dating Jaylen would complicate things," I say, leaning into Cooper's shoulder. "What if I picked the wrong movie or the wrong place to eat and he played bad?"

"Dating straight men is so strange."

"My career needs my full focus right now. Since being single, things are going good for me."

Cooper cocks his head back. "You're unemployed," he says, serving me a dose of reality I didn't order. "Speaking of which, are you sure you don't want to come and work for me again at the café?"

He's kind for asking, but I need to figure this out on my own. "You and I both know I can't memorize that many variations of milk alternatives. Besides, I really have to see this tattoo apprenticeship thing through."

"Good. You're much better at drawing a latte than making one."

We stop at the row of food trucks selling beverages. Cooper takes the lead and orders us two hot teas while I continue to spiral into a pit of despair. It's always a pit of despair; just once I'd like to spiral into a ball pit or something fun.

Jaylen's playing amazing hockey and I've never been so dedicated to finding an apprenticeship. I like how things are with us right now; I don't want to risk messing it up. That's what's so fun about the beginning part when you first meet someone. It's a free fall, and you can't yet see the bottom—you can't yet fathom the damage when you eventually crash-land. I feel faint and brace myself on Cooper's arm. He grabs our teas from the vendor and leads me out of line.

"You and Jaylen have been talking for a while now and you've found a couple possible apprenticeships. It's time to give him a chance. My therapist says that fear of abandonment or intimacy is the primary cause of self-sabotage," Cooper says. We secure a bench on the outskirts of the hustle and bustle of the event.

"Your therapist? You mean the part-time spin instructor, part-time life coach you're fucking?" I snap back playfully.

"Don't do that." He waves his finger at me. "We're focusing on your issues."

"Jaylen got us tickets to the game next weekend." I pivot knowing the promise of a few free tickets will distract him from his psychoanalysis.

"About time. I was starting to wonder whose dick I had to suck to get some tickets to a hockey game," Cooper says loudly as an elderly couple walks past us. Their necks practically snap as they whip their heads around toward Cooper in shock.

"It's a beautiful day, isn't it!" Cooper says to them with a jazz-hand wave. They nod awkwardly and quickly shuffle on their way. "Speaking of dicks to suck, here comes yours. Although it looks like he's switched teams midseason." Cooper points up the road into the crowd.

I turn my head to find Jaylen waving me down from across the street. He holds a large sack of unshucked corn and is covered in various flags and rainbow stickers—including one on his chest that reads Sounds Gay, I'm In!

"Where did you get all those stickers? You look like my college laptop," I ask Jaylen, looking him over.

"This place is awesome. Everyone's handing out free samples.

Someone named Danni even gave me all this free corn. I love it here." Jaylen proudly lifts the bag in his hands to show off his free produce like it's a pet fish he won at the carnival. Apparently, no amount of money earned will diminish the thrill of free swag, or free food.

Cooper eventually has to leave to get back to his café, leaving Jaylen and me alone with time to kill before his autograph signing. We eat at a few food trucks and listen to some live music before heading back to meet Maya.

By the time we get to his booth, there's already a long line of Rainiers fans waiting to get a selfie with the superstar. Cheers ring out as he waves to everyone while taking his spot in front of a Rainiers-branded backdrop. He welcomes the first person in line with a wide smile and handshake.

I stand back near the information booth to stay out of the way. I watch Jaylen pose with fans, not once taking a bad photo, and realize that I'm not the only one who finds him handsome. Jaylen has movie star looks, and while he's notorious for his brilliant playmaking, by the twentieth fan interaction it's apparent that it's also a well-known fact that he's as handsome as they come.

I watch as he enthusiastically talks to everyone, taking time with each person to make sure they feel seen. He humbly accepts compliments but gives his teammates all the credit. By the end of the day, Jaylen has been personally invited to at least ten different farms for family dinners, two weddings, a bar mitzvah, and a college graduation.

I'm so entranced by Jaylen that I don't notice Maya slip right next to me. "Turns out lesbians really love hockey." Maya tugs at her thick knit wool sweater, wrapping it tighter around her body and crossing her arms over her chest. It's been a long day and her walkie-talkie is still shouting at her. She turns it off.

"I only care about the opinion of one lesbian," I say.

"Look around." Maya motions to the crowd of people. "This

place is still packed. We had record attendance this year, and we raised three times the amount of money we thought we would today. Thanks for bringing him."

"That's amazing, Maya. This is an incredible event. I'm so proud of you." I lean into her. She wraps her arm around my shoulders, and I tuck my head into the crook of her neck. I can feel the relief release from her body as she lets out a deep sigh. This event has consumed much of her attention and energy for the past few months; she had a lot riding on its success.

"Thank you. And for the record, I think he's cool," she says quietly.

Maya might be hard to win over, but she will always give credit where credit is due. Not only did Jaylen follow through on his end of the deal, but he also made a real effort with my friends, and he showed up for our whole community.

I squeeze Maya a bit tighter as we continue to admire Jaylen's hospitality from a distance like proud lesbian moms.

"He's just my friend," I remind her.

"Is that what we're calling him now?" Maya raises an eyebrow.

"Better than what the media is calling him. 'The comeback kid.'" I do my best sportscaster impersonation.

"Be warned, your friend over there really likes you."

"How do you know?" I pull back from Maya, embarrassed by my eagerness to ask and my desperation to know the answer.

"He wrote me a check today for the largest single donation we've ever received." Maya's tone is serious, and in that moment, I wonder how serious my friendship with Jaylen might be.

# TWENTY-ONE

## Lucy

JAYLEN:

Lucy is Mars in Gatorade? What possible effects does this have on my game?

LUCY:

the universe has bigger issues than your lack of knowledge in astrology

JAYLEN:

Good! Wait until you see the jerseys tonight for Pride night in action. It's going to be like if the Care Bears were violent.

LUCY:

good luck delusional bear

JAYLEN:

Thanks Grumpy Bear.

Cooper drags Maya and me through an arena packed full of prideful Rainiers fans, eager for the game to start. We are minutes away from puck drop, a fact Cooper has been shouting at us for a while now as he attempts to encourage us to move faster through the crowds. Instead, we stop for drinks, and Cooper huffs. He wants to watch the pregame show, the player introductions, the opening face-off; he might not have paid for these tickets, but he's determined to get his money's worth.

Cooper is the only one of us who has ever been to a Rainiers hockey game. Correction: he's the only one of us who has ever been to *any* hockey game before tonight. Maya quickly grabs our drinks off the counter and we head to our seats.

I've been watching some of Jaylen's games on TV, mostly to see how powerful my good-luck texts really are. If I was smart, I would find a way to monetize this—although, I think it might be all in Jaylen's head. Not that I would ever tell him that; I prefer the excuse to talk to him, and of course, the free tickets.

To Cooper's relief we make it to our seats as the lights dim and the pregame show begins. Music blares as a light show commences on the ice. For a sporting event, this is very theatrical. The crowd stands as the MC bellows out the starting line. Jaylen Jones bursts out from the bench and onto the ice with force. He gets the loudest applause—most of which comes from Cooper shrieking like a Swiftie who was chosen for the concert ticket presale.

After the anthem, Jaylen readies himself at center ice to take the opening face-off, and the crowd settles back into their seats. Our seats are great. They're near center ice, about twenty rows up. I have the perfect view of the ice, and the Rainiers' bench.

The atmosphere is electric, and energy is palpable. I have never been a sporty person, but after that pregame show I'm ready to chug my beer, crush the can against my head, and get into a verbal altercation with a fan of the opposing team.

"Screw it, I'm going to come out and say it. The fact that he got us all tickets to the Pride game feels kind of homophobic. Did he assume we're all gay?" With great suspicion, Maya takes in the arena's atmosphere.

"We are. And this was the first game that finally worked with all our schedules," I say, reminding her of the coincidence.

Tonight, the Seattle Rainiers are celebrating the LGBTQIA+ community by hosting a Pride-themed night. The arena is festive for the evening, with rainbow flags lining the giant scoreboard that hangs over center ice. And by the look of it, lots of fans are joining in on the celebration by wearing various rainbow-branded hockey merchandise.

"I'm not complaining. All the gay hockey boys in one place," Cooper says, waving to a guy at the end of our row.

Maya, however, is still taking in her surroundings, likely calculating the facility's carbon emissions.

"See anyone you know?" I ask.

"Not yet, but we passed a lot of Subaru Foresters in the parking garage on the way in so it's only a matter of time," Maya says, looking up and down the rows of fans. "Oh! There's Danni!" Maya offers an overexaggerated wave across the arena to get her attention.

Since watching some of Jaylen's games, I've picked up on the basic rules of the sport. Well, I know that each team is trying to score while simultaneously attempting to knock the heads off each other. Jaylen has been helping me learn some of the more complicated stuff.

One time I asked him if it was okay to bump into the goalie. He called it goalie interference, and then proceeded to talk about it for an hour. Eventually I had to ask Jaylen what was up with all the fighting just to get him onto another subject.

The three of us are at the edge of our seats watching the game. Our eyes are wide as we follow the fast-paced play up and down the ice, mesmerized by the players' movements. Two players come crashing into each other against the boards and stay there well beyond the play, rubbing their bodies against each other in an aggressively erotic display of passion. Even after the whistle, they cling to each other.

"Who knew hockey was so homoerotic?" Maya remarks softly to no one in particular.

Cooper leans across my lap. "I did," he quickly replies.

"Did Jaylen spank you like that when you two hooked up?" Maya points to the bench where one of the players is skating off the ice and is greeted by encouraging butt spanks from his teammates as he shimmies past them to find his seat.

"No, but I wish he did." I hover in my seat, leaning forward to get a better look at the team's bench below us.

"Can you ask him to get me whatever popper the players are sniffing?" Cooper asks.

"Those are smelling salts—and unless you're trying to run through a brick wall, I suggest you avoid them." My nose still burns from the smell.

"Sorry, did you say something? I was too distracted by the guy at the end of the bench deep-throating that water bottle." Cooper points across the ice to the opposing team's bench where one of the players leans over the side squirting a water bottle into his eager mouth.

"They all shower together naked in an open room. Do you think they've explored each other's bodies?" I ask.

"They should, for the convenience factor alone," Maya says.

"God, I love hockey," Cooper says breathily. We all share a laugh.

During a break in play, a group of beautiful women make their way into the row below us. They are all dressed nicely in expensive-looking non-team-branded outfits, with shoes that click loudly against the cement floors and handbags that look like they cost more than my rent. If I didn't know any better, I would assume it was a sorority sister reunion, but I know they're the girlfriends and wives of the Rainiers players.

I suddenly feel stupid wearing the Rainiers crewneck I victoriously thrifted last week. I pull at the ratty sleeves of my worn sweater like I pulled on the hem of my crop top at that restaurant weeks ago, worrying that I'm wearing the wrong thing again.

"This must be the section where they put all the hot people," Cooper says loudly as the women find their seats. They look over and giggle.

I lock eyes with the one on the end. The woman sweeps her long honey-blond hair out of her face as she holds her stare on me long enough to make me wonder if she knows about me. *Did Jaylen tell anyone about us?* No. She must recognize me as the girl who painted the mural.

The woman simpers at me, and I'm convinced that she's Hannah, Wells's wife. Jaylen's told me about her. I awkwardly lift my hand to wave, but Hannah is already sitting in her seat with her back turned to me. I can feel Maya's eyes burning a hole into the side of my head.

"Say it," I say softly to Maya. I then brace myself, expecting a comment about how different I look compared to those women, and how I'm nothing more than a good-luck text to Jaylen. That the second my luck runs out, I'll never hear from him again. I would look so out of place sitting in that row, and I know it because I'm still out of place sitting behind them.

"Nothing. Just don't go bleaching your hair again," Maya teases, gaze still on the women.

A couple years ago, after a bad breakup, I bleached my hair in my bathroom and fried off all my ends. I ended up needing a pixie cut. It was so bad that I looked like Alice Cullen for months.

"Blond didn't really suit me anyway," I say. I'm not watching the game anymore; I'm staring at the row of perfect women in front of me.

During the first intermission, I spot Anna from marketing walking up the stairs approaching us. I panic, worrying I've done something wrong, but quickly remember that I haven't been painting here in weeks.

"Lucy! I saw your name on player tickets at will call tonight. Can't say I recommend dating a player, but I do respect the hustle for free tickets in today's economy." Anna slides into the empty row where all the significant others were sitting.

"Oh, we're not dating. I'm a good-luck charm." I peer around, making sure my voice isn't loud enough for others to hear.

"I'm familiar with the BDSM community," Anna says, holding up a hand. "No need to explain."

"Oh my god. It's not a sex thing!"

Anna couldn't care less. She continues on. "Listen, the execs were thrilled you completed the mural without becoming an anecdote on *1,000 Ways to Die*. Everyone loves your art." She leans over the seats in front of us.

"Really? I didn't get much feedback from you, so I wasn't completely sure. Actually, I don't think you gave me the correct email. I've been trying to reach you. I would love to get a reference letter from you, if possible," I say.

"I don't really have time to shoot the shit, Lucy. Someone just mistakenly posted an incriminating video of themselves on Instagram Stories rather than sending it directly to their sneaky link and now I have to convince the public that 'Daddy Long Leg' is his well-known innocent nickname and not what he calls his dick. Do you want to paint more murals for us or not?"

"Yes," I blurt before she has time to become so frustrated that she revokes the offer.

"Great! I'll be in touch. Don't call me." Anna pops up out of the seat and turns on her heels, disappearing as quickly as she appeared.

Looks like I'm painting more murals at the rink. While I'm not thrilled to be putting so much of my focus on painting, I am relieved to have secured some income for the next little while. This incoming money should be enough to hold me over until I hear back from tattoo artists about my apprenticeship applications. And if nothing else, it's more art to add to my portfolio.

I can't wait to tell Jaylen after the game; he'll be thrilled to see me around the rink more. He says an in-person good luck is always luckier.

# TWENTY-TWO

## Jaylen

Tonight is an important game; a win would move us up into first place in the division. Reaching the top of the chart is the perfect way to ring in the New Year. Some of the guys are already staring at me as I fuss with my mouth guard. Chomping it like a stale piece of gum isn't soothing my anxiety like I hoped it would.

The crowd is overwhelming me, the lights are too bright, and it feels like I'm at the end of my shift and not the beginning. I haven't used an inhaler since juniors, but I skate over to the team's equipment manager and politely ask him to grab my just-in-case inhaler out of my cubby. I discreetly take a puff on the bench followed by a sniff of smelling salts, and then I'm ready to hit the ice for the face-off.

When my inhaler doesn't offer the immediate relief I was hoping for, I try relying on muscle memory to get me through my shift. I lose the face-off, get hammered into the boards, and turn the puck over in the neutral zone all in the span of forty seconds on the ice. The Squids get on the board first, and I know it's my fault.

I don't even look at Coach Pete as I skate off the ice and find my spot on the bench. The team's assistant coach comes over and gives me a firm pat on the shoulder, which I find more patronizing than encouraging. I continue to struggle to catch my breath on the bench despite the moment of rest it offers my lungs. My chest is tight. I readjust the straps on my chest protector several times over before I'm up for my next shift.

I finish the second period with no shots, no hits, and a dash one. Back in the locker room, guys refuel with coffee, energy drinks, slices of pizza, and whatever else they need to keep their energy up.

Wells is out of his equipment and biking in the corner of the locker room to keep warm between periods. He's clocking more minutes than usual tonight because I can't seem to get my shit together.

"I've never seen someone sweat so much in my life," Lamber says as he walks past Wells sweating his ass off on the bike. Lamber rips open another mustard package and slurps it down in one squeeze. He tosses the wrapper in his cubby next to a pile of them.

Wells wipes his face with the towel hanging around his neck and tosses it at Lamber. "And I've never seen someone eat so many of those things. You're not supposed to enjoy them," he says, getting off the bike. Wells changes into fresh gitch and quickly gets his equipment back on before the coaches are back in the room, chatting to the team.

While everyone around me goes about their regular in-game rituals, I haven't moved. I haven't even taken off my helmet or gloves. I sit in my cubby staring at the team crest printed on the middle of the carpeted floor in a daze.

Calendar days don't exist to hockey players; only game days, practice days, and off days make up our lives for most of the year. But today is January 16. It's a day I wish I could forget. A day I wish was a meaningless number written on the whiteboard in our locker room.

I can't believe it's already been five years, but then again, my life has hardly slowed long enough for me to give it much thought at all. A fact that sends a crippling pit of guilt into my stomach. I sit in my stall quietly.

Out of the corner of my eye, I see Soko toss a skate guard at Wells to get his attention. He discreetly points to me with a questioning shrug. Wells shakes his head. The guys know I'm off my game tonight; everyone knows. It's one of those games where not even a good-luck text from Lucy could save me. These games plagued my potential for years until I was left with nothing but a PTO.

"You good, JJ?"

The deep voice startles me out of my misery. I look up to see Wells ready to hit the ice again. I glance around the room to find all my teammates ready with helmets and gloves on to step out for the third period while I've barely moved.

"Yeah, all good," I say, not wanting to raise any alarm.

During my second year in the league, I had what was described by reporters as a horrendous fall from grace. There was speculation I was injured, even that I was dealing with substance abuse problems—rumors that not only hurt me as a person, but also my value as a player.

But I've been playing so well, so consistently these past few months. I thought I was done having games like this. If my last two periods are any indication of where I'm at with my consistency struggles, then I expect to read some horrible things about myself online tonight.

I battle through the last period trying to keep the puck on my stick. I struggle to read plays I can normally see blindfolded. The rest of the game feels like riding a rough wave. Right when I find my footing, I am once again swept up into a turbulent sea. The final buzzer sounds and after thanking my goalie for the win, I sulk off the ice and down the long tunnel to mope in my locker cubby alone.

I shed each layer of equipment desperate to escape the constant squeeze I feel around my lungs. Nothing offers an immediate release and I continue to take sharp, shallow breaths as I linger dazed in my stall. With my head hung, I press my eyes shut and try to escape myself.

The locker room is empty by the time I leave. If I'm lucky, the team's family room will be cleared out and the other team's bus will be long gone from our parking lot as I walk out to my car. The last thing I need right now is to pass everyone on my way out. I can't rally a happy face—not even for the fans. All I can think about is how badly I played, and how everyone saw.

As I'm leaving the authorized-personnel-only area of the rink, Lucy quickly rounds the corner. She runs over, waving me down.

"How did you get down here?" I ask, looking around for a security member escorting her—or worse, chasing her.

"Please, it was easier than sneaking backstage at Warped Tour." Lucy's mood is light and cheery, much like everyone's mood leaving the locker room tonight after the win.

I'm embarrassed that she's witnessing me like this. It's bad enough she had to watch my performance tonight; now she has to see me upset with myself too. I'm not sure what she's after, sneaking down here to meet me. I'm not focused on finding out; I'm looking for the nearest exit.

"Were you supposed to come get me or was I supposed to meet you down here?" she says, jogging my memory.

I bring my palm to my forehead. While I wallowed in self-despair, I completely forgot about meeting her and her friends in the stands after the game. I didn't think it was possible, but now I feel even shittier about myself. "I'm sorry, I forgot. I got caught up with treatment after the game."

Water from my intentionally long shower soaks into the white collar of my dress shirt. I wipe the back of my neck with a silk tie gripped in my fist. My hands weren't steady enough to button the top buttons of my shirt. For the better I leave it undone; tonight's poor performance is suffocating enough.

"No worries," she says cheerfully. "We ran into some friends at the game, and Maya and Cooper headed out to the beer hall with them." Her cheeks are flushed, maybe from the cold, or maybe she had a couple drinks.

"Cool." I eye the exit behind her. The longer we chat in this hallway, the higher the odds are of me running into a staff member or coach. I want to get home and pull the covers over my head.

"I wanted to see your face when I told you that you'll be getting more in-person good-lucks. The team wants me to paint more murals around the rink," she says, smiling out the corner of her mouth. She's excited, and she should be. It's good news; if I weren't in such a horrible mood, I would be able to match Lucy's excitement.

"Great." My eyes dart around the rink, making sure no one is coming.

"Yeah. So, are you going to give me a ride home or make me take a scooter in the rain?" She knots her arms into a tight cross over her chest, standing there like a roadblock preventing my quick escape.

Not only had I completely forgotten to meet her up in the stands after the game, but I also forgot part of our arrangement included driving her home tonight. One quick stop and then I can get home and bury myself alive under my sheets.

Coach Pete's voice projects down the hall, and it's getting louder.

"Right. Let's go," I say, making a quick beeline for the door with Lucy tucked tightly by my side.

The silence in the car is palpable. I don't know what to say; I forget how to make small talk. My chest feels constricted as I tighten my grip on the steering wheel. My ears are still ringing from the polarizing change in moods between the crowd celebrating the Rainiers' win and the tense car ride back to my apartment. Finally, Lucy breaks the silence.

"What's going on?" she asks, with an uncharacteristic uncertainty in her voice.

I keep my focus on the road. It's pitch-black outside tonight, except for the blurred streetlights distorted from raindrops gathering on my windshield. "I don't know." The words fall from my mouth so low they're almost indistinguishable. I don't think I can talk without crying. I'm also worried that if I talk too much, I won't be able to breathe again.

"Did I do something? Is this about the wave I tried to start during the second period? I knew I shouldn't have done that. It was lame, wasn't it? There's something about a live sporting event that possesses your body into thinking the wave is a good idea." Lucy forces a laugh. She turns and stares quietly out her window.

"It's not the wave, Lucy. It's not you."

I'm blocks away from her apartment and she's digging through her purse. She fumbles with the contents as she practically dumps its entirety out on her lap.

"Everything okay?" I ask, peering over.

Loose tissues, candy wrappers, lip gloss, a lighter, and a few paintbrushes spill from her bag. She keeps digging.

"Yeah, I'm sure my keys are hiding on me at the bottom of this bag," she says with slight panic in her voice.

I'm not sure what more could be hiding in her bag; it looks like she's packed everything imaginable. I look away, not wanting to get worked up over the increasing mess she's making in my passenger seat.

"I can't find my keys. They must have fallen out at the game. Can we go back to the arena really quick?"

I shake my head. "Um, no, I can't go back there right now. I'll grab them from the lost and found tomorrow."

Lucy doesn't pry. "Okay. Well, hopefully maintenance is still up."

"How long will that take?" I try my best to sound unbothered, but my voice is stuck on monotone. I can't deal with all this right now.

"Bobby is great. I'm sure he'll be over in no time." With the phone pressed to her ear, I hear the call go straight to voicemail.

It's late. Most people are asleep right now. I can't leave her on the sidewalk late at night in the rain waiting for someone to show up with the master key. I know I'm feeling pretty down on myself tonight, but I'm not that shitty of a guy.

"Do you want to come over? Until you get it all figured out."

"Yeah, sure. Cool." Lucy repacks her purse and stares out her window.

The rest of the car ride is silent with all my focus on getting us back to my place safely. My vision is tunneled again, and despite the air-conditioning blasting, I still feel flushed.

I'm stuck on mute the entire way up to my unit. I walk like a zombie to my closet.

"I'm not trying to be dramatic or anything, but you're starting to freak me out," Lucy says, following close behind. I keep my mouth shut while I begin changing out of my suit. I still don't have the words to express myself. "Are you sick?" she adds.

Finally, I stop what I am doing and look over at her. I'm half-undressed, but Lucy pretends like she doesn't notice. She keeps her focus on my face, which is limp and void of any emotion. I let out a long sigh. "I played really bad tonight," I say, drawing my lips into a tight line.

"Oh," she says, like my answer caught her off guard, and for once she doesn't have anything smart to say back. I drop my pants and she cranes her head toward the ceiling while I slip into sweatpants. Following me into my kitchen, she leans against a countertop while I rummage through my fridge. "But you guys won," she adds warmly.

I can't stomach any of it, so I shut the fridge door. "We did, but we didn't deserve the win. I was dash three and took a bad penalty."

"If it makes you feel any better, my friends and I didn't even notice."

"It's fine. You don't get it." I leave her in the kitchen while I head to the living room. "You don't have anything in your life with this kind of pressure," I say dismissively as I slump down on the couch. I'm frustrated with myself, and I'm struggling to express my pain without taking collateral.

"I can relate to work stress. Trust me." Lucy sits next to me. I know she's trying to give me some perspective, but I'm so closed off it's hard to accept.

I kick my feet up on the coffee table and toss my head back, slouching into a position that allows me to fully expand my lungs—yet my breathing still feels shallow.

"Not like this. If I don't perform, then I could be gone. I will lose everything again." I stare up into a pot light on the ceiling until my vision is distorted with black spots every time I blink.

"Jaylen, I want to put permanent art into people's skin for a living. One bad move and *whose* becomes *who's* or a portrait of someone's beloved dead dog becomes some random dog."

"I would take one bad Yelp review over twenty thousand people booing me," I say, wallowing in self-pity.

I feel shitty when things are going well for me, like I'm an undeserving recipient of good fortune, but just as much, I feel shitty when things go awry, like I should know well enough to prevent it. No matter what, I feel an insatiable guilt for existing.

Lucy grabs my hand, and the connection is warm enough for me to finally look down. "I only heard cheers tonight," she says softly.

She's being kinder than I deserve, and this goes well beyond her scope of being my good-luck charm. I'm sure I'll pay bigtime for this postgame pep talk.

Lucy's head tilts to the side as she squeezes my hand. She's still not letting go. It hits me that she's seeing me at my worst tonight, and yet she insists on checking on me.

I've tried my best to respect her determination to remain unattached and single as she figures out her career, but I'm not sure I'm strong enough to fight off my urge to love her right now. The only self-defense against her I can rally is to be a dick, and it doesn't feel great.

"I'm sorry, I don't know why I said any of that," I say. I sit up and grab my chest. "It's hard to breathe. Like someone is squeezing me. Everything looks out of focus." There's a panic in my voice that scares me. I need to pull it together, but my breathing is labored again. Lucy starts rubbing my back, but I can't stop thinking about the game, about her, about Cam. Every breath I draw is heavier and louder than the last.

"I think I know what's going on here. I'll be right back." Lucy disappears into the kitchen. With my eyes pressed shut, I hear the ice machine clang and she quickly returns with a couple ice cubes in hand. She places them in my palms. "Squeeze these," she says.

I hold the freezing ice cubes in my hands as they melt into my palms, the fridge water dripping out of my grip and onto the area rug beneath my feet. Drip. Breathe in. Drip. Breathe out. Drip. Breathe in. I feel the cold burn against my skin and for the first time in what feels like hours, I can escape my mind. I can breathe again.

"Where did you learn that?" I ask, examining my wet hand for some magic pill, but it's only water.

"My mom started having panic attacks after my dad left us. If you don't have ice handy, you can try sucking on really sour candy. Anything to trick your mind into focusing on something else long enough to calm down." Lucy sits back down on the couch next to me—closer this time.

"Panic attack?" I've heard the term before, but never knew

what it meant. I assumed it was an expression people used when they were stressing over something. The way Lucy speaks makes it seem serious—clinical even. I've never struggled with my mental health in the past, at least I didn't think I did.

"Shortness of breath, tunnel vision, tight chest. That's a panic attack. Sounds like you've had a few tonight. You should talk to someone about it," Lucy says.

While her concern is gentle with the well-intended suggestion, it's still embarrassing. "Yeah, sure. I can bring it up with the team doctor," I say, wanting to forget about the entire thing.

I don't feel weak or broken. I'm in incredible shape. I've played through a fractured foot before; labored breathing feels like a silly reason to see the team doctor.

"Good. Panic attacks can be really debilitating." Lucy leans her head against my shoulder. "How do you feel now?" she says, her tone a bit lighter.

With the weight of her body propped against mine, I feel more stable than I've been all night. And I'm prepared to sit like this as long as she lets me.

"Better," I say.

My head feels clear, and I'm more present than I've been all night. I was so determined to avoid everyone all game, but now that I'm with her, I don't want to be left alone anymore. I lean in even closer to Lucy. She makes me want to forget about tonight's unforgiving sixty minutes of hockey, or even face them. It's a confusing feeling, but I know one thing for sure: I'm glad she lost her keys.

"Good, but if you're still feeling a bit anxious..." Lucy says, sitting up. She squares herself up to me. "You should close your eyes and visualize a place that makes you happy." She closes her eyes and takes a deep breath. Her chest rises and falls as her cheeks swell into a grin. I wonder what place makes her happy and wish I could be there with her.

"I don't have to. I'm already there."

I can see her so clearly right now, like I did the first night she ran into me. She's something good and I need to grab on to her before she's gone. I move a chunk of her hair off her face and push it behind her ear, wondering how anyone so scrappy can look so angelic. She tips her head up to me, slowly blinking her eyes open. They're strikingly green tonight. I can't hold back anymore. The words practically fall out of my mouth. "I can't keep pretending I don't want to kiss you."

"Then don't. You've never been good at it anyway."

Lucy grabs my face, and I latch on to her, making sure she doesn't slip away again. Being this close to her is like coming home after a long road trip, and kissing her is like crawling into bed. Even the thought of her makes me feel less lonely. I pick her up and bring her into my bedroom.

I fall back on the edge of my bed with her straddling my lap. Watching Lucy run her hands up her body and over her tits until her nipples poke through her shirt has me momentarily wondering if I've passed out from lack of oxygen or if it's all really happening.

Lucy slowly lifts her shirt up over her head until she's topless. I dive in, cupping one bare breast in my hand and putting my hot mouth over her other nipple. Her piercing tickles my tongue. I feel it harden even more in my mouth as I run my tongue back and forth.

I push Lucy's hair out of the way and kiss her neck. She hums. I tip her onto her back and kiss my way down her body. From near her belly button, I look up at her, waiting for permission to pull her pants off her hips. She nods at me, lifting her hips, and I finish undressing her.

She pulls my shirt over my head, and I slowly make my way back up her body, kissing her until I reach her mouth. Her nails dig into my bare back, and it feels almost as good as the pressure of my dick pressed between her bare legs. She trembles beneath me as she bites down on her bottom lip.

"I want you so bad," I say. I've thought of this moment every night for months—since I messed it up last time. I need to show her that I can take care of her, that I know how to please her.

"Fuck me, then." She says it like a dare—like she knows her taunting drives me wild.

"I've thought about you for months." I rush to get my pants off. As I'm leaning over the bed, opening my nightstand drawer to grab a condom, Lucy reaches for my hand and stops me.

"I've got an IUD and I haven't been with anyone else since our night together in the hotel. So, you're fine."

"Okay. Same." I nod, trying to act like I didn't get even harder at the thought of feeling her bare. "Whatever you want, I'll do it for you. I want you to feel good." I sound needy, but I don't care because I do need her, so badly.

Her knees fall apart, and I take in the sight of her. I open my mouth and let the spit I've gathered on my tongue drip down onto her pussy. She watches as my fingers firmly rub up and down over her clit, spreading my spit around. Her mouth parts and she gasps for air.

With my dick in hand, I spit on my head and stroke it up and down a couple of times, making sure it won't hurt when I slide inside of her. Glancing down, I ask, "Are you ready?"

Her eyes narrow, and her top lip curls. "Fuck me already, Jaylen. I've waited long enough."

I watch her face as I slowly guide my cock inside her. We gasp in unison. She's even tighter than I remember. I thrust hard and she tosses her hands over her head; I quickly pin them in place with some force.

"Tell me I'm a good girl," she begs with a breathy voice as I fuck her. Lucy's cheeks are flushed as she looks up at me with pleading eyes.

I laugh nervously at her request, thinking she's teasing me. Lucy grits her teeth at me, like she means it. Her nails dig into my hands, so I feel it too.

"But you're not. You're naughty and that's what I love about you," I say, thrusting into her harder. I adjust our positioning, taking her legs and putting them over my shoulders. Her body bounces from each thrust. Lucy throws her head back and moans. I never knew sex could be this selfless. I want it to last forever. I want to make her feel like this all night.

"Turn over." I use my most authoritative voice. I want to see her from behind. "I mean, if you like it like that," I quickly add, in a less threatening tone.

Her face lights up, and she does as she's told. As she turns around, I plant a firm slap on her ass. She gasps as my palm makes contact. We're already so in tune because she's on all fours before I can even ask her to bend over for me.

I spread her legs farther apart and she arches down even lower to the bed. I guide myself deeper inside her pussy than I thought possible.

"Tell me if it hurts too much." My breathing is labored while I try to keep my composure and last long enough to impress her.

She looks back at me with pleading eyes through heavy eyelids. "I want it to hurt."

I nearly bust right there, but instead, I grab her hips and thrust into her, my body smacking against her ass.

"Don't stop," she cries out. "I'm going to come." She pants. I feel her clench around me and her body shake. I finish a few thrusts later, deep inside her.

When it's over, I gently kiss up her bare back and take Lucy into my arms. She rests her flushed face against my warm chest. She leans into my body and I wrap my arms around her to stabilize her. We're both sticky with sweat. I tip her chin up and kiss her on the lips.

"I like your art," she says, still panting. She tilts her head over toward my wall where I've hung the stolen Lucky Thirteen sign. It's the first thing I see in the morning and the last thing I see at night.

"It reminds me of you."

She smiles, giving me a playful shove off her. "Let's order some food and eat it in bed," she says sluggishly as she crawls under the duvet.

And in that moment, I know I'm in trouble, because I would do anything she asks of me.

# TWENTY-THREE

## Jaylen

My eyes peek over the top of the magazine as I look around the waiting room. The glossy pages crumple beneath my tight grip. We've been waiting long enough for me to read the gossip mag from front to back. I even completed the color analysis quiz—I'm a deep autumn. And possibly deeply unwell. I'll know soon enough. The no-electronic-devices signs taped on every wall and stern receptionist keep me from checking the time on my phone.

When the team doctor recommended this psychiatrist to me, I figured she would have made sure the whole process was a bit more confidential than this. I thought I would be escorted through a back door or the doctor would make a house call—guess not. I pull my hat lower over my forehead.

"Relax." Lucy digs her elbow into my arm. "No one here knows who you are. You're not a celebrity, you're a hockey player." She snatches the magazine out of my hand.

"A mentally ill hockey player, apparently." I fold my arms over my chest and sink lower in my chair.

The receptionist calls out my name, and I physically flinch. I "Shh" through my teeth, looking around to make sure no one has their phone out to snap a picture of me. I'm finally thankful for the sign. Lucy gives me an encouraging pat on the bum as I head back to the doctor's office.

Inside, Dr. Patel sits behind a large wooden desk buried beneath leather-bound books. He sits about ten books tall and has a mustache that puts my pathetic Movember muzzy attempt to shame. His outfit is as monochromatic as the front and back book covers that frame him in his desk.

His office looks like what would happen if you gave a hoarder unlimited access to a Barnes & Noble. There are piles on the floor, on his desk, and stacked up in the shelves that run from the floor to the ceiling behind him. I figure if I'm going to trust anyone with my mental health, it should be the person who's read that many textbooks on the topic.

Dr. Patel pulls a folder off the top of a stack of books and flips it open. He glances up at me as I make my way into his office and then back to the paper. "Jaylen, is it?" He motions me to sit in the chair across from him.

"That's me." I take a seat, sitting tall enough to try to get a peek at what he's reading. Before he snaps it shut, I catch a glimpse of a singular piece of paper. What will my folder contain by the time I'm done here? What more is there for people to say about me?

He takes out a legal notepad and digs for a pen in the top drawer of his desk. Finding one, he holds it up like he's hailing a cab. "Ahh, I'm always losing these. Now, please, let me know what brings you into my office today."

"It's not a big deal. It feels a bit dramatic to even bring it up." While I stall, Dr. Patel sits patiently among his books. His silence is more probing than any follow-up question he could ask. I clear my throat. "I think I'm having panic attacks. It's possible I've been struggling with them for a while now, but I thought they were nerves. I would turn over the puck, or my shot would miss the net, and suddenly I would find myself keeled over on the bench hyperventilating. I had a really bad one a couple weeks ago and it freaked some people out—myself included."

Dr. Patel begins jotting down notes that I'm sure will be used to bulk up my folder. "Heart palpitations, sweating, shaking, shortness of breath, tingling..." he says, listing symptoms I'm all too familiar with.

"Don't forget dizziness," I interrupt.

"Do you know what could have brought on these intense feelings of anxiety?"

"Beats me. Was hoping you'd have some answers for me."

If I knew what was making me feel like this, I would have put an end to it a long time ago. I wouldn't have let myself hit rock bottom—jobless, released from a PTO, sneaking out of my hotel room without leaving my number for Lucy because I was so embarrassed with what I became.

So far, therapy is nothing like hockey. I'm used to everyone else telling me what's wrong with me—I'm not defensively aware, I have no consistency, I'm not a team player. This is the first time someone is asking me to identify the problem.

"Any trauma in your childhood I should know about?" he asks.

"I have two older sisters who used to dress me up like a girl and push me around the backyard in a wheelbarrow chanting 'Princess JJ' well into my preteen years."

"Tell me how that made you feel." He jots down more notes.

"Included. They didn't pay much attention to me otherwise." I catch myself gripping on to the arms of my chair like I'm hanging from them. I slowly release my grip and wiggle my fingers.

Dr. Patel continues writing, despite my tight lips and cursory responses. "Okay. Any bullying, head injuries, or death you have experienced throughout your life?" he asks like he's reading off a checklist.

"All of the above. How am I doing? High score?" An awkward laugh bubbles out of me.

"I'm not keeping score." He uses the end of his pen to scratch his bald head. "Your parents, are they divorced?"

"Worse, still together." I laugh at my own joke. Dr. Patel makes notes, and I instantly stop. *Who do I think I am, a stand-up comic? This is so embarrassing.*

I know how stupid I sound. I have an awesome family, my childhood was great, my life is blessed—why doesn't my body know that?

Dr. Patel's forehead wrinkles. "Should we try digging a bit deeper?"

"Shallow is fine," I say. I appreciate what he's trying to do— dig up some deeply buried painful memory—but the cause is obvious—my job is stressful. I can't make mistakes, and I've made a lot of them.

His face softens. "You're under a lot of stress at work." It's his first observation.

I'm far too exposed for direct eye contact, so I stare out the office window hoping to escape, but the view is solid gray. It's painfully overcast today. "Being a pro athlete is stressful, and being an underachieving pro athlete is excruciating. Between the in-game panic attacks and postgame blues, it's hard to find the joy I used to feel playing hockey. Things were better for me for a while, until they weren't."

He stares me down, like my diagnosis is written across my forehead. "Based on the information you've shared with me today, and the emailed forms you completed prior to this appointment, I'm writing you a prescription to help with your anxiety and depression."

Anxiety *and* depression. I thought I was here for panic attacks. I think about objecting to my diagnosis, telling him he's got me all wrong. All my teammates would agree, I'm the easiest-going guy ever. I get along with everyone. I never complain. I'm only mean when my job calls for it.

"Are you sure? Because, not to brag, but I'm a pretty outgoing guy. And for the most part, I really love my life." I don't want to question his expertise, but he could be wrong about me.

"Anxiety and depression do not discriminate, Jaylen. It can affect anyone, sometimes even those you would least expect. It's nothing to be ashamed of. Think of this medication as an integral component of your training regime. Does that sound reasonable?"

I nod. "Like making sure I eat enough protein, drink enough water, and get enough sleep."

"Exactly. In addition, I recommend talking to a therapist about what possible triggers are leading to these panic attacks." Dr. Patel scribbles down the names of a few therapists he recommends and hands it to me.

"Isn't that what the barber shop is for?" I joke, looking over the list as if I would recognize any of the names.

"Is your barber a licensed therapist?" Dr. Patel interlocks his hands on the desk, his elbows bumping into books as he wiggles forward past a pile of encyclopedias on phobias, trying to maintain eye contact.

"Not in the technical sense."

"Then no," he says flatly.

I leave the office with a prescription slip in hand, therapists listed on a loose sheet of scrap paper like restaurant recommendations, and another appointment scheduled a month out. It wasn't as scary as I thought it would be, nothing like being called into the general manager's office after a slew of poor performances.

Back in the lobby, Lucy is curled up asleep in her chair snoring with her mouth open. I gently tap her shoulder and she wakes with a full-body jolt and a gasp. "I'm resting my eyes." The receptionist glares at us.

"Looks like I'm an overachiever on and off the ice. I have both anxiety and depression." My joke earns a giggle from Lucy, which makes the stares coming from strangers in the waiting room worth it. It's nice to have found someone I can be myself around. She wasn't freaked out over my panic attack, or this appointment, or even my diagnosis. She's looking at me like she always does—like I'm still the same person.

Lucy stands up to slow clap. "Wow, congratulations. Welcome to the club. We've been expecting you, but we were too sad to tidy the place up for your arrival. Hope you like microwaved melted cheese on saltines." Lucy gives me a formal curtsy.

I laugh even though I'm not following her joke. Guess now I'm the rookie and she's the vet.

"Too niche?" she asks.

I hold up my prescription. "No, fluoxetine."

She grabs it out of my hand and reads it over. Between keyboard clicks we hear the receptionist groan and recognize we've overstayed our welcome.

"Nice! Hopefully it works for you. If it doesn't, then your doctor will help you find something that does." She tucks the prescription in my pocket and throws up the hood of her jacket. I do the same as we dart out into the parking lot in the rain.

"Thanks for coming with me today," I say as we get into my car. "And thanks for being so cool about this. I was really freaked out when he told me I was anxious and depressed. I was like, 'Could an anxious and depressed person do this?'" I point to my face and give a big full smile. "Apparently they can." The rain drops ricochet off my car loudly as we hide out together before heading back to my apartment.

"It was nothing." Lucy pulls back her hood and tousles her shaggy bangs. Behind her hand I can still see the bashful expression she's hiding.

"It's not nothing. I probably would have kept pushing through the panic attacks and playing until I collapsed on the ice if you hadn't intervened." I wipe a raindrop off her cheek with my thumb.

Since our night together in my apartment, Lucy and I have

been seeing a lot of each other. I've been giving her rides to and from the rink whenever I can while she paints another mural—this one much larger and in the concourse of the facility.

"It was really difficult to see you suffering that day and I wanted to help. I'm proud of you. Is that totally cheesy to say?" Lucy grimaces.

"I'm used to people telling me they're proud of me, but it's nice to hear it from you. Especially with something like this." I start the car and pull out. I've got the rest of the day off, and Lucy and I plan on spending it in bed together watching anime—and not thinking about what deeply buried trauma lurks within me.

"You're just so *relentless* on and off the ice," Lucy teases.

I throw my head back and laugh a deep cackle. "More like deeply flawed."

"A painting without flaws lacks all character. I find your cracks deeply endearing," she says, staring out the window.

I bite down on the flesh inside my cheeks and merge onto the highway.

# TWENTY-FOUR

## Jaylen

Staring into an empty suitcase is nothing new, but the act of leaving for long road trips has become more burdensome since Lucy came into my life—and bed every night I'm in town. Life in a hotel can be lonely. At least I can count on the guys to drag me out of my room for a nice team dinner. Lucy's good fortune doesn't stop at hockey; I've yet to lose credit card roulette and have to pay for dinner this season. I carefully lay a few suits into my open Tumi.

"I'm so nervous I think I'm going to crap my pants." Lucy barges into the bedroom with two cups of hot coffee in hand. She hands me a mug while sipping the other.

"Is coffee really the best choice then?" I say into my mug.

Ignoring me, Lucy does a spin and strikes a pose. "How do I look?"

My eyes go directly to her tight graphic T-shirt, which reads Fuck the Patriarchy. This isn't the first time I've seen this shirt on her, but it's a bold choice given her schedule today. She has an interview at a tattoo shop this morning. I haven't had to interview for a job since selling ICEEs and popcorn at the concession stand in my local rink back when I was fourteen. Still

I'm pretty sure you can't wear a shirt that says *fuck* across your protruding nipple rings.

"Honestly, you look like you would cuss the shit out of someone for being rude to their barista and then put your cigarette out in their latte. You look really cool."

"That's exactly what I was going for." Lucy takes another sip of her coffee while motioning to my open suitcase. "All packed for the road trip?"

"I think so." I lean over to take inventory. Suits, ties, shirts, underwear. "I forgot socks. Want to grab me a couple pairs?" I ask.

Lucy tugs open the top drawer of my dresser. "Dress or regular?"

"A couple of both." I wait for her to toss them over, but she must not have heard me because she's still hunched over the open drawer.

She looks so good from behind that I check the clock on my nightstand to make sure we have enough time to fit in a quickie before we both leave. I ditch my coffee and approach her with plans to ditch the rest of my clothes too. Before I can come up behind her with a playful squeeze, she turns around.

That's when I notice what's in her hand: a worn memorial card.

The picture of a lanky boy with curly dark copper hair and bright blue eyes on the front. It's a candid shot of him laughing. He looks so young, yet the photo isn't that old, is it? Below the photo are the dates May 3, 2000–January 16, 2020. I forgot I had that buried at the bottom of my drawer.

We stare at each other for a few beats, waiting to see who will make the first move. Most people keep their skeletons in the closet; mine are in my sock drawer.

"Who's Cameron?" Lucy moves in small, slow motions as if not to spook me. She sets her coffee down on my dresser and holds up the card in both hands.

I think about lying to her, making up some excuse about how I didn't know it was in there, and that he was some distant friend of a friend. Will she still like me once she knows the truth? Will I still like me if I keep lying to everyone? I've held this secret in shame for so long that I'm not sure I have the strength to carry it any further.

"Nobody now." My answer is as bitter as the black coffee she made this morning.

I'm not mad that she found it. I should have gotten my own socks if I didn't want her to see it. I can't remember if I knew that it was in there or not, but I'm almost relieved Lucy has it. Finally, someone outside my immediate family knows about Cam.

"Kind of seems like he was somebody," Lucy says.

I kept Cam a secret mostly out of the shame I felt for abandoning him, but the guilt over missing his funeral was only amplified as my game continued to slip away from me. I collapse on the edge of my bed. I'm tired of hiding, because no matter where I go, it finds me.

"That's my... He was my... That's Cam. We were best friends growing up, until our lives went in opposite directions. I was drafted into the NHL, and he got involved with a gang and into hard drugs. I didn't make much of an effort to stay close. He died of an overdose, and I chose my hockey game over his funeral. My mom mailed me that memorial card because she thought I would want one to remember him. Feels more like a reminder of how shitty I am. Maybe I like to keep it around because of that."

Once I open my mouth, it all comes pouring out; I didn't know I had so much to say. No one's ever asked, but if anyone is going to be real with me, it's Lucy. She'll tell me I'm a piece of shit, and I hope she does.

"It made the move," Lucy says, sitting down next to me on the edge of the bed.

"I can't bring myself to throw it out. Now you know what's wrong with me. Feel free to tell all the reporters. I'm sure they'll love this sappy story. They can even rescind all their substance abuse allegations they wrote about me that year. I can see the headlines now: 'Jaylen Jones, not a shitty player because of drugs, but a shitty player because he's a shitty person.'" I try to laugh it off. Sometimes it's easier to laugh than it is to cry.

Lucy isn't laughing. Instead, she grabs my hand and holds it tight. "The tattoo initials... CB?" She peeks up at me from under her bangs.

"It's him."

She exhales with a quiet whimper. "How long are you going to punish yourself for this?"

"I'm not sure I have a choice." I stare up at the ceiling, wishing I could fold myself up into my luggage and zip it shut.

There is *never* any time. I don't have the time to sort through my feelings over this—just like I didn't have the time to go to the funeral. I don't even have the time to have this conversation with Lucy right now because I'm wheels up in an hour.

"Bullshit. You always have a choice. Do something about it," she says, dropping my hand.

"Like what? Cam is dead. I made my choice then and I need to get over it. I need to keep playing well so I can get a contract extension or a long-term deal," I say, matching her no-bullshit tone.

I haven't had another panic attack since I went to see Dr. Patel—at least, not as big and debilitating as that one after the Pride night game. My medication is working. I've been among the top five in the league for points all season. I don't need to change anything, not right now.

"Could this be why you're struggling with panic attacks?" Lucy says, looking into my eyes with a softer expression.

Dr. Patel has encouraged me to reflect on what triggers could contribute to my anxiety and depression. We've established that my job is a major stressor, but he still thinks there's something else I'm keeping buried inside. This isn't Cam's fault—it's *my* problem and it feels selfish to make his death about me.

"They're not nearly as bad as they used to be," I snap defensively.

Once I get a better look at the obituary in Lucy's hand, it starts to click together.

I started experiencing the tightness in my chest after Cam died, but I assumed it was part of my grieving process. Then when I couldn't get back into the flow of my game, I figured I was struggling with the pressure to perform. Somewhere along the way, the shame from not being there for Cam and my guilt for letting everyone down on the ice blurred together.

"You remember that game, the one where I had a panic attack?" I ask. Lucy nods. "It was January sixteenth." I hunch forward, covering my face with both hands.

She rests her hand on my shoulder. "Did you tell your psychiatrist about this?"

I shake my head. Dr. Patel keeps reminding me to talk to a therapist. It's uncomfortable. It's messy. It's disgraceful. It's things I never want to be again.

"You should talk to him. If you do, I'll go with you again. We can face it together." Lucy rubs my back, but my whole body feels numb.

Depression is a lonely island. The further I pulled away from people, the more stranded I became. Then Lucy came along and helped me get back to civilization, but no matter how far I've come, the things that once haunted me on the island eventually followed me here.

I think I can trust her, and maybe I should. I was scared about seeing my psychiatrist for the first time, but now it feels like another part of my training regime. Physical therapy, weight training, stickhandling drills, and psychiatrist appointments. I guess I can squeeze in a therapy visit into the mix. I'll at least think about it.

"I think you only like going to those appointments with me because you like to steal the magazines from the lobby," I say, still trying to fight the tingles that fill my nose before I inevitably start to cry.

Lucy laughs into my shoulder and stays there, resting her head against me. We lean into each other with heavy sighs. "You can't save your friend, you can't bring him back, you can't turn back time and show up for him, but you have a lot of money and resources and a huge platform. Say something with it," she says.

I think about how much fun I had at Maya's event meeting everyone. I've always been one of the first guys to volunteer for any charity initiative. When I was playing poorly it offered me a much-needed escape from the game. The people we helped never cared how many goals I scored in a season; they were just grateful for a fun distraction—and so was I.

Still, doing something on my own feels daunting. It's exposing myself to criticism I'm not sure I can handle. It's not like I have everything figured out. I've barely got a grasp on my game, like I'm waiting for Lucy's luck to run out and I go back to being the league's biggest letdown.

"But what do I have to say?"

"You said a whole lot to me right now. You have to start being honest."

"With the media?" I grind my teeth, nauseated by the thought of the headlines. I can't give them fuel, not when I'm a free agent soon. I'll never sign a long-term deal if teams know about my deepest character flaw.

"With yourself," she says.

My eyes well up as I tip my head back, trying to stop my tears from spilling over. I close them tightly and several tears escape down my cheeks. I feel them drip from my jaw. My chest rises and sinks with each labored breath. "I don't know what to say," I whisper through a quivering lip. My voice is raspy as I take deep breaths to calm myself. The tears have stopped, but Lucy still takes me into her arms. I bury my head against her neck.

"Would you ever consider starting a nonprofit?"

I pull away, drying my face with the inside collar of my shirt. "You think I could do that?"

"Absolutely. I know Maya would link up to bounce ideas around with you. She's connected to just about everyone in the nonprofit space in Seattle," Lucy says with an excited hum.

My wheels are turning; I like her idea. "And you think that will help me finally get over it?" I sit taller.

"No." Lucy shakes her head and I shrink down again, practically folding over. Like letting go of an untied balloon, I deflate. "It's not about getting over it. It's about learning to live with the loss and finding ways to honor Cam," she adds.

"Do I deserve that?"

"You're a good person. Even if you listen to music loudly in public spaces and don't hold the elevator for people." She playfully knocks her elbow into my side, near the tattoo she gave me.

"I love you, Lucy." The words fall out of my mouth like I've been saying them for years, like it's no big deal. I say it like I'm asking her to pass me the remote or plug my phone into the charger for me. The thought of loving her feels so deeply embedded into my DNA, it's nostalgic. Like it had been buried in me the whole time and I needed a little reminder as to where I hid it.

Looking into her eyes right now, I remember the love I've always wanted. I long to be the person she sees in me. I love her; I'm sure of it. I don't expect her to say it back to me, and I don't need her to either. Her knowing is enough.

Lucy's eyes go wide as she chokes into a coughing fit. She composes herself. "Thanks" is all she gets out of her mouth before she lunges at me with a passionate kiss.

# TWENTY-FIVE

## Lucy

"You *New Girl*'ed him?" Maya gasps, bracing herself against my work-in-progress mural. The news of Jaylen's "I love you" is clearly just as disorienting for her to hear as well.

"Careful!" I shout, tugging her arm and pulling her off the wet paint. Her hand narrowly misses the Rainiers' logo. I put the finishing touches on its snowy mountaintop this morning while the sun played peekaboo through the clouds. I toss Maya the rag slung over my shoulder, and she wipes her hand clean.

A few strangers pass by on the shared sidewalk and I subconsciously tuck into the brick wall to hide. They pay us and our personal conversation no mind. I feel a bit like a zoo animal on display while painting this giant mural on the outside of the arena's north end entrance. This exhibit closes soon, and I hope to wrap up this last team commission and finally get that yes I'm so desperate to hear from a tattoo shop. The apprenticeship search is tireless—and so far, fruitless too.

*As if I didn't have enough on my palette, let's add one perturbed BFF to the mix.* I thought telling Maya about the nonreciprocated "I love you" blunder was the right thing to do. Surely my most responsible friend would say something sensical like *It's too early for love* or *You did the right thing*. Instead, Maya is giving me the reaction I expected from Cooper. She's still standing there looking at me like I threw a compostable cup in the trash bin.

"I panicked. What was I supposed to say?" I've replayed the moment over and over in my mind and every time I think about saying *it* back to him, I panic all over again.

Maya throws her hands up in the air and my soiled rag flies along with them. "'I love you too, Jaylen,' would have been fine."

"I don't know. Feels a bit desperate. Jay and I aren't even dating." My eye contact drops sheepishly, and I begin painting over the handprint smudges Maya left on the mural. I know I don't have much of a case here, but that doesn't stop me from getting defensive.

Jaylen was open and vulnerable with me last week, and I shut him down with a kiss. It's not like it was the first time I've ever heard those words, but usually it's been awkward or said after a few too many drinks and forgotten by morning. I could tell Jaylen meant it by the way he kissed me after. He kissed me like it was the first time again. How you kiss someone when you don't know if there will ever be another one.

Maya enjoys a smug laugh, tilting her head back as her shoulders shake. "Jay? You gave him a nickname? Oh, you're totally dating. This right here is typical Lucy behavior. It's how I know for a fact that you two have *been* dating." Maya's new microbraids shimmy as she shakes her head at me.

"What's that supposed to mean?" I spin around, wielding my brush. I'm more defensive than I should be, but it feels like getting called out at Club Purple Haze for dating around too much all over again.

"It means you always do this in relationships. You sabotage yourself. If you're not ignoring the signs that your girlfriend clearly has a secret boyfriend, then you're looking for a reason to bail on someone great when things get serious." Maya talks far too loudly for such a private conversation. I feel naked on the sidewalk in my paint-stained clothes.

"I don't know if I'm ready to tell Jaylen that I love him. I didn't think it was that serious. I'm just trying to paint my murals while I wait to hear back about my applications. I had an interview at a shop in Capitol Hill and it went well," I brag, hoping to change the direction of our conversation. I also heard back from the shop on Capitol Hill the next day. They went in a different direction, but I keep that painful news to myself.

I'm not dwelling on the loss because I heard back from Hunter Gunn; I have an interview with her in a couple weeks. Jaylen doesn't know that the position with Hunter Gunn is in LA, because I haven't exactly told him. It hasn't come up in conversation. I'm sure I'll tell him—eventually. I drop my brush among my mess of supplies and grab a seat on a nearby bench. I've been painting since dawn and Cooper should be here soon with our lunch. "Like a picnic," he called it. I sit down on the public bench and practically step in a wad of dried chewing gum.

"And that's great, but you've said 'I love you' to plenty of people before Jaylen. You tell the new barista at Brewed This Way that you love them all the time," Maya says, sitting down next to me.

"Because they remember how I take my coffee and what type of muffin I usually get." My deflection is lazy at best, but most of my focus is being used to analyze my progressing mural. *What should I tackle next?* More highlights on the beer cans; maybe some condensation for a pinch of realism. This mural is already shaping up to be my best one yet.

"I don't think you should say it if you don't mean it, but be real—you and Jaylen need to have a conversation. You can't avoid him forever, especially not painting here," Maya says in a softer tone. One warm enough to melt my layer of frigid defense.

She's right; I should text Jaylen. I've been able to avoid him for a bit while he was on a road trip with the team, but he got back early this morning around 2:00 a.m., and I'm expecting a text once he's up—which could be any minute now. My stomach is in knots and it's not the hunger.

"The stakes feel way higher with Jay than they've ever felt with anyone else." I have no choice but to be a bit more vulnerable with Maya. I'm running out of time before I have to face Jaylen, and I could really use her advice.

"You deserve to be loved, Lucy." She reaches for my hand.

The words practically knock me off the bench. I squeeze her hand so I don't fall over. It seems like such a simple concept. One that I can grasp in my head—but when it comes to my heart, I'm not so willing to accept it.

"Thank you," I whisper. I cough into my fist, clearing my throat. "I think I am a bit freaked out."

Maya nods her head somberly. "I get it. Jaylen's your first serious partner in forever. He's like the first guy you've dated without a suspended license. He doesn't even have a criminal record."

"He has a bed frame and multiple bath towels," I add. Not only is Jaylen's criminal background clean, but he's also a homeowner, has health insurance, and has a pension. He has his shit together, which for whatever reason raises the stakes in our relationship greatly.

Maya's face contorts. "I don't know how you date men."

"I've dated enough bad ones to know when a good one comes along."

"So, you do know how you feel about him?" Maya's eyebrow raises slightly. "Maybe you aren't ready to tell him you love him. Do you at least like him?" Maya asks.

"I'm scared to admit how much I like him. I don't even want to say it out loud in case I jinx it," I say. My phone vibrates in my pocket and we both feel its ripple against the bench. I startle but try to play it off as if I don't notice—it continues to buzz.

Maya gives me a nudge. "You're not going to jinx it, but you will push him away if you keep ignoring his calls."

"Then I should take this." I excuse myself and dart around the corner of the building for a bit more privacy. Must be serious because he usually texts.

Once I'm out of sight and earshot, I pull my phone out to see that it's not a call from Jaylen, but one from an unknown number. There's a lump in my throat. Most people see "unknown number" and think a telemarketer is trying to reach them about their car's warranty. I don't even have a car, but what I do have is a dad who changes phone numbers as frequently as he does jobs, and addresses, and moods.

I haven't seen him since my senior art showcase when he showed up drunk and caused an embarrassing scene. He called me a couple of weeks after the event from an unknown number with some excuse and the empty promise of a lunch date in the near future. My dad is good at making promises and even better at breaking them.

I can't help but have a visceral reaction at the possibility of hearing his voice. I've completed two murals for the Rainiers, and I'm about halfway through the third. Did he see the pictures I posted of my work on social media? He's never cared about my art before. Most people would send a call from a person like that to voicemail, but I always wonder if he is calling to apologize.

I answer the call—I always do. I came out of the womb programmed to destruct, tripping over my feet in a rush to reach the conflict. I wish I was strong enough to hit Ignore, but it gets tiresome pretending I have any self-restraint.

"Lucy!"

Unfortunately, I was right—it's him.

"How have you been?" His tone is far too vibrant and upbeat for someone who abandoned their wife and six-year-old kid, for someone who never paid any child support, for someone who never showed up to any of his daughter's art events, for someone who has never made much of an effort. His carelessness with my feelings causes my chest to tighten.

"I'm good, I… I'm surprised you called me." I wince at myself.

"Why? I call you all the time." His vibrant tone quickly runs its course and he's already annoyed with me. "My boss has me working a job near the city later this month. I'm wondering if you wanted to grab lunch with your old man. It's been too long, kiddo," he says.

I'm so caught off guard by the use of my childhood pet name that I almost don't notice he's finally asking me to the lunch he promised more than three years ago.

"What do you think?" he asks before I have a chance to respond. I can practically smell the Budweiser on his breath through the phone.

"I don't know. I've been really busy—" I start feeding him an excuse, but he cuts me off before I can finish explaining myself.

"Come on! I'll pick the spot." Before I can say no, I hear shouting in the background from his end of the call. My dad yells something indistinguishable back. "Look, I got to go, but I'll text you the details soon." He hangs up.

By the time I can process what happened, the call is over. Like being thrown back into my art, I worry that seeing my dad will put me back in harm's way. Although, if I can pick up a brush again, then I can face him too. I still have time to prepare myself for our reunion, or come up with a good excuse to skip.

My phone dings in my hand, but it isn't my dad texting me the details of our upcoming lunch; it's a text from Jaylen.

JAYLEN:

Are you free? I've missed you.

Today must be the day where the things I've been avoiding finally catch up to me.

LUCY:

I'll be over after work.

"Let me guess, it was our favorite ally?" Maya asks as I approach. She's sipping the sustainable fair-trade loose-leaf tea she made Cooper buy for his café.

Cooper is sitting beside her, joining us with a lap full of lunch from the café. Rather than get into the details of the call with my dad, I nod my head.

"We're meeting up after work." I keep my response vague, not waiting to provoke one of Cooper's dramatic gasps. Which is inevitable once I tell him I didn't say "I love you" back to Jaylen.

"You need to bring him to the café. It would be great for business." Cooper hands me a coffee and half a sandwich.

"He's not some show pony for me to parade around town, Coop," I say with my mouth full.

"I know, he's a stallion," Cooper says with a snarl, earning an eye roll from me. "If you're not going to bring him around, then you can at least paint one of your beautiful murals for me. One of Lady Gaga's body from the 'Stupid Love' music video with my face on it." Cooper strikes a pose more suited for *Vogue* than the wall of a coffee shop.

"That's going to cost you big," I say, though I probably owe him at least one pro bono commission.

Maya's phone chimes. "Well, well, well. If it isn't Lucy's boyfriend, Mr. Rainier himself." Maya flips her phone for Cooper and me to see a text from Jaylen Jones. I gave Jaylen her number and Maya has put him in contact with the right people so he can begin creating his nonprofit.

"Boyfriend?" Cooper gasps.

There it is. Like a puff of steam, it sizzles my ears and scratches my brain.

I can't help but chuckle; the commotion of it all makes me bashful. "You didn't hear? Looks like Team Jacy is about to be official." I say it jokingly at first, but I'm taken aback by how tickled the whole thing makes me feel. The dread I built up all on my own has been extinguished and I can't wait to finish up for the day and face the unsaid.

# TWENTY-SIX

## Jaylen

JAYLEN:

Have you seen my Seattle
hoodie?

LUCY:

the green one?

JAYLEN:

Yeah!

LUCY:

no srry good luck tn

I woke up this morning exhausted from the week's travel schedule. In the last six days I've been in three different time zones. Adjusting to time change is one thing, but facing off against some of the most highly skilled and lightning-fast teams this road trip drained what little mental energy I had left. The season is long, and spring feels the longest. The games were hard-fought battles, and luckily, we left with more wins than losses.

We ended the trip in Chicago, where I was welcomed home by my own personal fan section of about fifty relatives. It's always a lively family reunion when you've got enough cousins to equip a twenty-three-man roster. Put them in Jones jerseys with beer in hand and you've got the loudest group in the whole arena.

As nice as it was being home and seeing everyone, I couldn't wait to get back to Lucy, the woman I told my entire family about. My sisters read it on my face like a billboard the second they saw me. One ear-to-ear smile as I glanced down at my phone reading a good-luck text from Lucy and they officially clocked me. "You're texting *her*, aren't you?" I couldn't shut up about her once I started talking.

I should be spending the day in bed trying to catch up on rest, but I haven't been able to sit still long enough to fall back asleep. I keep thinking about Lucy. She's on her way over now, and I hope she gets here soon. I've already ironed my shirt three times. If I have to wait around much longer, I'm going to burn a hole through it.

As I fuss with my hair in the reflection of my microwave, the door opens. She's rushing in, apologizing for being late. Her hands are full of painting supplies and various reusable cups, which she dumps on the floor near the door like a weight lifter dropping their bar. I walk over and give her a big hug. The second she wraps her arms around my waist, my anxiety melts away.

"I missed you," I say, taking a deep inhale of the top of her head. I missed the way she fits into my arms, the way she smells. I swear I wasn't gone that long, but it feels like forever since I've seen her.

"I missed you too. Although, I think I'm getting really strong having to carry stuff to and from the rink on my own." Lucy steps back, rolling up the sleeve of her T-shirt as she flexes her muscles at me.

"Looking buff." I humor her by squeezing her bicep, and to my surprise, it's pretty firm. "I want to hear all about your last interview." I help move her bags out of the doorway and inside my apartment.

"It was fine. A good practice run for my upcoming interview with Hunter Gunn. That apprenticeship is mine," she says passionately. Her face contorts into a worrisome expression, souring like she's taken a candy in her mouth. "I mean, as long as I don't do that thing where I get nervous and ramble about the time I accidentally ate an entire magic mushroom chocolate bar and when I finally came to I was making balloon animals for children at the farmer's market. I made two hundred dollars in tips that afternoon." She hops up on a kitchen bar stool and leans her torso over the granite island countertop, getting comfortable.

"I'd say that's a strength."

She's been working so hard lately between the murals and her job applications and interviews. She's even started selling her work online while she waits to hear back about the tattoo apprenticeships. Her passion is contagious, and it's really sexy to watch her go after what she wants so fearlessly.

"Do you need a ride to the interview? I can skip my pregame nap and drive you if you want," I offer, wanting to support her with this as much as possible.

"No! I mean, you'll be traveling for away games. Maya said she would drive me." Lucy fidgets with her fingers, twirling her rings like she's aggressively sharpening a pencil.

She seems a bit on edge. I lean back on the counter across from her, extending the space between us. I hope she isn't mad at me.

"I didn't hear from you as much this past week. Is everything okay?" I grab an apple from the overflowing fruit bowl on my kitchen island. It makes a loud crunch as I bite into it.

"Everything's fine. It was an eventful week." Lucy grabs her own apple out of the fruit bowl and fidgets with its sticker. "A drag queen burned her wig off during a very believable performance of 'Girl on Fire' during a show at Cooper's café. Then Maya had this clothing-swap meetup thing, but it was just a bunch of lesbians exchanging slightly different variations of the same plaid button-up. If I start wearing a lot of plaid button-ups, please know I did not join an axe-throwing team," she rambles as she twists the stem of the apple until it snaps off.

I set my half-eaten apple down on the counter behind me. The reason I was so nervous to see her today is because I think I might have laid it on too heavy the last time we were together. She usually FaceTimes me while I'm on the road, but this trip she was always too busy anytime I tried to call.

I want to make sure we're cool, but I don't want to create an issue if there isn't one to begin with. Relationships are new to me, and I don't have the experience to know how to handle this situation. Wells would probably tell me to say what's on my mind, but I'm not trying to tell her she'll look like a sexier Kurt Cobain in her new plaid shirts.

"I freaked you out with the whole 'I love you' thing, didn't I?"

"Noooo." Lucy drags the word out for a dishonest number of syllables.

"I've never had a serious girlfriend before, so I don't know all the rules. I'm guessing it was too soon to say that to you," I say, despite the fear of rejection. I step forward and lean on the countertop, getting closer to her.

"We're dating?" Lucy asks, her face giving no indication of whether or not she's joking.

"Well, yeah," I say matter-of-factly. My head tilts to the side as I look her over for any visible signs of a head injury. She looks fine, which means she must be joking. We've been inseparable for months. She makes me coffee every morning. I scratch her back every night. We're already more than halfway through watching every *Naruto* episode.

I know I don't have a whole lot of dating experience, but there isn't a doubt in my mind that we've been dating for a month, minimum. At least that's what I've been telling my friends, family, teammates, and Cheryl, the lady who does my dry cleaning.

Lucy finally cracks a smile. "It seems everyone already knew we were dating but me. Aren't you supposed to ask me first? Did we agree to be in an exclusive relationship and I missed it?" Lucy slides out of the chair and slowly walks up to me, stopping close enough that I can feel the heat of her body.

"Hmm, I guess not. Was I supposed to formally ask you? We spend every night I'm home together. You have a toothbrush here. You've stolen at least three of my sweatshirts already." I pull her into my arms.

"Four," she says, resting her head against my chest.

"Four?" I pull back, my eyes widened. "We *better* be dating or else I'm concerned you're stealing from me."

"Everything in here is too big and heavy to lift alone. Although, I have stolen a couple of T-shirts in addition to the collection of sweatshirts." She stands on her tippy toes to kiss my neck.

"And let's not forget that we at least like each other, right?" I find a casual way to bring up the unreciprocated "I love you" from the last time we were together. I'm not usually one to interrupt a kiss on my neck, but I hope this time she's more receptive to having a discussion about it.

"Right. I like you, Jaylen. I really like you." Her big round hazel eyes look up at me, sucking me in. She has a bit of dried paint in her hair that I assumed was a new dye job at first glance. I gently scrape it out of her hair for her.

"Good, so you're my girlfriend. I mean, Lucy, will you please be my girlfriend?" I ask, humoring her with pleading hands.

"No," she quickly replies, flashing her signature cheeky little-shit grin that I love so much. She loves to give me a hard time, but I take it with great pleasure. Before I can grab her in my arms, she darts away, escaping to my bedroom like it's a game of tag and now I'm It.

It's game on as I quickly catch up to her. I wrap my arms around her body and tackle her onto my bed. She giggles in my grasp as she tries to wiggle her arms free.

"Say you're my girlfriend. Say it!" I shout, tickling her ribs.

"Okay. I am. I am. Of course I am!" she laughs as she fights me off.

She gets her arms free and cups my face, tracing over my bottom lip with her thumb. I quickly part my lips and let her thumb slide into my mouth, playfully biting it until she slides it out and down my lip.

"Say it like you mean it this time," I demand.

She licks her lips. "I'm your fucking girlfriend, Jay." She quickly breaks into a smile. "You know, in actuality, we've probably been dating for at least a month without me notic-ing," she says, biting down on her full bottom lip.

I shake my head at her stubbornness, in disbelief at how lucky I am to have a girlfriend as cool as her. I move in slowly for a kiss. Her soft lips part as she kisses me with passionate force. I immediately want more.

She pulls her mouth back. "Hey, since you're officially my boyfriend, you wouldn't want to come to my birthday dinner at my mom's, would you? I know it's really lame to ask, but it feels like something you do with a boyfriend." She holds her breath as she awaits my answer. Her body is tense beneath me.

I'm honored she asked. She might not have said "I love you" back to me, but sometimes people say it in different ways.

I don't know much about Lucy's family, but she talks fondly

of her mom, and about as fondly as you would expect an older sister to speak of their younger brother. It's her relationship with her dad that remains a mystery. In some ways, Lucy wears her heart on her sleeve—literally, her tattoo arm sleeve says a lot about her. But there's a lot she keeps guarded. All I know is that he left when she was little, wasn't around when she was growing up, and doesn't check in much. This dinner at her mom's house could give me more insight into her life, her childhood. It could bring us closer together.

"Absolutely. I would love to go with you," I say eagerly. "I mean, I would *like* to go with you." My lips spread in a sly smile.

Laughing, she wraps her hands around the back of my neck and pulls me in close. "I would love for you to come." She coos, humming on the word *come*.

I slowly trace my hands up her body and lace my fingers through the back of her hair. "I like the way you say that."

Her eyebrow pops, and she smirks. "Love?" she teases.

"Come," I say, biting my lip.

She laughs even harder. "So, you wouldn't mind if I hopped in the shower then? I'm still covered in paint from today." She bats her eyelashes at me like it was more of an invitation than a request.

"I should come with you. You know, to conserve water." I've been half-erect since she stuck her finger in my mouth, and now that the thought of her naked in my shower is on my mind, I can't think of anything else.

I follow Lucy into the bathroom, where she makes me watch her slowly undress while the water heats up. I try to touch her, but she pushes my hands away. First her shirt, then pants, then underwear, until she's naked in front of me. She runs her hand over the front of my pants, and my hard dick jerks against her touch.

"I've really missed you," she says, with her hand still pressed against my cock.

"Show me how much you missed me." I unbutton my pants and slide them down to my ankles along with my underwear.

Lucy drops to her knees, and I rip my shirt off over my head. She takes my dick in her hand and licks it from the base all the way to the tip while looking up at me. She teases me, swirling her tongue around my hard tip while I tug on a handful of her hair. My eyes roll in the back of my head as she takes it all in her mouth. Her hot wet tongue presses against the bottom of my shaft and she sucks as her mouth slides to the tip. I use my hand on the back of her head to guide her up and down my cock.

"You look so pretty with my cock in your mouth," I say. She moans with a full mouth. It feels so good that it's selfish and, in that moment, I want nothing more than to feel her come all over my dick. "Get up," I say, tugging on the back of her neck.

We step under the showerhead, soaking our bodies in hot water. I grab her by the waist and pull her into me, kissing her in the steam. She makes good use of the oversize standing shower as she leans back against the wall and props a leg up on the built-in bench.

I get to my knees for a better view of her pussy. I slowly slide my hand up the inside of her thigh and she bites down on her lip, suppressing a moan. She's slick and hot between her legs. I bring my mouth to her for a taste.

She squeezes her tits together as my fingers slowly push inside her. "You fucking love this, don't you," she moans.

My head nods like a bobblehead on a dashboard. I struggle to find my words. A breathy "yes" is all I get out.

I stand up and turn her around, pressing the front of her body against the shower glass. I stand firmly behind her, gripping her hips. We both have a foggy view of ourselves in the mirror across from the shower. "Look at yourself. Look at how good you look," I say, pointing to our reflection.

I take my dick in my hand and slowly guide it inside her

from behind. She's so tight from this angle. As soon as I get inside her, I know I'm not going to last long. I reach my arm around and start rubbing against her clit. She whimpers as I thrust harder and harder until I'm right there.

"I'm coming," she says, gushing into my hand and all over my cock.

I keep fucking her until I feel the tension in her body release. Only once I know she came do I allow myself to finish inside her.

I gasp. "Fuck, I love you, babe." The words fall out of my open mouth before I can catch them. That's the thing with "I love you"—once you've said the words, they'll keep finding their way out of your mouth again and again.

# TWENTY-SEVEN

## Lucy

My fingers pry open the yellowed aluminum blinds as I peer out the window. I search down the long stretch of neighborhood for any sight of Jaylen's pricey foreign car. The car worth more than most people's salaries around here stands out as the engine revs rounding the corner to my childhood house.

"Will you get away from that window? I don't need Kayleigh-Anne from across the street getting sight of you and coming over here trying to sell me essential oils again," my mom says in a shrill voice as she finishes setting out a variety of potato chips on the living room coffee table. "It's going to take a lot more than a dab of peppermint to get your brother out of my house." She brushes her hands down the front of her blouse, patting out the wrinkles.

I drop the blinds back into place with a noisy rustle and step back. Grabbing a chip from the same bowl I used to vomit in as a small child, I chomp like a hamster, waiting nervously for Jaylen to make his way up the driveway. I'm not worried about Jaylen making a bad impression with my family—he's media trained. I am worried about my mom embarrassing me, or my brother asking Jaylen if he can take his car for a joyride around the block. Between deep breaths, I use my pant leg to clean the potato chip grease off my hands. *This is what it feels like to let people into your life, Lucy.* It's uncomfortable, but I like Jaylen enough to endure it.

The doorbell rings and I rush to the front door before my mom can answer it. I slip in front of her, blocking her out of the way.

Jaylen dressed up—even for him. His shirt has a collar and his jeans look starched. Someone has got to hide that iron from him.

The entrance fills with the smell of his best cologne. I give him a hug so I can get a better look at the sides of his head, because I swear he got a fresh fade too. Jaylen wants to make a good first impression.

"Holy shit, you're Jaylen Jones," my brother, Lucas, says.

I didn't know he was standing behind me—he must have crawled out of the depths of his room past all the dirty dishes and empty Doritos bags while I wasn't looking. His hands are still clawed from the controller he grips twenty hours a day. Lucas squints; all that screen time has done irreversible damage to his corneas.

"You'll have to excuse my little brother—he's not fully house-trained," I say, welcoming Jaylen inside.

I turn to Lucas, scowling. Without hesitation Jaylen extends a hand toward him. Miraculously, Lucas knows what to do with it.

"I can't believe this. I thought Lucy was lying about you. I owe someone twenty bucks." Lucas whips out his phone and takes a quick selfie with Jaylen. I try to swipe his phone from him, but he runs back down the hall to his bedroom.

"Amy," my mom introduces herself, shaking Jaylen's hand. "It's really nice to meet you. My daughter tells me you're the one who hit her in the face with a puck." My mom is no bigger than me, but I watched her build our back deck from scratch one summer. Her firm shake jostles even the biggest hockey player.

"Mom!" I snap.

"What, I can't give him a bit of shit? I made that face so forgive me for being protective over it." My mom grabs me by the chin and gives my head a playful shake. She plants a wet kiss on my cheek that I quickly wipe off.

"I told her she could shoot one at my face so we were even, but she refused," Jaylen says.

"She must really like you then." My mom briefly looks over at me to make eye contact. Turning her attention back to Jaylen standing in our entrance, she says, "Come in, come in. Make yourself at home."

In the living room, my mom sits down in a weathered chair for an uncharacteristic moment of rest. Scooping her hair up into a messy bun, she leans in toward Jaylen, presumably getting ready to tell him embarrassing stories from my childhood. As the two of them make friendly small talk, my brother re-emerges with his phone held up in an extended hand. He's on FaceTime with someone.

"Guys, I'm not lying! It's him." He turns the camera on Jaylen.

This time I'm quicker and I snatch the phone out of his hand, ending the call. "Can you behave? Or do I have to tie you to a tree out back? He's a regular guy," I say, ready to slug my brother in the gut for already making this dinner weird.

"Regular guy? Dude, he's practically leading the league in points. He barely fits through the door frame to our house. Look at him, he's so handsome he could be on the cover of *World's Hottest People* and the entire edition would just be him and Zendaya." Lucas snatches the phone back from me.

"He's not wrong. They've asked," Jaylen butts between us to add. I swat him away with my hand. Jaylen has to be nice to my family, but I don't.

"Lucas, put that damn phone away, or I'll pull up the old videos from your failed gamer YouTube channel," my mom says. The threat works; he tucks his phone in his back pocket and slumps down on the couch with a loud huff.

My mom pops up and heads into the kitchen to check on dinner in the oven, and my brother sees his opening. "You play NHL 25 on Xbox?" Lucas asks, peering over me at Jaylen. He raises his hands and twiddles his thumbs as if he's holding an invisible video game controller.

Jaylen nods and I clue in. They're trying to dip so they can play video games together.

"Go," I say, pushing Jaylen off the couch.

"Only for a couple games." Jaylen leans down and gives me a kiss on the cheek. Lucas gags behind his back.

"Yell for help if Lucas starts being weird," I whisper. My brother makes an unamused face at me.

Lucas jumps up and the two head down the hall. "You know I *was* on the cover once," I overhear Jaylen brag to him. Jaylen must be really loving this ego stroke, and who am I to deny them their fun?

With dinner almost ready, my mom sends me to grab the boys. As I pass my childhood room, I find Jaylen peering around. I quietly watch him from the entrance. He's looking at the paintings hung on my wall—the ones from my senior art showcase. I wanted to burn them in some sort of fire ritual after I ruined everything that night, but my mom insisted on holding on to them. She pulled them out of our basement and hung them on the wall before today's birthday visit.

Jaylen leans in, getting a closer look at three paintings that hang in a row in my room. The series is titled *Finding Home*. The first is a painting of my childhood trailer, which we lived in until my dad left us homeless. The second, the shelter we stayed at while my mom got back on her feet. The third, this house, which she bought and fixed up on her own so no one could ever take it from us. These paintings were the most vulnerable

I had ever been with my art, and I haven't had any interest in opening myself up like that since.

"Looking for something?" I say.

Jaylen startles, turning to find me standing in the doorway. "Sorry. I used the bathroom and when I passed by your room—I couldn't help myself. Did you paint these?" He tucks his hands into his pockets and turns his attention back to my art. Approaching, I stand beside him, staring at the reminder of the worst day of my life.

"I did. They were for my senior art showcase. I was supposed to be a painter, but that obviously didn't work out. I haven't really looked at these since that night," I say.

We stand side by side in a time capsule of my childhood. My walls are still decorated in the black-and-white-checkered pattern I hand painted in high school. The green bedding, the posters on my walls, and all the old sketchbooks stashed in every drawer in the room remain preserved.

It feels weird being in here with Jaylen. If we had met in high school, we would have hated each other. Although, I guess we've always been this different. I lean into Jaylen, and he wraps his arm around me.

"Want to talk about it?" he asks softly.

"There's not much to say. I was supposed to meet a bunch of important people in the industry that night, but my dad showed up drunk and caused a big scene. I never made it to the introductions. I was so mad at him that I stopped painting for years, until I got that commission at the rink. Probably for the best I gave it up anyway. Tattooing is the future I want." I sit down on my bed, curling my legs up into my chest to comfort myself from the painful memory.

"I'm sorry that happened to you. It's painful when your career doesn't pan out the way you envisioned." Jaylen sits next to me.

"It's all in the past now. I finished up the last mural at the rink and my focus is fully back on tattooing. I know an apprenticeship is close."

"You're really talented. Whatever you choose to do, I love looking at it." Jaylen rests his hand on the small of my back.

I stare across the room at the painting of my first home. I can almost smell the stale beer and burnt Hamburger Helper. It's hard to believe so much chaos could fit in such a tiny space.

"It's really serendipitous seeing these paintings tonight... I heard from my dad for the first time in years last week. He wants to meet up for lunch." I grab an old stuffed bear and begin to pick at its matted fur.

I never talk about my dad with anyone. I can't even mention his name around my mom, or she'll break out into hives. Maya and Cooper don't know the full extent of my family history, and Lucas wouldn't understand—his dad's a different brand of deadbeat. Jaylen's dad, on the other hand, sounds perfect. They're close and really love each other. Maybe Jaylen can help me figure out what I'm doing wrong.

"Coming from someone who really regrets blocking an important person out of their life until it was too late, you should go and hear what he has to say," Jaylen says, gently rubbing my back.

"You think?" I slump forward even more. I'd fold myself up into oblivion if it meant not having to think about the unresolved conflict festering between the two of us, but what do I know about a healthy father-child relationship?

"I can go with you if you want."

I lean my body against him, anchoring myself to his side. It's the only thing holding me back from running out of here and not stopping until I'm back at his apartment, safe from any old memory looming in this room. Jaylen's lips press gently into my temple for a kiss, and I decide I can brave the rest of the evening.

"I got you something for your birthday." Jaylen gets up and reaches into his pocket.

"You didn't have to get me anything." I toss my bear to the side and scoot to the edge of the bed eagerly.

"That's what everyone says, but no one means it."

I close my eyes and hold out my hands. Jaylen plops a small velvet box into my palm and my heart drops into my ass. I open my eyes and they bulge out of my head like I'm waiting for the optician to blow a puff of air into my eyeball.

"Don't worry, it's not *that* type of box. I would never propose to you in your childhood bedroom. I would do it in the middle of a live stadium sporting event in front of seventy thousand people so you would be too embarrassed to say no," Jaylen says. Jokingly, I hope.

"How romantic," I say sarcastically. "This isn't smelling salts, is it?" I add, eyeing the black box.

"Open it." Jaylen nudges my arm.

I slowly tilt open the lid. Resting on a bed of velvet is a gold thirteen pendant attached to a gold box chain. It looks exactly like the thirteen we stole from the tattoo shop that night together. Jaylen's jersey number. My flash tattoo. Our stolen sign.

For the first time, I don't know what to say to him. I have no clever or cute rebuttal, no sarcastic quip; I just sit with my mouth open looking at the most thoughtful present a partner has ever given me.

"You hate it! It's totally lame, isn't it?" Jaylen reaches for the box, but I pull it into my chest, guarding it with my tight grip.

"I love it, Jay," I say, turning away from him to get another look.

"I hope it's as lucky for you as it's been for me. It really changed my life. I can't imagine not having it. The thirteen sign we stole, of course," he says.

Jaylen takes the necklace from the box as I gather my hair up off my neck and turn my back toward him. His arms wrap around my chest as he lays the necklace against the skin of my collarbone. His hand tickles my nape when he fumbles with the clasp.

His present isn't lame. It's a bit cocky, a bit romantic, and a bit awkward. It's one hundred percent Jaylen and it's perfect.

# TWENTY-EIGHT

## Jaylen

JAYLEN:

Hypothetically speaking, if you were gifted a Jones jersey would you find that cool or lame?

LUCY:

cool...would you sign it for me? hypothetically speaking of course

JAYLEN:

I'll make it out to my biggest fan.

Lucy:

Ha! I mean I do know all your strengths...and weaknesses...

Jaylen:

Not fair. They're both you.

Lucy:

lol good luck tn jay!

My knee bounces up and down at an aggressive pace as I inch even closer to the edge of the bench. I'm about to carve a divot in the rubber matting if I don't stop digging the toe of my blade into the floor. I hang my head, and unsuccessfully try to hide behind the blade of my stick. Anything to shade myself from the glare of the arena's spotlights. Anything to hide from this crowd.

A lot has changed since I've last been in this arena. The view is so different I hardly recognize it. The visitors' bench gives me a whole new angle of the ice, and the time that's passed since I last played here gives me a new perspective.

This is my first time back in New York since I left without a qualifying offer at the end of last season. Booed off the ice with more volatility than anything thrown at the visiting team. I was already the enemy before I ever played for another team.

My entire body is tense as I await the first TV timeout. Like an incoming fist, I brace myself for the punch. The lights dim. The emotional music is loud. A video begins to play, and my eyes are glued to the jumbotron knowing what's to come. I hold my breath when the tribute video starts with a shot of me in the crowd at the NHL draft. Eighteen years old in an ill-fitting suit and a petrified baby face. Soft and green like lush grass until it is cut.

I take a sharp, shallow breath. And another. Until I find myself practically panting as I hear my name being called, and I watch the video of myself slipping into the Skyliners jersey for the first time. I'm expecting to be showered with boos at any moment from all the fans in attendance tonight. Or maybe they've all sneaked in with eggs tucked under their red sleeves and it will soon begin to rain yolk on me.

I stop my wandering mind and center myself with a deep

breath. *I am more than a draft pick.* Deep breath. *I am more than my stats.* Deep breath. *I am more than a hockey player.* Deep breath.

I finish my mantra—a helpful trick I've learned in therapy—and summon the courage to take a peek at the crowd. To my surprise, the Skyliners fans are on their feet for the first time tonight. The video plays on, shockingly with enough highlights to fill two minutes of excitement and accomplishments. Most of which I had previously forgotten about or picked apart in game film until there was nothing left to celebrate.

I thought watching the highlight reel was going to trigger a massive panic attack, but it isn't. Therapy must be working because as I watch the rest of the video of myself, I don't think about all the times I messed up wearing that jersey. Instead, I'm proud of myself for surviving that difficult period in my life.

Clawing my way back to reach my full potential may have earned back the fans' respect, but realizing that life is so much more than stats and achievements was the only way I could have done it.

It's a quick bus ride back to our hotel after the game. Rather than jetting off in the private plane to the next city tonight, we're sticking around while we play the local teams. We'll face off against the New Jersey Stallions in a couple of days, completing our series of games in New York and New Jersey before finally flying home. I've had my go-to order from my favorite local bagel shop three times already on this road trip, and I plan on going back for fourths tomorrow morning.

Wells and I walk into the hotel together following Soko and Lamber. The two of them whisper back and forth, sharing devious looks and passing off laughs—no doubt plotting an epic night out after tonight's win. I look the other way. My bed and a phone call with Lucy are calling my name.

A small group of players slowly gather in the lobby to decide their plan for the night or say good-night and head up to their hotel rooms. Soko and Lamber, on the other hand, suspiciously head for the elevators.

Wells jogs ahead to catch up to them. He drops his arm around Lamber's shoulder. "Where are you boys off to tonight?"

"Soko's going to shave my back," Lamber shares casually.

Wells's arm drops and so does his face. "Tell me that's the name of a trendy club or at least some viral internet challenge?"

"It's a challenge for the razor," Soko says, laughing. "He's hairy like big bear." He pets the back of Lamber's suit jacket like it's the beloved family pet.

Lamber shrugs. "I can't reach the middle of my back by myself."

Wells sighs, drawing his lips into a thin line. "I gotta stop asking so many questions," he says to himself, shaking his head.

Soko and Lamber squeeze into a full elevator, while Wells and I wait for the next one. "What about you? I'm grabbing a late dinner with some of the Skyliner guys." Wells angles himself toward the hotel bar on the other side of the lobby. "Want to join, or do you have body-hair-removal plans too?"

New York City is still the only road trip stop he'll hit up after a game. Wells still has a lot of friends in the city from his early years on the team here. I know—I used to be one of them.

"Maybe next time." I press the up button once the elevator doors fully close. "I'm helping Lucy prep for an interview tonight."

Wells smiles as he looks me over from head to toe. "It suits you."

"Staying in?" It's suited me for a while. I'm getting too old to be playing hungover, or guilty as we call it in the league.

"Being in love." He teases me. You know it's true love when those who know you best take notice. His observation makes me blush, and I dart into the open elevator doors to hide my embarrassment. "Just promise me I get to be the best man at your wedding," he adds.

"I mean, you're already the best wingman," I shout to him before the doors close.

★ ★ ★

I'm already calling Lucy before I reach my room. She answers my FaceTime on the first ring, greeting me with an eager hello and welcoming smile. In an instant, no matter the distance or which hotel-branded linens wrap me up at night, I'm suddenly home, or at least right where I'm supposed to be. Being in love feels a lot like always being in the right place at the right time.

"You played well," she blurts out with bubbling excitement. She's at her desk surrounded by an art supply mess so chaotic there's no need to ask her what she got up to tonight.

"More importantly, we won." A PR answer slips out as I hold my phone up in one hand and use the other to loosen the tie around my neck.

"It's me, Jay. You can brag a bit." Lucy brings an oversize mug to her lips and blows on the steam.

I set my phone on the desk, but keep my eyes on her. "I played well. I felt even better, no panic attacks," I say, quickly slipping out of the rest of my suit and into pajama pants.

"Good. I know you were worried about tonight."

I climb into bed with my phone in hand, watching Lucy tuck her hair behind her ears as she stares at me through the screen. She's looking at me like she wants to crawl into bed with me, and god I wish she could.

She presses her eyes shut and opens them with newfound determination and focus. "Can I show you my portfolio for the Hunter Gunn interview tomorrow?" she asks.

"I'd be honored."

She jitters with passion as she gathers up a stack of work off her cluttered desk. "I've got all my best work in this binder. I may have included too much, but I'd rather be overprepared," she says as she begins flipping through the pages. From simple script to intricate geometric. Gray realism to vibrant illustrative. Bold traditional to delicate fine line. It's a collection of work that will no doubt land her the apprenticeship she so badly wants and obviously deserves.

I gawk at the screen as she flips through each page. "You're so talented. You've got this interview on lock."

Some of it I've seen lying on her desk or posted on her social media. I've had the privilege of being with her while she created a few pieces. Seeing it all together is like a time stamp on our relationship. I've known her since the original mural sketch, liked her since the destroyed raven, and loved her since the CB tattoo. It's all there in her portfolio.

As she sets the binder back on her desk, her phone, which had been propped up in front of her, falls on its side. Suddenly, Lucy isn't in view and instead, I see the easel in the corner of her room. Painted on the propped canvas is a hockey player, but not just any hockey player—it's me.

"What was that?" I ask, bringing my phone closer to my face, squinting to get a better view.

Lucy is quick to turn her phone upright so I can't see it anymore. "Nothing. It's stupid. Just a doodle."

"Was that me? Come on, show me."

"It's so bad. It's embarrassing. I did it in like ten minutes while I was watching the game." Lucy delays before sheepishly turning the camera's view. She's painted a close-up of my face as I line up to take a face-off. It's as detailed as a photograph, and as vibrant as real life.

"That took you more than ten minutes." She's good, but as arguably her biggest fan and someone who previously monitored the rate at which she painted a mural, I would know she's not that fast (luckily for me).

She flips the camera back around to her but averts her eyes from my face and any potential reaction I'm offering up. "Nine periods, six intermissions, and too many pre- and postgame interviews to count if you must know," she admits, biting her thumbnail.

"You painted? For fun?" I tease.

"For love," she coos. "I think I might be a hockey fan." She smirks before baring her teeth in a snarl and pumping her fist by her side.

"You being a hockey fan is believable—it's an incredibly violent sport. But a painter? I thought you weren't a painter. Your words. Not mine."

Her head tilts upright as if she accepts the position being bestowed upon her. "I've been feeling more like an artist lately," she says.

"That suits you. You should bring your portfolio when we see your dad next week. I'm sure he'd love to see it."

Her eyebrows pinch as her whole face grimaces. "Maybe."

*Shit.* I shouldn't have brought it up. I know I'm feeling nervous about meeting him, but by the look on her face, she might be more nervous than me.

Based on what I know about Lucy's past, we both had very different home lives growing up. My parents have been happily married for thirty-five years. I can't help but think of my dad bringing me to the local rink for public skating every weekend as a young kid. When I first took an interest in hockey, my dad was determined to help. He learned how to skate right alongside me. He wasn't a natural at it like I was, and by the second session I was teaching him. Despite my dad's Bambi legs and embarrassing falls, it was still nice to know he was willing to strap knives on his feet and get out on a hard, frozen surface to be supportive of me.

My mom was the one who made the hockey dream become a reality. She did every team fundraiser possible to help us afford the cost of registration. We were almost always the only Black family, and they protected me more than once from hurtful fans and nasty opposing players. My sisters even got into a few fistfights outside the rink in my honor. I won't give them the satisfaction of admitting it, but they were the ones who taught me how to fight.

My dad, mom, and sisters were my first teammates. I couldn't imagine my life without them. I feel sorry for Lucy that she has a strained relationship with her dad. I know not everyone grew up with a great home life like me, but I know Lucy's heart. She's the most confident person I've ever met, tough as nails, and loyal as hell too. I can't imagine someone not wanting to be a part of her life as much as possible. I know I do. I think this lunch could really turn things around for them and then she could have the relationship she deserves.

I yawn, not due to boredom or because I find our conversation uninteresting, but because being around her puts me at such ease it's easy to relax myself right to sleep—even after games. I prop the phone up on the pillow beside me and tuck my hands under my head.

"Sleepy?" she says, picking up a pencil and twirling it between her fingers.

It's midnight here, which means it's only 9:00 p.m. in Seattle. Lucy will still be up for a few hours, but I can hardly keep my eyes open. I settle deeper into my pillow, pulling the covers over my shoulders. "Will you stay on the phone with me until I fall asleep?" I say before another yawn cuts me off.

It's my favorite postgame routine. We stay on the phone with each other until one of us zonks out and the other finally hangs up. Lucy nods and the last thing I see is a fresh piece of sketching paper move across the screen. The sound of her pencil striking against the sheet puts me to sleep.

# TWENTY-NINE

## Lucy

I pick at the white paper napkin in my hand, tearing it into tiny specks of paper confetti that scatter across the table. We've been waiting for seventeen minutes and counting for my dad to show up to the small diner on the city's edge. Despite selecting the time and location, he's running late with no courtesy text to assure us he'll still arrive.

Jaylen sits close beside me in the booth, eyeing my deteriorating napkin. After the final tear, he slides his fresh one across the table into my restless fingers.

My attention is glued to the entrance of the diner as if I am willing my dad to walk through the door with my glare. Condensation pools on the linoleum tabletop around my untouched ice water. A pile of menus sits stacked in the center of the table where the server dropped them for us.

Guilt represses what's left of my appetite as I remember how far Jaylen had to drive us to get here. I try not to think about how terrible I'll feel if my dad doesn't show at all.

Right when I'm about to call the game, the bell above the door chimes. It's my dad, Rodger. He spots us at the booth and after a tip of his head, he casually walks over.

He is more weathered than I remember. Everything from

his frayed hat to his stained work boots is covered in a layer of black grease. The last I heard he was working on an oil rig in Alaska—another reason Maya wasn't my first choice for this lunch date. The two of them would have likely engaged in a heated debate about the ethics of oil drilling, or worse, the impact of absent fathers on young girls. I'm pretty confident Jaylen's never read up on family dynamic research. Plus, he is too polite to be judgmental.

My dad slowly slides into the booth as if he wasn't twenty minutes late to the lunch he planned. I decide I'm not going to hold it against him and drop what's left of the napkin to say a very awkward hello. Before he even says hi, my dad leans out the booth to flag down a server and order himself a beer.

He quickly glances over at Jaylen from the corner of his eye. "I didn't know you were bringing a friend." He smells of petrol and stale beer, a familiar scent that practically teleports me back to my miserable childhood. I shiver in my seat.

"This is my boyfriend, Jaylen," I say, introducing a partner to my dad for the first time.

Jaylen extends his hand across the table, but my dad reaches for the menu instead. The server brings my dad his beer and I ask for more time to look over the menu. My dad ignores my request and places his order, forcing Jaylen and me to scramble and quickly make a choice.

"How ya been?" my dad asks, his eyes shifting around the room.

"Um, things are really good. I quit my job at Come As You Are Ink and recently finished a few painting commissions for the Rainiers, but I'm waiting to hear back about tattoo apprenticeships. I just had an interview for this really amazing opportunity, so fingers crossed," I say, leaning in to engage.

The two of us have so much to catch up on, and luckily things have been going really well for me these past few months.

It has taken me years to find my footing after college, but I finally feel like I'm on the right path.

"You still at that museum?" he interrupts me. He drinks about a quarter of his beer in one pull and tries to flag the server for another. He looks as familiar as ever with his nose in a glass.

"No, that was my internship my senior year of college. I'm trying to be a tattoo artist now." Our food arrives and I begin tearing apart my hot French fries.

"She's an amazing artist. You should see some of the stuff she's made recently. Her paintings and sketches are beautiful," Jaylen says between bits of food too hot to eat.

I appreciate his enthusiasm, because trying to connect with my dad right now feels like painter's block. I've been talking to a lot of brick walls lately, but at least they've left me inspired.

"More tattoos, really? You spent all that money on a college education only to get a felon's job." My dad tries to pass off his rude remark as a joke, but no one laughs. He stares down at his plate and begins eating his burger.

Jaylen looks over at me, but all my energy is focused on not crying into my plate of food. I suppress my pain, not wanting to cause a scene. I unclench my jaw to speak. "What about you? Still at the oil rig?" I try to keep the conversation going and decide it's probably best if we don't talk about my stuff any longer.

"Between stuff right now, but that's not your business." He shifts around in his seat. We eat in silence, until he drops what's left of his hamburger and finishes another beer.

The tension between the two sides of the booth hangs like a heavy rain cloud threatening a downpour, but I risk the rain. "If you're in town for a while, you should stop by the rink. I painted the big mural out front, and a couple inside too. They're really cool, took me forever. I guess I could show you pictures of them on my phone, but it doesn't do them justice. We can grab lunch after you see it? There's a great sushi place—" It's a bit desperate, which would likely be embarrassing if it wasn't so heartbreaking. I hear the pleading in my voice, but my dad can't even be bothered to listen.

He cuts me off. "I'll check my schedule. Look, I'll cut to the chase. I'm in a tight spot right now. I don't get paid until the end of the month, but I'm way past due on some bills. It wouldn't be too much of a bother to help your old man out, would it?" He continues to completely ignore Jaylen and keeps his eyes deadlocked on me.

I drop a cold fry from my hand. I'm disappointed, but I'm not surprised. Ever since I agreed to go to lunch with him, I've been waiting for this moment: The moment where he would come up with some elaborate excuse and cancel or completely blow me off and not show up. The moment where he does something to let me down. And here it is. It came late—but it hits equally as hard.

"I'm sorry to hear that, Dad, but I don't have enough to give you anything. I have rent, student loans, and insurance. I'm between jobs too. I can't." My hands are balled into tight fists resting on my lap. I dig my nails into the flesh of my palms, but don't feel anything—any deeper and I will penetrate my skin.

"Bullshit," he snaps, pounding his fist against the table. The silverware clatters together as it ricochets from the force.

My body involuntarily flinches. I close my eyes tightly and grind my teeth. My jaw muscles flexing under the strain. I wish I could evaporate.

He's not even trying to hide the fact that he's annoyed with me—disgust is painted on his face. "You've got your nice little Rainiers job and a rich boyfriend. You've got money."

Jaylen looks over at me; I'm not sure if he's more shocked at my dad's behavior or at the fact that I'm letting him talk to me like this. If it were anyone else, I would lunge out of my chair and scratch their eyes out for being so inappropriate, but he's my dad so I am catatonic.

"I'm sorry. I can't help you." My words come out as a whisper. I continue to stare down at my lap, hoping he'll drop it. I can't tell him no for a third time without bursting into tears. I am literally unemployed at the moment while I wait to hear back from tattoo shops. My emergency savings of a thousand dollars is down to four hundred and fifty dollars. One vet bill, one toothache, or one broken phone could put me in the negative. I'm trying to be financially responsible, but I don't want to be a bad daughter either.

"Fucking worthless, stupid and lazy just like your mother." He says it quietly enough not to cause a scene, but loud enough for me to hear. My heart sinks, and for a moment I believe him.

Jaylen's body goes rigid as he stares across the booth. "You have no idea, do you?" he says, his top lip curling in disgust. For a moment I worry he's about to ask my dad to go toe to toe at center ice.

"What are you talking about?" my dad snaps at Jaylen, trying—and failing—to match his level of disdain.

"You're clueless. You don't know anything about her. You don't know how talented she is. You don't know about her amazing friends. You've never met her cute yet mildly psychotic cat. You don't know anything about your daughter and it's your loss, because she's incredible. And you know what, it's not *because* of you—it's *despite*," Jaylen says with conviction. He pulls his wallet from his back pocket and unclips a folded mound of cash. He throws a few hundred-dollar bills at my dad and stands up. "That should cover the food and you can get a clue with the rest."

I slide out of the booth, but before I leave, I look my dad dead in the eyes—the ones everyone says I got from him. I want so badly to tell him to leave me alone, to give him a piece of my mind, but I am frozen, paralyzed by his glare. I open my mouth to speak, but I can't find the words. Jaylen offers me his hand, and together we walk out of the restaurant.

In the safety of Jaylen's car, I bury my face in my hands and sob. "I'm so sorry. That was so embarrassing."

He rubs my back and lets me cry. "It's okay. He's the one who should be embarrassed, babe." I know Jaylen's trying to make me feel better, but it offers little comfort right now.

With a deep breath, I will myself to get it together. I lean back in the passenger seat and close my eyes while I wait for my tears to dry up. "Sometimes I can't help but think about how much easier my life could have been if he just loved me. Is that pathetic?" I ask candidly. I don't expect an answer. I only want to get the feeling off of my chest, and hopefully it will leave my body altogether.

"No. Of course not." He wraps his arms around me and I fall into his chest.

Try as I might, I can't stop the tears. I've been holding them in longer than I've realized, and now pressed against Jaylen's warm cotton T-shirt I finally have something to catch them.

I'm not crying because my dad was mean to me—he's always been mean to me. I'm crying because I know that was my last chance at a normal relationship with him. I'm old enough now to know that he will never be the dad I need, and that realization feels like mourning.

"I think I may have given you bad advice about reconnecting with your dad. Some people aren't worth it," Jaylen says.

"Is that why you did that for me back there?" I pull away from his embrace, sweeping my palms across my cheeks. No one has ever stood up to my dad like that. I didn't know it was possible. Judging by the look on my dad's face when Jaylen told him off, he didn't think anyone would ever have the guts to try.

"I did it because we're a team. I'm not going to let anyone treat you like that," Jaylen says.

I sigh. "You're a good teammate, but you can't protect me from everything." I shake my head, covering my mouth with the sleeve of my sweater. I look out the passenger window in time to see my dad's truck speed down the road and out of sight. Luckily, Jaylen's windows are tinted so dark that I'm safe from sight.

Jaylen's head drops back, relaxing against the headrest. He gazes over at me and says, "You're right. But I can love you the way you deserve every second you let me."

It's likely the sweetest thing anyone has ever said to me, no matter how naive of a proclamation. I decide it's time to let Jaylen in a little bit, let him see behind the curtain for a moment.

"The tattoo here," I say, unzipping my hoodie to expose my bare shoulder. I point out the little wishbone sitting atop my exposed skin. "You asked about it that first night we met. Basically, every wishbone, every birthday candle, every 11:11, I wished for him. Or I guess a better version of him. I know, I'm so stupid. Sounds childish after all this." My head slumps against the cold window.

Jaylen leans over and softly presses his lips against the top of my chilled shoulder, kissing my tattoo. His lips are warm, and his touch is comforting. Like a child with a wound that aches for the loving kissing of someone they trust, his kiss makes me feel better.

"I would never think you're stupid." Jaylen is settled in his seat, like he's ready to stay parked at the diner, comforting me for as long as I need. He looks at me with no expectations and lets me cry. He gives me the room I need. He lets me be.

"I love you." I say it with the type of confidence I wish I always had, because I wish I felt the same way about myself as I do him. Despite my initial effort to hate Jaylen's guts, I could never get away from him. I didn't want to say it back to him last time—even though I knew I loved him then—because I didn't believe he could mean it. I didn't think he really saw me, but after today I know he's looking. *At* the ugly parts and not *past* them. And I say it because I do love him.

Jaylen's left dimple makes an appearance. "Thanks," he says. I whack his arm with a huff. His smile grows even wider. "I love you too." He takes me into his arms. "I know you're going to hear back about the apprenticeship any day now, but I want you to know that you're welcome to come to Chicago with me for the offseason. You can stay the whole time, or for as many visits as you want," he adds.

Guilt instantly poisons the mood. I have to tell him that the apprenticeship with Hunter Gunn is in LA. At first, I didn't see the point. It was such a long shot, but my interview went so well that I already have a follow-up one scheduled. Jaylen's holding on to my hand for dear life, while I'm tugging away.

I want to tell him right now that there's a chance I have to move, but everything is so perfect between us. I don't want to be the one to ruin it. And for what? What if I don't even get the job?

"That sounds nice," I say instead. I want to follow Jaylen wherever, even to boring Midwest suburbia. He holds me and everything is perfect in his arms.

I'll deal with the truth when it becomes a reality.

# THIRTY

## Jaylen

LUCY:

would you still love me if i was a worm?

JAYLEN:

I'd be the fish swimming after your hook.

LUCY:

good luck today...i know it's not a game but figured you could still use some

JAYLEN:

Thanks, I need it!

We kick off practice with some easy laps around the rink. The boys like to joke that it's the Indianapolis 500 on ice, but I don't feel much like joking today. I've got too much on my mind to banter *and* skate.

Once shooting drills get underway, I begin to find my flow. A lot of players hate practicing—not me. I find the repetition comforting. Not only am I getting the most out of practices lately, but my new off-ice routine is clearly working. Last week I was awarded the NHL's first star after tallying six goals and four assists in four games. It took me years to understand that training doesn't end when I leave the rink; for me, it includes my therapy and medication.

Unlike a structured NHL practice, the game of hockey is unpredictable. It's wild, and erratic, which means I need to be as controlled and calm as possible. I need to be able to predict and intercept the game. My panic attacks and depression had previously hindered my ability to keep my head in the game. Since getting help, I'm better equipped to handle what's thrown my way. However, there is one last thing weighing on my mind today, and after practice I'm getting it off my chest.

I skate hard into the corner, fearlessly fighting for the puck. I lose it to the defender, who saucers it up to their winger and into the neutral zone. The next group of guys step up and the drill restarts.

"Come on, JJ. You're not going to let an old guy like me take you off the puck that easily, are you?" Wells chirps, nudging me with his elbow as we make our way back into the neutral zone.

"You might not be fast, but you're strong as hell, dude." I huff, catching my breath.

"Other than my unbeatable dad strength, is everything good? You seem a bit distracted this morning. Unless you let me take you off that puck in the corner on purpose, in which case, thank you. I need all the help I can get."

We stop in front of the bench and each grab a squirt of water from the bottles lined up on top of the boards. I lean against them, taking some weight off my feet.

"I've got an interview after practice with the team reporter, Nichole." I slide off my glove to wipe the sweat off my brow.

"Life of a superstar." Wells shakes his head and laughs. "Do you think she would let me contribute a quote?" He takes another drink. The sweat from practice is dripping down his cheek and we're only one drill deep.

"It's not that kind of article. I'm launching a nonprofit foundation and the team is helping me announce it," I say.

"That's awesome, man. Let me know how I can help." Wells squirts water all over his face and shakes it off like a wet dog.

"Thanks. I'll tell ya about it tonight at the party." I grab one last squirt of water before tossing the bottle on the bench, ready to rejoin the drills.

"Hey, Wells!" Coach Pete's voice carries over from center ice. "You going to work any other muscle besides your tongue this practice?"

Wells throws his arms up in overexaggerated outrage. "What about JJ?" he shouts back.

"I'll leave you alone when you're the NHL's first star of the week," Coach Pete says before blowing his whistle for the next group to start the drill.

Wells covers his mouth with his glove and says discreetly, "Guess he's never going to get off my back then." He smacks the top of my helmet playfully and skates off.

As practice comes to a close, Coach Pete calls the team to center ice. "Good job today, boys. We got a couple of days off before the playoffs start, so let's rest up and stay hungry. Let's get the most out of these practices so we're ready for game one. I'll see you guys tonight at the team dinner."

The team finished the season second in the Pacific Division, a long way from their last-place finish a few seasons ago and even better than last season, when they narrowly missed out on a wild-card playoff spot. We are currently riding a hot streak into the playoffs, which start later in the week, but until then, we are all headed to a team dinner tonight. The owner of the team has organized a low-key event for the players, coaching staff, and significant others to gather and celebrate our accomplishment. I'm picking Lucy up later tonight, but first, I have to sit down with Nichole.

Nichole is waiting for me outside the team's locker room. I'm usually the first guy on the massage table after practice ends, but today I skipped postpractice treatment and showered in record time so I could get out and get this part of my day over with.

I don't hate the media. I understand that they have a job to do, and that job helps promote the team and the sport, but that doesn't mean I enjoy the spotlight. When you've had a famously polarizing career like mine, you know which reporters are only in it for the clicks and views, and which ones have enough integrity to get the story right.

Nichole is employed by the team and has agreed to write a story that does me justice. I trust she'll make me sound good.

"Should we grab a seat in the media room?" Nichole says discreetly.

I don't want to be rude to her, but I hate the media room. The lights, the backdrop, the chairs all facing the podium. Even if it's only going to be her and I in the room today, I would rather chat anywhere else.

"Can we sit in the stands instead?" I ask.

I follow Nichole up the stairs, and we find seats near center ice. While she gets herself set up for the interview, I stare down at the clean, glossy ice. The overhead lights reflect off the freshly flooded and untouched sheet like a mirror.

Nichole presses the record button on her phone. "Ready when you are." She rests the ball of her pen against a fresh piece of paper in her notepad.

I take a swig of my BodyArmor and brace myself.

"I'm officially launching Cam's House, a nonprofit organization helping to provide shelter, food, and therapy for youth experiencing homelessness in Seattle. This week we're handing out personal hygiene items to Tent City camps." The words come out exactly as I've rehearsed them.

One answer down. I release the grip on my drink and dry my sweaty palms on the tops of my thighs. As much as I've always hated postgame press conferences and intermission reports, at least I could spew the same regurgitated lines over and over. This is different. I'm not talking about getting pucks deep or giving it a hundred and ten percent—I'm talking about Cam.

"What inspired you to launch Cam's House?" Nichole continues to jot down notes on her pad of paper while never breaking our eye contact.

"Teen homelessness, drug abuse, and mental health crises are serious issues facing the community here." I give the rest of my prepped PR answer. I deliver it with the same cadence I would when reciting a response to a beat reporter at a postgame presser. Like when Bob from the *Times* asks in a roundabout way who was responsible for the team's loss, and I have to dance around the answer. Over the years I've gotten good at the dance, so good that I'm subconsciously shutting Nichole out right now.

Nichole drops her pen and sets her notebook to the side. I continue to shift around in my seat, tearing at the label on my drink.

"Everything you've said so far about the initiative is really powerful, but if you're comfortable talking about it, I would love to know about Cam."

I knew the question would come up—I just hope I say the right thing. "Cam was my best friend growing up. We played youth hockey together as kids. One time when we were ten, this asshole on the other team yelled at me to go back to Africa. Cam beat the wheels off that kid and almost got himself kicked out of the league. He was always the first one to be there for his friends, like he was on standby, waiting for you to need him. We ended up drifting apart as we got older, and he got wrapped up in being there for friends who didn't have his best interests. He could have used a charity like this. Actually, he would have been the first one volunteering to help hand stuff out to those in need. He died of an overdose in 2020."

"I'm sorry for your loss, Jaylen." Nichole gives me a second to gather my composure.

I relax into my seat, staring down at center ice like it's a hypnosis spiral. Voices carry down the hall and suddenly people are filling the rink.

"Shoot, that was today," Nichole says under her breath. "The team is holding their monthly public skate this afternoon. We can move over to the media room for more privacy." She tosses her belongings into her tote bag.

I continue watching the public skaters. The ice is no longer unmarked. It's littered with couples gliding in pairs, adults holding up small children learning to balance on blades, and kids racing as they weave in and out of other skaters.

I try to hold myself back from saying too much about Cam; I don't want to jeopardize my opportunity to sign a long-term deal this offseason, but at the same time I want to honor Cam with the truth. And I want to honor myself.

"I missed his funeral. I had a game, and I missed his funeral for it. I can't tell you a single play from that night. I can't even tell you the score, but I still live with the regret. I haven't been playing with a nagging injury all these years—I've been playing through regret," I say, still looking down at the ice.

Nichole doesn't say anything; she only listens.

As I watch the public skaters, I notice two young boys ripping around the rink, laughing uncontrollably as they spray ice up on each other. Then I see a father and his son clinging to the boards as they step out on the ice for what is clearly both their first times.

"Do you remember the first time you ever skated?" Nichole asks.

The question catches me off guard, but still, I don't need much time to recall the memory. It's one of my favorites. "Yeah.

I kept telling my dad that I was going to fall if I let go of the boards. Finally he said, 'You'll never skate if you don't.'"

"That's pretty solid advice."

"What's crazy is that no matter how good you get at skating, sometimes you still fall."

"But you keep getting up."

In remembering my father's advice, I realize I have a platform; what good is a voice if I don't speak? I'm having an undeniably successful season, and the more I've lived my truth, the more I've reached out to others, the better I've gotten. If this team doesn't want me for who I really am, then another one will. And even if they don't, I'm done hiding. It was never luck that pushed me out of my funk—it was healing.

I tell Nichole everything. I tell her about the pressure to never miss a game, and the guilt over my choice to give in to that demand. I tell her that the pressure to live up to my draft status caused crippling panic attacks until I sought help for anxiety and depression. Then I tell her in great detail about my new charity initiative and how I hope I can honor my friend and be there for kids in the way I couldn't be there for Cam.

I spill it all and don't stop to worry about what others might think of me, including my peers. I don't have the security of a long-term contract yet, but I don't care if the Rainiers don't want me after I tell my truth. This is who I am—on and off the ice. When I sat down for this interview, I had no intention of talking about my own mental health and the challenges I am learning to face, but I feel better having done it.

By the end, Nichole shakes my hand and assures me she'll deliver a story that does me justice. She thanks me for my honesty and commends my bravery. I accept her praise, even though I still feel unworthy of it.

When I finally get into my car, I let out a deep breath of relief from the fact that the interview is finally over. Then I turn on some Phoebe Bridgers for the drive home.

# THIRTY-ONE

## Lucy

JAYLEN:

Good luck at your second
interview today babe.

LUCY:

oh...that is nice i see why you
like it

JAYLEN:

Maybe mine will be just as lucky.

LUCY:

let's not get carried away

I quickly pull my bangs back and clip them into place before
frantically running a lint roller all over my little black dress.
With its white collar and cuffs, I look like a slutty Wednesday
Addams. I slip into my heels and head out the door before I
have time to second-guess my outfit for tonight. I'm headed

to a dinner with Jaylen and his team, and I just received his "I'm out front" text a couple minutes ago. I don't want to keep him waiting.

"You look amazing," Jaylen says as I slide into the passenger seat of his car.

I lean over the center console to steal a kiss from his lips before I can thank him or return the compliment. I can't believe how much I've missed him, and it's only been an afternoon apart. As we kiss, Jaylen is careful not to dishevel my hair, a chivalrous gesture that I hope he ditches later tonight.

We pull away from each other and I wipe my lip gloss off Jaylen's lips with my thumb. "And you look handsome. You know I love it when your top buttons are unbuttoned." I run my fingers down his exposed neckline, tickling his chest. I'm feeling playful tonight as I make eyes at him from across the car.

"I know. I did it on purpose." He blushes. Jaylen rests his hand on my thigh, giving my bare leg a squeeze. I grab on to his hand before he can pull it away, forcing it up higher on my leg, his fingers sneaking under the hem of my dress.

"We have a bit of time, don't we?" I glance over at the car's dashboard display. We're on time, but when have I ever cared about that? I look into his eyes; they darken.

Jaylen leans into me and whispers in my ear, "I always have time to make my girl feel good." His breath tickles my neck and sends goose bumps all over my body. He forces his fingers into my mouth while maintaining eye contact. I get them all wet for him.

I quickly shimmy in my seat, sliding my thong down to my ankles and spreading my legs for him. Knowing what comes next, I practically giggle. Jaylen runs his hand high up my leg until his fingertips brush against my clit. My pussy throbs as he firmly rubs his hand back and forth, touching the perfect spot.

He places his free hand around my neck. "Is this okay?" His voice is firm, in control.

I nod, looking up into his eyes. He squeezes my neck and my eyes roll into the back of my head on a moan.

His movements become firmer, faster. "Just like that," I whisper hoarsely. He continues to touch me the way I like it until I come all over his hand.

Jaylen pulls his hand out from between my legs and brings his fingers to his mouth for a taste.

"Should we go back to your apartment?" I adjust my underwear back into place.

Jaylen kisses my forehead. "Soon. First, we have to go to this stupid dinner." He shifts his car into Drive, and we speed off before fashionably late becomes late-late.

Jaylen leaves his keys with the valet and grabs my hand as we head inside together. The upscale bar is overflowing with men with broad shoulders, toothless smiles, and nice butts. Most of them have a beautiful partner linked on their muscular arm. For now, everyone is standing around chatting, but the bar leads into a fancy restaurant with tables set for the sit-down dinner to follow.

I can't remember the last time I attended a private event that wasn't one of Maya's charity fundraisers. For once I'm a guest and not a beneficiary.

A few more people trickle in behind us, but the room is already filled with a buzzing hum of chatter.

"Come on, I want to introduce you to everyone," Jaylen says.

Wells and his wife, Hannah, are gathered around a circular bar in the middle of the room talking with Lamber. I've briefly met Hannah a couple of times at games, since my friends and I are usually seated in the same section as the players' significant others. Sometimes her kids are with her. She strikes me as the type of mom who always volunteers at the school, but still knows how to cut loose with her friends on the weekend, like life and its delicate balance come naturally to her. A woman with a maturity and sophistication far beyond my reach.

Before Jaylen can introduce me to the group, Lamber turns his head slightly, peering at me out the corner of his eye. Without hesitation, he says, "Two glasses of champagne, and what do you guys have on tap here?"

"I'm not sure," I say, laughing off the confusion. This isn't the first time I've been mistaken as an employee when I'm really a guest.

Jaylen clears his throat. "This is my girlfriend, Lucy," he says, in a threatening voice.

"You're Lucy. My bad." Lamber throws his hands up in defense.

Suddenly, a server steps in offering up a tray of hors d'oeuvres. It doesn't take me long to notice that she's wearing a black dress with a white collar and cuffs—the same black dress that every other woman working the event is wearing. Face-to-face with my outfit's mirror image, I begin stuffing my mouth with whatever tiny appetizer the woman is offering as she passes through the venue.

"We were just talking about the playoffs," Wells says, interrupting the awkward silence. "It's official—we're playing the Dallas Stampeders."

"Lucy," Hannah says, turning to me, "I haven't seen you at a ton of games this season. Will you be attending any playoff games?" Her eyes dart back and forth between me and Jaylen. She seems protective, but I'm not sure of which one of us.

At every game I've attended, the row of wives and girlfriends is packed with familiar faces. I guess it's unusual for a girlfriend to miss a game, but I haven't been in an official relationship with Jaylen all that long.

"It's my schedule. I started selling my art online to make extra cash and I'm the most creatively productive in the evenings. But it sounds like I'll have to make it to a playoff game," I say.

When it's convenient with all our schedules, I take Maya and Cooper to the game with me. Maya has become quite the unlikely die-hard Rainiers fan. Even going as far as to form an official queer fan group, the Rainbow Rainiers—they have carabiner merch and everything. Just as much, I've been enjoying watching the games from home while I paint. Maybe I can sit with Hannah next time.

"Playoff hockey is the best," Wells says enthusiastically.

"I'm surprised you remember. The last time you played a playoff game your stick was made of wood." Lamber chuckles at his own joke. Wells and Jaylen narrow in on him with unamused glares. "I'm going to go find Soko. Hopefully he's got some edibles on him because I need them to get through this boring dinner." Lamber excuses himself.

Wells and Jaylen commiserate about Lamber before getting into a discussion about the Stampeders' defense.

"I love the dress." Hannah sweeps a handful of soft blond curls over her shoulder, revealing a small flower tattoo hidden behind her ear.

"Thanks. I thought it was vintage, but looks like I thrifted someone's old uniform." Looking around for someone dressed like me, I spot a server and wave her down. She quickly passes tall crystal champagne flutes to the group.

I take a drink, hoping the bubbles will settle the knots in my stomach. "Cute tattoo. Part of the reason why I'm working on my art so much is because I'm trying to get a tattoo apprenticeship," I say, trying to find common ground.

It's not like me to struggle so much with meeting new people, but I really want to make a good impression. Just as I start to feel out of place again, Jaylen's warm hand links with mine. It's a reminder that he brought me with him tonight because he wants me here. I belong, and his tight grip on my hand is exactly what I need to almost believe it.

"I thought you were a painter. Your murals are amazing, by the way. Would you ever take a personal commission? Because I know some hockey wives who are looking for a meaningful retirement gift for their husbands and I think your art would make the perfect gift," Hannah says.

"Really?" I drop Jaylen's hand.

"Absolutely. And not only retirement, but even Christmas or milestone gifts."

I think for a moment, taking a mouthful of bubbly while I let the idea marinate. "I'm not sure I'll have the time."

"Let me give you my number in case." She motions for my phone.

As Hannah enters her number into my contacts, Jaylen interrupts. "We should go make the rounds before we all have to sit down for dinner. Save us a spot in there?"

Wells flashes him a thumbs-up.

I wave bye to the two of them as Jaylen drags me back into the crowd. I hadn't thought about doing more commissions, especially not sports-related ones. The murals ended up being a lot of fun to create, but I won't have time to take on projects like that once I get a tattoo apprenticeship.

"I want you to meet Groot," Jaylen says.

"Let me guess, another nickname?" I need a glossary to keep up with everyone.

"His real name is Calvin Moore. Guy's an absolute giant, plus his goaltending is out of this world."

We stop in front of a lanky guy about as tall as a tree with beautiful shaggy hair. I used up the last of my goldilocks paint on him and his lemon-chiffon-highlighted locks. The entire time I painted I wondered what elaborate expensive hair-care routine he followed. Now that I'm inches away, I realize it's likely good genes.

"Groo, this is Lucy." As Jaylen introduces me, I come to an unfortunate discovery.

"Oh my god. They were yelling 'Groo' this whole time? I thought everyone in the stands was always booing you. I briefly joined in at one point. I'm so sorry," I say, shaking his hand. The boys laugh at me.

Groot is with his fiancée, Katie, who proudly shows off her new engagement ring. "Oh wow! It's like a paperweight," I blurt out, feeling a bit dizzy from my first glass of champagne. I hold up Katie's hand toward the light to get a good look at the massive rock engulfing her dainty finger. For a moment, I wonder if I'm being tacky, but figure anyone with a Ring Pop–sized diamond is wearing it to be admired.

"Thank you." Katie's hand drops back down to her side like a wrecking ball from the sheer weight of the stone.

A server stops by offering drinks, which I gladly accept. Katie, on the other hand, politely declines, turning to me to say, "I'm pregnant." She rubs her tiny belly, which looks like no more than indigestion rather than pregnancy.

My mouth agape, I say, "Shit. What are you going to do?"

Katie's eyebrows pinch together. "Have the baby during next season and then the wedding the following summer just as we planned."

It finally dawns on me that my peers are *trying* to get pregnant, and I quickly wrap up the conversation before I shove my foot any further down my throat.

Once we're out of earshot, I ask Jaylen, "Can you believe they're getting married? Talk about teen bride."

Confusion consumes Jaylen's face. "Groot's like twenty-six."

"Do you think their parents know?" I ask, shocked at their infantile age, fetuses really.

"Yes, and I'm sure they're really happy for them." Jaylen places his hand on the small of my back as we make our way to the next couple.

After meeting a few other couples on the team, I learn that twenty-six is quite old in hockey years. By twenty-six, a hockey player should have a wife, two dogs, a kid on the way, and at least one major surgery. Most of the players I meet look even younger than twenty-six and are already married with kids.

It reminds me of the time I visited upstate New York with Cooper after graduation and met all his hometown friends, most of whom were already getting married or knocked up. Meanwhile, Cooper and I were trying to come up with creative ways to sneak drugs into music festivals and figure out how to cook frozen pizza without burning our shitty apartment down to the ground.

I have yet to have an existential crisis over my age, but quarter-life crises are common and Jaylen and I are both twenty-five. Part of me knows that this is a serious relationship that will someday lead to a life I never thought possible. A life where I'm someone's wife; someone's mother. I know Jaylen can give me that life, and eventually I want it all. But there's another part of me that feels out of control, and it's making my heart race. My dress feels like a boa constrictor wrapped around my body. Sweat beads form on my nose and my legs begin to wobble like spaghetti.

"I need to pee." My eyes dart around the room desperately searching for a restroom.

"Now? We're about to move into the restaurant for dinner," Jaylen says, waving across the room at Wells.

"I'm not risking another UTI. I'll catch up with you." I see the bathroom across the room, and I shove my half-empty champagne flute into Jaylen's empty hand before quickly weaving around dinner guests to reach the door. I lock myself in a stall to catch my breath away from all the diamond engagement rings, photos of babies, and talk of summer wedding plans. It's tiring work being on your best behavior all night, and for a second I can relax and not worry about saying the wrong thing.

The silent retreat ceases as the sound of my phone vibrating startles my eyes open. I fumble with the broken clasp on my purse. It's Hunter Gunn. I answer the call with trembling hands. My second interview for the job went really well, but I try not to get my hopes up in case she's calling to tell me she went with someone else.

"Hello?" I sound like the final girl in a horror movie calling out to my killer.

"Lucy! This is Hunter Gunn. I'll get right to the point. You got the apprenticeship." She says it like she's announcing a radio contest winner live on air.

"What! I mean, I don't even know what to say." I'm in shock. I waited so long to get this call that I almost lost faith it would happen for me. Now that it is, I can't believe it's real.

"Say you'll get out here right away. I can't wait to get started working with you."

"Yes! I can't wait either. Thank you so much." The hysteria in my voice is matching that of an Oscar-winning actress at this point. I need to get off the phone before I start thanking my mom and friends for their unwavering support. *What is this emotion taking over me? Am I going to cry?* I don't think I've ever cried happy tears, only depressive sobs howling over Radiohead's most upsetting tracks.

"I'll be in touch. Look out for an email with the contract. Chat soon."

Before I have time to let out a celebratory scream in the stall, I hear the clicking of a herd of heels stomping their way into the restroom.

The bathroom door creaks open and someone with a heavy vocal fry says, "Did you see she's dressed like a waitress?"

I freeze with my hand on the door's latch. The thought of confrontation twists my stomach like a wrung-out cloth. I don't want anything to sour my mood. Instead of leaving the stall, while the tap is running, I jump up on the toilet seat and crouch down like a school-age child hiding from a bully.

"It's secondhand, and she looks amazing." I recognize the voice talking this time; it's Hannah's.

"Second Hand? I've never heard of that brand." The gossip continues in a variety of voices.

"I heard she's a lesbian," someone else says.

I try to peek through the door's crack, but my view is too obscured to see faces.

"Did you know Jaylen was into emo girls?" Vocal Fry asks.

"Emo?" I whisper under my breath. I'm a lot of things: heavily tattooed, broody, depressed, queer, always running late… She might have a point. With my hand cupping my ear, I continue to eavesdrop on their conversation.

"She seems nice, but I've known Jaylen for years and he is not the relationship type." I feel lightheaded when I hear Hannah's voice again.

"Player?" someone asks.

"No, he's totally boring. Hockey is his love. But Evan says it's serious, so maybe men can change," Hannah says.

"No way. It will fizzle out by the end of playoffs, and then he'll be like every other single guy enjoying a slutty offseason."

"They always do."

And just as quickly as they entered, the group exit the restroom, leaving my confidence devastated. I finally jump down from the toilet and stumble out of the stall, wiping the tears from my face before they can smudge my makeup—because I spent way too long getting my eyeliner perfect to ruin it. I pull myself together enough to brave dinner.

As I rush out of the bathroom, a man dressed in black with a white apron around his waist tries to hand me a tray full of drinks. "Bring these to table five," he says, pushing the tray into my arms before I have the chance to object.

Luckily, I waited tables to offset the cost of college tuition. I balance the tray in my dominant hand with ease, and while looking very much the part, I strut off to find the fifth drink-less table. I had every intention of dropping the tray quickly and running away before anyone could notice, but then I hear a familiar screeching vocal fry coming from the end of the table. Hearing someone posing a statement as a question triggers my better judgment. I slam the drinks down with a splash, right in front of my bully.

"Hey! Careful," says Vocal Fry, checking her dress over to make sure it's spotless.

"Sorry, guess I'm feeling a bit emotional tonight," I say with as much attitude as I can muster, and I turn on my heels and dart off to find my seat before someone asks me about tonight's dinner specials.

Wells and Jaylen carry the conversation for the entirety of the dinner. Jaylen explains his new charity and Wells and Hannah gush about their girls. Leaving me to retreat into silence.

Part of me is incredibly excited for my new job—my dream job—but another part of me worries what it means for Jaylen and me. The apprenticeship with Hunter Gunn means moving to LA; this is exactly why I shouldn't have gotten into anything serious while I was trying to focus on my career. It complicates things.

Jaylen's going to hate me when he finds out that I've been lying to him about this job. I never found the right time to tell him it's out of state. Even if by some miracle he still wants to be with me once I come clean, our relationship is so new and fresh that we could never last long-distance. Not with his travel schedule. Not with my upcoming workload. I'm not stupid. I heard those girls; Jaylen wants a slutty summer. He's a superstar NHL hockey player; of course he does.

"How's your food? Is everything okay?" Jaylen asks discreetly.

"It's great. Everything's fine." I pick at a hangnail underneath the table, turning something superficial into a much deeper wound.

# THIRTY-TWO

## Lucy

The car ride back to Jaylen's apartment is so quiet that not even the sound of the radio can drown out the silence. I sit on my words, holding my breath until I'm red in the face and white at the knuckles. I dig through the glove compartment in search of some chewing gum. If I don't occupy my mouth, I'm afraid of what might come out of it.

Sitting on top of the owner's manual and a stack of fast casual restaurant napkins is a stick of women's deodorant. I snatch it up and confront Jaylen on impulse.

"Whose is this?" I ask. The girls in the bathroom were right. He is a player, and I just found incriminating evidence.

"It's mine. Women's deodorant works better. You can use it if you want," he says, only glancing over momentarily to see what I'm holding.

"I'm fine. I put some on before I left my apartment." I shove the deodorant back in the glove box and drop it for approximately one second before deciding that I'm not ready to let it go. "Let me see your armpit," I demand.

"What?"

"Let me smell it." I lean over, lifting Jaylen's arm and taking a big whiff. "Okay, it's women's deodorant." I settle back into my seat with my arms in a knot across my chest.

"Is everything okay?" Jaylen's grip on the steering wheel tightens as his body tenses up.

"Are you a player?" I decide that I need to know, no matter how much the answer will hurt me. If he's incapable of loving anything other than hockey, then what's the point of telling him that I'm moving to LA? He doesn't have to wait until after the playoffs to dump me; he can get it over with right here, right now.

"Yes, forward. Center if you want to be specific. Think of me as the distributor..." Jaylen begins to mansplain hockey to me.

By now, I've watched enough hockey to not only know what his role is, but to know when he isn't doing it properly. "That's not what I mean. Are you incapable of loving anything other than hockey?" I interrupt.

"I love you. You know I love you. Where is this coming from? Did I do something tonight?"

We stop at a red light, giving Jaylen the opportunity to look over at me. I'm straining my face, eyebrows pinched, as I gnaw at the inside of my cheek like chewing gum. His gentle eyes disarm my tough exterior, and I confess what transpired in the bathroom. "No, I overheard some of the girls in the bathroom tonight talking about you."

"Well, what do they know? They don't know me. I certainly don't remember all of their names, I'll tell you that much." He chuckles.

"It was Hannah."

Jaylen's laughter dries up and his Adam's apple bobs as he gulps. "I'm not sure why she would say that. Last week I told Wells how excited I was to bring you back to Chicago with me this summer."

"Let's drop it." I feel stupid for getting caught up in my own insecurities. I know I have to tell him about LA, but I don't know how. With my arms wrapped around my own body in a tight embrace, I watch the city speed by. The silence consumes the conversation for the rest of the drive back to Jaylen's apartment.

In Jaylen's closet, he helps me unzip the back of my dress, and I slip it off my shoulders, sending it to the floor in a pool around my feet. He averts his eyes away from my body like he's avoiding me as he changes into comfy clothes. I pull on an oversize shirt and help him unclasp the gold chain from around his neck. It's a tiny moment of intimacy that sends a twist of guilt into my consciousness.

We're face-to-face, inches from each other, when he grabs onto my waist, stopping me before I can pull away. "Listen to me for a second. Hockey was always the only thing I had room for in my life, but that was before I met you. I didn't think someone could fit into my life. I never felt like I had the space for it. This whole time I was saving that space for you. I've been waiting for you," he says.

My grip on his chain releases, and the necklace drops to the floor. I stumble back, struggling to breathe like I've been punched in the gut. His fierce display of love sends me into a panic.

"I'm moving to LA." My confession comes out as a whisper. There was probably a better way to tell him the news than blurting it out, but I didn't trust myself to keep it in any longer. I was bordering on making the move and texting him as I touch down in LAX.

"I don't understand." Jaylen looks at me, waiting for answers. I already know mine will disappoint.

"The apprenticeship with Hunter Gunn is in LA."

His confusion turns into elation, and he reaches out to rub my arm. "You got it? That's amazing!" His face sours as he realizes what that means for us. "Wait, why didn't you tell me it was in LA?" He's hardly mad. He's acting like I accidentally forgot to grab milk on my way home.

"This job was a long shot for me. When it started to become a possibility, I didn't know how to bring it up," I say, turning away.

"You moving to LA isn't ideal, but you can still come visit me in Chicago this summer. And I'll go visit you when I can. Between FaceTime and texting, I'm sure we can figure it out. I mean, it's just an apprenticeship. You'll move back to Seattle in a year once it's done." There is so much enthusiasm in his voice. His confidence is irritating; it's like he's used to things working out for him.

He has no idea what I've gone through to get this opportunity. If he knew what it meant to me, he would never diminish it like this; he's acting like I'm going away to summer camp. Like my career is juvenile and temporary.

"Just an apprenticeship?!" I cock my head back, his unsavory comments warranting the crazed look in my eyes. "It's my career. There's no moving back once it's done."

A tattoo apprenticeship can last anywhere from a year to three years. By then I'll have established a clientele, a reputation at the shop, and a life in LA.

I leave him standing alone in the closet with the dumbfounded look painted on his face as I stumble back into his room hoping to hide under the heavy duvet. I'd much rather be crushed by a million duck feathers than continue this suffocating conversation.

"Hold up. Since when are you moving away and never coming back? Don't you think this is the type of thing we should discuss together?" He follows me into the bedroom.

"Apprenticeships are hard to get. I always knew there was a possibility that I would have to move away for my career. This is why I didn't want to get into anything serious. You're the one who kept pressuring me to be your good-luck charm." Heat rises to the tips of my ears.

"Oh, so it's my fault. I tricked you into falling in love with me."

"That's not what I mean," I say under my breath. I slump down on his bed, my head hitting the pillow just in time to close my eyes and release the built-up tears. They stream down my cheeks onto the silk pillowcases I gifted Jaylen for Valentine's Day because they're softer for his curly hair.

"Lucy, I don't love the fact that you kept this from me, but I also would never want to be the reason you turn down an opportunity like this. We can make it work. Go for the apprenticeship and then we can talk about what our future together looks like after that. Even if you're in LA, we should at least try to make our relationship work." I feel his weight hit the end of the bed as he plops down near my feet.

"Athletes are good at motivational pep talks, and apparently even better at having a fun offseason." I turn on my side away from him. I pull the heavy covers over my head. He can't talk me out of this; I won't let him.

"Is this about what Hannah said?" Jaylen asks, tugging on the bedding. "Will you talk to me?" His voice shakes.

"I'm going to sleep." My voice is muffled as I hide my face.

"You don't get to be mad at me right now. If anyone gets to be mad, it should be me. Not only did you not tell me about moving to LA permanently, but now you won't even talk about a long-distance relationship. Why can't you accept that you've changed my life and I want you in it forever?" he says, his voice pleading. It's a heartbreaking Hail Mary.

I snap out of my failed attempt at an early bedtime. I throw the blanket off my body and hop out with a newfound jolt of energy. I barge into the bathroom, angered by the guilt he's feeding me. I'm already too full of it myself. Jaylen's quick to get to his feet, following me into the bathroom.

"I'm not your manic pixie dream girl! I have my own life to live. I can't hang around, following you and your career. Especially when you don't even know where you're going to end up playing next season. This is my dream and I need to chase it," I say leaning over the sink, splashing water on my face.

"What the hell is a manic pixie dream girl? We don't all have a liberal arts community college degree with a minor in women's studies."

I face him with water dripping from my chin. "It was queer theory! You're trying to make me feel bad about taking this job. You're an asshole," I say, toweling off.

"And you're a coward."

We may know how to love each other, but that means we know how to hurt each other too. The words escape our mouths before we have time to process the inevitable: we are having our first fight as a couple. Even though I know it's happening, I can't stop myself from engaging. I can't walk away. I can't back down.

"You think because you stood up to my dad that suddenly you know what's best for me?" I look up at him through a raging glare, meeting him in the door frame. Resentment bubbles in my stomach. The cracks in my tough exterior threaten to give under the threat of vulnerability.

"No, of course not. I thought we were a team and now you're bailing on us." His voice breaks getting the words out.

My bottom lip quivers. I'm seven years old at the top of the Seattle Great Wheel and I can't breathe. When did I become unreliable and unreasonable like my dad?

"I should leave. I have to leave." My voice trembles. I know how ridiculous I sound. I'm standing here in nothing but his oversize T-shirt and my underwear. My toothbrush is lying on his bathroom counter, my half-finished book is propped open on his nightstand table saving my page, the yogurt I like is stocked in his fridge, and my Pepto-Bismol is stored in the cabinet above the sink. I can stomp out of his apartment as dramatically as I want, but I will remain.

"Don't." Jaylen reaches for my arm, but I recoil from his touch.

"I need some time to think about what I want to do." I fidget with the hem of my shirt. I hold my stare up toward the ceiling to prevent more tears from falling down my face.

"Sure. I'll make us some popcorn and I'll dissolve your melatonin in the hot tea how you like it. After a good night's sleep we can come back to this tomorrow morning and figure it all out." Jaylen heads into the kitchen and rummages through a cabinet for tea bags.

I follow him, stopping in the doorway. "No, Jay. I need some space to myself to think about this. And you're not an asshole. You're a great guy—to a fault even. I think I'm the asshole," I say, fighting back tears. With a deep breath, I gather myself enough to grab my dress and slip on some pants.

"Lucy," he calls for me.

I hug my crumpled-up dress like a child clinging to their beloved stuffed animal, desperate to be soothed.

"I love you, but you're being cowardly. You can't keep doing this sometimes-y bullshit with me. I'm willing to be there for you, no matter the distance. If you walk out on us right now, then I know you wouldn't do the same for me." Jaylen is emotionless. I've never seen him so despondent.

I don't say anything; there's nothing left to say. Instead, I do the only thing I know.

I leave.

# THIRTY-THREE

## Jaylen

In the late morning after pregame skate, I get a text from Nichole letting me know that her article on the launch of my charity initiative and my mental health struggles is going live on the team's website.

I'm too distracted by my mental preparation for the game to give it much attention. I figure people will find something negative to say about me, and I don't want to get stuck doomscrolling through the tired and uninspired insults. Not to mention, I don't need that kind of negativity before going into today's game against the Dallas Stampeders. But once I wake up from my pregame nap, curiosity gets the better of me and I reach for my phone.

The article has gone viral, met with overwhelmingly positive feedback.

The city, the fans, the ones who matter, everyone has nothing but kind and encouraging comments for me. Even some of the hockey reporters who had previously posted that I was past my prime, injury stricken, a lost-cause bust, are changing their tune and singing a praise of perseverance.

I have close to a hundred text messages from friends and family. Everyone read the article and wants to let me know how proud they are of me and my honesty. The team's group chat is still blowing up; all the guys want to know how they can help with my charity. Guys have offered to donate money or make appearances at future events for Cam's House. Whatever I need, they all want to help. I can't wipe the smile off my face no matter how hard I try—my cheeks are starting to hurt.

As I scroll to the bottom of my text message notifications, there's a text from Lucy. She must have sent it to me minutes after the article went live. I pause briefly before opening it, not wanting it to throw me off my big game. I need to be focused, and Lucy is the only person capable of knocking me off my feet.

Ultimately, I open the text. I'll only spend the entire game wondering what she sent me if I don't.

LUCY:

> great article jay. i'm not stalking you online or anything, but i get a notification when something is posted about you...ok i think that might be the literal definition of online stalking but I'm glad i didn't miss this article. i know some people say you're relentless but i think you're awesome too.

> i doubt you need it anymore but good luck tonight...

The sentiment is nice, but it's not the text I wanted to read. It's been two weeks since our fight, and this is the first I've heard from Lucy. Since she stormed out of my apartment, I've tried to keep my head down and focus on what's going on in my life. I kept myself occupied with the playoffs and the charity, but I still think about her constantly. She must be getting ready for her big move to LA—or maybe she's already there.

My hand hovers over the keyboard wanting to say a million things to her. But I don't say anything at all.

Rushing into the offensive zone, I chase the loose puck into the corner, where I battle with a Dallas Stampeders defenseman for possession of the puck. I'm nearing the end of my shift. My legs burn and my lungs feel like they're going to burst, but the cheers from the crowd let me know there's blood in the water.

For a split second I think about heading back to the bench for a line change, but when I see Soko—the team's one-timer specialist—skating up center ice to his go-to spot at the point, I decide I'm going to be the one to feed him the shot.

I can't let up, no matter how hard I'm huffing through my mouthguard. We're still down by a goal with ten minutes of play left in the third period. These are the moments I train for. Not the first thirty seconds, but the thirty seconds after that. When I'm stuck out on the ice for a long shift and need to find a way to keep playing through the exhaustion to get a shot on net—or better yet, score a goal.

I battle the puck loose from the Stampeders' possession. Faster than you can yell "shoot," I feed Soko a tape-to-tape pass with enough weight behind it to make his one-timer sound like an explosion firing off the blade of his stick. The one-timer finds the back of the net, glove side top shelf. No goalie stood a chance against that bullet.

I jump into Soko's arms and let out a lively, "Fuck yeah, Soko!" Fans are on their feet cheering so loudly that I can hardly hear myself shout celebratory profanities. Soko's locked in my tight embrace and surrounded by the rest of our teammates.

"Let's go, Gucci!" Lamber shouts at Soko from the bench.

It's right back to business after the tying goal; we can't let the excitement take our heads out of the game in a moment like that. The team is already dialed back into play, while the fans remain loud as ever, still on their feet.

The time on the clock is dropping fast, and I and the rest of the Rainiers want to finish this one in regulation. We have the momentum, we have the crowd, and we have the new and improved Jaylen Jones.

I'm back on the ice, hungry for my first goal of the game. I know this goalie, Eino Lampi. They call him No Light Lampi because the odds you're lighting up the goal light behind his net are slim to none. He's big and fast and an absolute monster in net. It's rare to get one goal past Eino Lampi, and if you get two in the same period, you should keep the puck.

Lamber gets control of the puck in the defensive zone. He hasn't been in the league long enough to know the true weight of this moment. Not every hockey player gets to play a sudden-death game seven, and even fewer get to win one. He has been solid on D this series and Coach Pete is rewarding the rookie with ice time in the last shift of the game.

Without an ounce of hesitation, he saucers a pass up center ice and catches the Stampeders' defense flat-footed. The sauce lands right on my tape, and I'm off as fast as my legs will take me. If you had told me at the start of the season that I would be staring down the best goalie in the league on a breakaway with seconds left in a tied game-seven playoff game, I would have said, *No, thank you.*

Not only would I have not believed that my game would be good enough to warrant prime ice time like this, but my psyche wouldn't have been strong enough to handle the pressure a moment like this carries. I can't remember the last time I was trusted to take the big shot.

This season, I've focused on simplifying my game. I'm always in position, my passes are tape to tape, I'm a good fast skater, and I have great vision out on the ice. It's the basics. It's not flashy, but it's reliable. My no-frills breakaway move is to rip a shot off before the goalie has a chance to know it's coming, but playing it safe isn't going to get us the win—not against No Light Lampi.

When you're out there, you don't even have time to think, let alone second-guess yourself. You get tunnel vision and suddenly you can't even hear the roar of the crowd. It's like you're using the full power of your brain to make your body perform unthinkable acts of physical talent. With no room left for your brain to hear or feel or think, you *do*.

I knew before the puck landed on my stick that I couldn't skate down center ice and shoot the puck at the top of the circle. With the clock ticking away, I skate harder than I ever have before. Without second-guessing myself, I'm faking right. Lampi bites. The goalie leaves the left side of his net wide open as he drops to his knees. I pull the puck to my backside. He watches me eye the wide-open shot. Lampi dives across his crease, but it's too late—even for someone as athletic as him. I'm flipping the puck over his blocker and into the back of the net so fast that it takes the goal light a few beats to finally illuminate crimson red.

The goal horn echoes through the arena, signaling the end of the game. I can hardly hear it over the roar of the crowd.

It's all over. We won.

The furious Finnish goaltender breaks his stick over the top of his net knowing their series is lost. I charge into the corner jumping up and crashing into the boards. Fans pound on the glass behind me, a thunderous roar that vibrates against the boards.

Lamber comes jumping into my arms, screaming god knows what in French. "Putain, ouais!" he shouts.

Elation courses through my body. "What a pass!" I say.

"Who cares about the pass. What about the deke? You finally dusted off those silky hands, JJ!" Lamber says, still tight in my embrace.

"Silky Hands, now there's a good nickname." The adrenaline chatters my teeth as I laugh.

"I'll call you whatever you want if you keep scoring goals like that." Lamber gives me a cheeky grin. It doesn't take long for the rest of the team to catch up and come crashing into us—a dogpile celebration of pure excitement.

Wells sits down next to me in the locker room. "Welcome back, JJ." He playfully tousles my hair like an older sibling man-handling their little brother. "That's a move I haven't seen from you since you were too young and stupid to know it might not work," he says with a wink.

"Yeah, well, a lot's changed this season."

I try to not think about how much I miss Lucy. I just scored the most important goal of my life in the biggest game of my career and all I can think about is how I wish she was here. How I wish I was going home to see her tonight.

Coach Pete enters the room with the giant chain in his hand. Everyone quiets and looks to me. "I think we all know where this is headed tonight. The hustler of the game goes to some-one who not only showed no mercy in the face of a two-goal deficit, but also showed courage this month as he bravely shared his story and struggle with anxiety and depression. We're honored to know you and relieved you're on our team. Way to go, JJ!" Coach Pete walks the player-of-the-game chain over to me and bestows it around my neck.

My teammates hoot and holler loudly. I bashfully accept their praise, but I'm just happy we won. When the announcers called my name at the start of the game, the fans got to their feet, and I swear I had the biggest ovation. There's no more hiding who I am out there—everyone knows, and it feels liberating.

# THIRTY-FOUR

## Lucy

I wake up on a pile of watercolor pages, my fingers still stained from a late night full of creative release. I don't know what time it is, let alone the day of the week. What I do know is that I've been painting at my previous college pace to try to keep up with my online business. I'll have to temporarily close my digital shop if the feeling in my finger pads doesn't return soon.

I'm not complaining; the distraction is welcome. It's been an emotional couple of weeks cooped up in my apartment. My therapist says I can't hide from my problems forever; I told her she shouldn't underestimate a competitive introvert. My therapist also says I need to call Jaylen—she might be right about that one.

Jaylen isn't the only person I've been avoiding—I've also been dodging Hunter Gunn's calls lately. She needs me to sign the apprenticeship contract, like yesterday. I keep saying I'm going to do it, but then I pick up a brush and suddenly I'm waking up face down in my paint palette.

I roll out of bed and begin cleaning yesterday's art mess when my phone vibrates against my nightstand. Expecting to see a message from Hunter Gunn reminding me to fill out my paperwork, I'm surprised to see a message from my dad.

I contemplate FaceTiming my therapist so I don't have to face the text alone, but she said I have to stop texting her memes and only use the number for real emergencies. Apparently, your favorite queer celebrity couple breaking up amid cheating allegations doesn't qualify as an emergency. A text from my dad doesn't seem like an emergency situation either, at least not until I know what he wants to say.

DAD:

> Kiddo, I owe you an apology. I was in a tight spot, and you know I wouldn't have asked if I didn't really need it. Anyway, I was able to get a loan off a buddy of mine and it's all good now. I'm in the city this morning. Want to grab some breakfast?

I shove my phone in my pocket, ignoring his text. Before I can decide if I want to tell him to fuck off or to drop dead, my phone vibrates again.

DAD:

> I have something to give you.

I have every intention of blocking him and never talking to him again, but that doesn't feel satisfactory enough. He needs to know he's hurt me. He needs to hear that I'm done with him.

I've been working with my therapist on finding the words I could never say to him. If I'm ever going to heal my old wounds, I need to stop pity-pouring salt into them.

★ ★ ★

He's there waiting for me in the booth at the back of the restaurant by the time I arrive, halfway through a soda and mull-
ing over the menu. I slip into the booth across from him and
bury my hands into my jacket pockets.

"You're late," my dad says.

"I wasn't going to come." I stare him down like a wild animal. Maybe just this once I won't get mauled.

The server stops by the table, but I tell him we need more
time. Picking up on the tension between my dad and me, he
quickly moves on to the next booth.

My dad reaches under the table and pulls out a medium-sized
canvas. It's wrapped in a plastic bag, but I still know what it is.
It's the fourth painting from my senior art showcase project—
the last piece in my series of four. It's the one of his old house.
I mailed it to him after he ruined my showcase; it was my way
of leaving art in the past.

I take it from his hands. Mostly to stash it under the table
before anyone else sees it.

"Why did you need to give me this?" I'm on high alert and
anticipate a cheap shot at my work or a dig at my mom any
moment now. He must have something diabolical planned for
me today if he brought this here with him because it's the most
interest he's ever taken in my art.

"I never got to tell you how beautiful it is, but it belongs in
a series. I think you should keep it with the others. If you still
have them." His words shake with a self-doubt my arrogant father seldom struggles with. His voice is clearer than usual, and
his eyes brighter. He looks less worn, like someone returning
from a vacation.

His kind words should make me feel good about myself, but
instead they piss me off. They're too little, too late. Like a bus
that never came—I found another way home.

"I don't have them anymore." I slide my legs out from under the booth and go to leave, but he reaches for me.

"Wait," he says, leaning out of his seat to stop me. "I saw your murals. You're making a mistake with this tattoo stuff. Don't give up on painting because of me. I've ruined a lot of things in your life, don't let me ruin this too." His voice is pleading and fast paced. He must know he doesn't have much more of my time left.

As a child I was powerless. My mom was too consumed by her own struggles to protect me, leaving me vulnerable. My dad had full range to jerk my emotions around every time he decided to finally show up. I'm done being scared of him. Someone is finally going to stand up for that little girl terrified at the top of the Seattle Great Wheel, and it's going to be me.

"What do you know about me or my life? You don't know what's best for me, and you never did." Saying the words feels like breaking through the surface of water after a deep dive. I take a long breath.

"You're right. I invited you here because I wanted to tell you in person that I'm sober now. I got my first chip yesterday—thirty days." He takes his hand out of his pocket and opens it to reveal a yellow chip the size of a silver dollar coin. "I understand if you hate me. I would hate me too. You don't have to forgive me, but if you ever want to let me start making it up to you, I'll be waiting."

Everything he's saying would be impressive if I hadn't heard it all before. This isn't his first time getting sober. For his sake I hope it's his last, but this is the impossible toxic cycle in which he lives. And I don't want any part of it anymore.

"That's really great for you, but it's too late for me. You can keep this." I hand the painting back to him. "I can't do this anymore. Don't contact me ever again." I get up and leave without looking back.

It's a firm boundary, but I'm glad to have set it. As the distance between my dad and me grows, I feel safer with each step.

I can't live in this purgatory with him anymore, stuck waiting for him to mess up and longing for him to make it up to me. I need to break this cycle before it breaks me.

Finally, light shines on the monster lurking in the shadows and suddenly he doesn't seem so scary. I have power over our relationship—over my life.

I decide to walk home in an attempt to clear my head. The weight of everything I have to do before setting off for LA has made me immobile, and I need to move. While my mind races between packing my things and signing the contract and saying goodbye to my friends and family, I see the Seattle Great Wheel in the distance. I continue on, heading in its direction. I'll watch a full rotation.

When I get there, I line up to buy a ticket. Why not? What's the worst that can happen to me at this point?

As I sit alone in the glass gondola dangling one hundred and seventy-five feet in the air, I realize it's not nearly as frightening as I remember. If anything it's peaceful. The sun reflects off the ocean below—the winter clouds must have left while I was cooped up painting in my apartment this month. The mountains are so sharp today they look digitally imposed. Or maybe I'm the one digitally imposed in the middle of a pristine, postcard-worthy backdrop. I feel like a fish being plucked from the ocean and dropped into a bowl for someone's kitchen countertop. Was Seattle always this colorful?

I sit back in my seat as the gondola rounds the very top of the Ferris wheel's rotation. I spot the hotel from that night all those months ago across the street in the distance. I remember looking out the hotel window upon the morning glow; it terrified me to look around. I was on the run. I didn't want to still myself long enough to see what I was running from, so I convinced myself I was headed toward something instead.

From this perspective, I don't want to run. I want to paint. I don't feel scared anymore. I'm inspired.

I want to disappear into the canvas the only way I know how. I have ignored texts from Hannah in my phone asking if she can pass along my information for commissions. I have un-read emails from the local MLB team. They want me to paint a similar mural of their players outside their locker room. And I have enough commission inquiries from my online shop to last me through the spring. I want to tell them I'll do it, all of it.

Then I remember that I owe Hunter Gunn a few signatures on paper and suddenly I can't picture myself signing them. I've been obsessively trying for a tattoo apprenticeship for almost two years; I haven't stopped to think about why I want it so badly. It's an incredible opportunity, but what if it isn't my op-portunity?

How long am I going to let my dad hijack my life? Today he finally paid attention to my art, even told me it was beauti-ful. I've waited my whole life to hear him say something like that. And now that he finally has, I know it doesn't matter what he thinks of my art. It doesn't matter if he loves it or hates it. Whether he shows up or ghosts me. If he says I should paint in-stead of tattoo. I needed to be the one who believed in myself and my work.

This is my second chance to make it as an artist, and every-thing I need is right at my fingertips. I'm the only one who hasn't been able to see that what I've always wanted was right in front of me this whole time.

As soon as I get off the ride, I call Hunter Gunn back. I tell her I can't do it. I can't move. I can't give up on painting. Hav-ing decided to see this through this time means I'm choosing to believe in myself.

It didn't take finally going to therapy for me to understand that I was self-sabotaging, but it has shown me that I don't have to live like this anymore. I'm still working on it, but being a work in progress feels a hell of a lot better than being a mess.

I can't believe I'm a painter again, and I can't believe I'm making more money doing it than I ever would have working at that job opportunity I blew after college.

I think of Jaylen, and his recent article where he bravely bared his heart. I want to call him immediately and tell him what I did today: standing up to my dad and going after what I want in life. I want to thank him for the inspiration—for the push. I want to take him out to Trolls Bridge for two-for-seven-dollar beers and I don't want to wait until two in the morning to kiss him this time. He probably doesn't want to talk to me anymore—he never responded to my text. I ran from him like I ran from painting when things got scary, but I have nothing left to lose, and I know what I want now. I have to try.

# THIRTY-FIVE

## Jaylen

Lamar greets me with a big embrace before we head inside the restaurant for a quick lunch. I have to get back home soon to nap and stick to the rest of my game-day routine. Initially, I tried to get out of this lunch. Lamar insisted, saying he's got something important to talk to me about. I told him fine, but he's paying.

He talks my ear off the entire way to our table and while we wait for the server, telling me about his flight into the city, and some kid from the WHL he watched play last night. I'm not the most engaging lunch date today, but luckily, Lamar likes to talk and carries the load of the conversation. I nod my head and add in an "oh yeah" every now and then.

After watching him chitchat with the server over the drink specials, I can't take it any longer. *Who cares if the beer is tap or bottled; pick something and let's go.* When someone says they have something to tell you, they should be obligated to do so immediately.

"What's going on? Is something wrong? Is my contract getting terminated?" I say, interrupting Lamar and the server. They stop talking momentarily to look over at me.

"Bring me whatever you recommend, and a water for him," he says to the server. She quickly disappears into the kitchen.

Lamar adjusts the collar on his sports coat. He's overdressed for lunch, but as far as I know he doesn't even own jeans.

He makes a face as he chuckles to himself. "Is your contract getting terminated? What's got you on edge? There isn't a team in the league who wouldn't want you for that measly deal you've got. You're so grossly underpaid right now, it makes me look like a bad agent." Lamar's bellowing voice carries throughout the tiny Creole restaurant—luckily it's mostly empty because he only has one volume.

"You got me an opportunity when I had nothing." No one thought I was going to have the year I did, myself included. Knowing that I still have my job, I try to relax a bit. Easier said than done, because I have no clue what he could possibly need to talk to me about so desperately that it warranted interrupting my game-day routine.

Lamar leans in. "And you turned that opportunity into a one-year deal. What a year it's been, huh?"

The server returns with our drinks and Lamar chats her up again about the lunch specials. I chug my water, hoping it will help my dizziness subside. He must sense my tension; I grip the glass so tightly, I'm about to crush it. He tells the server to give us a minute.

"If everything is fine with my contract, then why are we here? No offense, but I've got a pregame nap to get to," I ask as soon as she's out of earshot again.

"Can't two grown men enjoy a nice lunch together?" Lamar indulges in a long sip of his drink.

"Not until you tell me what's up."

He puts his glass down. "You can calm down. I called the restaurant ahead—they're bringing out some pasta in a to-go bag for you. I won't take up much more of your time, but I wanted to see your face when I told you in person."

"Lamar." My shoulders drop with a sigh. I'm about to stand

up, walk around the table, and give him the Heimlich if he doesn't spit it out already.

He smirks. "The Rainiers want to extend you to a multi-year deal. Eight years, sixty million dollars to be exact. With a no-trade clause too." He leans back in his chair, taking another long drink of his beverage.

"Goddamn." I'm too stunned to say much else. It's not the hundred million I dreamed of years ago, but somehow, it's even better because I fought so hard for it. It's a lot of money, and it's going to do a lot of good for Cam's House.

"I was hoping you would say that. This is obviously being done in good faith, since you can't officially sign anything until free agency. But you're finally getting that big long-term deal you always dreamed about. Congratulations, JJ." Lamar reaches across the table and grabs my hand. Enthusiastically shaking my arm up and down, he tugs me up out of my seat and we both embrace in the middle of the restaurant. After a few solid pats on each other's back, we settle back down in our seats.

I wipe my hands down my face, discreetly drying my eyes. "Should I wait until free agency to see if there are other teams interested? What about LA?" This is the first time in my career I have any type of leverage; what if I don't want to stay here?

"What about LA? Owner is cheap, team sucks, and they've had three different head coaches in the last five years. Listen, as your agent, do I think you can get more money somewhere else in free agency? Maybe. But as your friend, I think you should take this deal. I haven't seen you like this since I first met you all those years ago in a cold rink up north. And I don't just mean how you're playing on the ice. You look happy."

I've known Lamar since I was sixteen, and he's always been real with me. Like the time I tried incorporating hats into my game-day fits; he said I was a pair of gators and a cane away from owning a chocolate factory.

"You're right. This season has been amazing," I say as the

server returns with a to-go bag for me and drops it off on her way to bring a plate of food to another table.

"Good. Now get out of here. Think about what we talked about, but don't think about it too much because you've got a big game tonight. You can let me know your decision tomorrow."

I'll do my best to listen to Lamar's game-day advice, but I've just been handed everything I've ever wanted only to be left feeling empty. I want to call Lucy and tell her she's making a big mistake leaving Seattle, but I can't stand between her and her big dream. So instead of celebrating this contract with the person I love most in the world, I'm going home to spend my whole nap tossing and turning across the giant void she's left in my king-size bed.

The game isn't going our way tonight. Tired and bruised, we're down by three at the top of the third period. The defending Stanley Cup Champions, the Nashville Ice Tigers, are merciless in their quest to eliminate us from the playoffs. The series currently sits at three games to one, in favor of the Ice Tigers.

Soko went down last game after a nasty slash from one of the Ice Tigers' grinders, and while the team is telling the media that it's an upper-body injury, the guys all know it's a broken hand. Even though Soko can still shoot better than half the league with a broken hand, there's no way he's ruining his career to play through it. He'll be healed up enough for the Stanley Cup final—if we survive this period.

Minutes into play, Lamber goes down after a blocked shot. He limps his way off the ice, right past the team's bench, and down the hallway to seek medical attention. Time is running out on our season and our two best rookies are both battered and broken.

As we break out of the defensive zone, Groot has already begun inching toward the bench as he waits for the official signal from the coaching staff. They motion him over with five minutes left on the clock and a three-goal deficit on the scoreboard. It's a bold move to pull your goalie for this long, but we're desperate for a lifeline.

My leg dangles over the edge of the board waiting for him to cross the threshold off the ice. With perfect timing, I simultaneously launch into play. I hurtle down the ice to catch up with the action. My teammates cycle the puck around the Ice Tigers' defensemen, waiting for a play to open up.

We catch them out of position and I slide into the slot. Before the Ice Tigers have a chance to box us out, I get a shot off, but their goalie juts his leg out just in time to stop my attempt. He's unable to control the rebound, and the puck lies loose in the crease. I crash the net, hammering the loose puck under the goalie's leg and into the back of the net.

There's hardly a celebration afterward—there's nothing to celebrate about a 3–1 score in a do-or-die game. Still, over twenty thousand faithful fans are on their feet, anxious to see what fate awaits their favorite team.

Groot skates back into his net as the ref drops the puck at center ice. I win the draw, and Groot heads off the ice in exchange for an extra attacker again. The puck is turned over in the neutral zone and the Ice Tigers are on the offense. A faithful wrist shot sends the puck into the back of our empty net. Now the score is 4–1.

It's the shot that ends our dream of lifting the Stanley Cup. The season is over, and we all know it. The time left on the clock is a formality—torture at this point.

My body feels too numb to be sad. Most of my sadness was tapped out that night when Lucy left. In comparison, losing the series doesn't feel like much. I was hoping we would keep winning games, and I could remain distracted by the intense, demanding playoff hockey schedule. Now I have to face reality. I'm going back to Chicago for the offseason alone.

I know I have to accept the eight-year deal with the Rainiers, like Lucy had to take the job in LA. I used to think something special brought us together, like fate or the universe or hockey gods. I thought we were destined for each other—and we were, but only for that moment in time.

I thought getting this long-term contract would make me happy. That it would finally prove that I was never a draft bust. Now that I have it, I realize the contract was never that important. I was never a failure to her; I was always just Jaylen.

# THIRTY-SIX

## Lucy

I wiggle my way through a swarm of disgruntled Rainiers fans. While everyone looks for an exit, I'm looking for a way in. I see a door propped open and slip through, going unnoticed among the crowd. Like a fish swimming against the current, I get bumped around by disappointed fans with their heads hung. The game is over, but I'm here for Jaylen. I need to show him something—if he'll even listen to me.

I catch a glimpse of the ice as I rush by; 4–1 is illuminated on the scoreboard, looming over the ice like a rain cloud. I dart into an overstuffed elevator and slap the lower-level button. A man in the corner looks me up and down with such disdain you'd think I was wearing an Ice Tigers jersey.

I look down at myself and realize that I'm covered in paint. It dawns on me that I haven't checked my hair in the mirror since this morning when I left my apartment. Between meeting my dad, turning down the apprenticeship, and painting all afternoon, I haven't had time for second thoughts.

When the elevator doors open, I take off running. The family room is around the corner, and if I hurry, I can make it before Jaylen leaves. As I'm catching my stride, I see a giant blur with SECURITY written on it speeding my way. The crowd hurries out of his way, allowing the security guard to barrel through as few obstacles as possible.

"Stop right there!" he yells, lunging toward me.

Suddenly I feel as if I'm being struck by a car. The security guard wraps his arms around me and tackles me to the ground to restrain me. I try to explain myself, but I've just had the wind knocked out of me and when I open my mouth only wheezing noises drain out.

"Let her go! She's my friend!" someone shouts.

His bear hug loosens and I grovel on the floor in agony, rolling around like a dog scratching its own itch.

"Oh my god! Are you okay? You took that hit like a champ."

It sounds like we're underwater. I slowly open my eyes to find Hannah hovering over me like an angel backlit by the humming fluorescent lighting. I prop my head up to find the giant security guard standing beside her.

"Believe it or not, that wasn't my first time being tackled by a security guard," I say. I slowly roll to my knees, pausing in a just-hit-by-a-car cat yoga pose to gather my bearings.

Hannah offers her hand and helps me to my feet. "She's with me," she tells the remorseful security guard.

"That was embarrassing." I hold the side of my head that ricocheted off the floor.

"Don't worry, I don't think anyone noticed."

I look up to find everyone in a fifty-foot vicinity staring at me in shock. Several people have their phones out ready to record a viral video of a deranged hockey stalker attempting to attack the team's superstars. I give an awkward wave before darting around the corner. Hannah's shoes click and clack as she follows me.

I brace myself on the wall out of view. I'm not sure if I'm queasy from the hit or nervous to see Jaylen. The sparkles on Hannah's jacket catch my eye and distract me from the pain. "Cute jacket," I say.

She does a spin. It's a custom bomber jacket with Caldwell

stitched across the back and her husband's number bedazzled on the arm.

"We have one for you, if you still…" She trails off, tugging on the sleeve of her coat.

"I'm not sure Jaylen wants me wearing his number anymore." I touch the gold thirteen pendant hanging from my neck. I haven't taken it off since he gifted it to me.

Hannah winces and offers me the drink in her hand, which I accept. While I start chugging what's left, Hannah leans in and says, "I'm sorry. Not only about Jaylen, but I know you were in the bathroom at the team dinner. Bianca can be so catty sometimes. I never meant to cause a rift between you and Jaylen. Hockey might be his first love, but it's not his only."

I wipe the back of my hand across my mouth. "It's fine. I was the one who let my own insecurities get in the way." What people think of me has never been my problem, but that night I felt so self-conscious and out of place. And worse, I let it get to my relationship.

"No, it's not okay. I'm pretty sure Mallory called you a lesbian too."

"That's not an insult…" I start to explain, but Hannah continues on.

"People already think the worst of us, but I promise we're harmless. I know how it feels to have people judge you and talk badly behind your back. Lots of people think we're all gold diggers," Hannah says.

I try to say the right thing by adding a dramatic gasp and a lengthy *nooo*, but Hannah waves me off and continues to explain herself.

"They do. They think that we're only with the guys for their money, following along behind them like a trophy wife for them to show off. I'm not. I've been with Evan since we had nothing. Since I was the one paying for his rolls of stick tape. I gave up a lot to make it work and I'd make the same choices a hundred times over."

"For the record, I don't think you're a gold digger. You're married to a handsome guy with full dental benefits and great seats to every Rainiers game. If I was going to call you anything, I'd call you smart."

She smiles. "Thanks." Her phone chimes loudly from her purse. She takes it out and silences the call. "My parents already want to know when we're going to be home for the offseason."

The sight of her phone jogs my memory. Jaylen and Hunter Gunn weren't the only people owed a reply. "Oh! I keep forgetting to text you back. I'll do the commissions. Pass my number along to whoever."

Hannah gasps. "Does that mean you're staying in Seattle? Wait, does Jaylen know? We need to find him immediately so you can go get the league's most desirable free agent and make him an offer he can't refuse." Her smile is encouraging.

"I don't know what that means, but I think you're wishing me good luck."

She links her arm in mine and brings me into the family room. Weaving through reunited families, I scour the room for Jaylen, but can't find him. I try calling his phone, but it goes straight to voicemail. As I peek my head in the bathroom, I hear a familiar voice.

"He's already gone," Bianca says, sitting in a chair in the corner of the room, sipping wine. "I overheard him talking to one of the guys. He said he could really go for a weird night—whatever that means. I can text you and let you know where we all end up going out tonight," she adds, in a way that feels like the closest thing to an apology she's capable of.

She didn't have to say anything to me. She could have ignored me completely and relished in my dismay, but I'm glad she didn't.

"I think I know where to find him. Thanks," I say, and run out of there like security is still chasing me.

★ ★ ★

I rush into Purple Haze and scan the room for Jaylen. It's dim and already filling up for the night. I see a bunch of Jones Rainiers jerseys, but no Jaylen.

"Great, *you* again. You can't bully me into turning the game off this time." The bartender throws a rag over his shoulder and leans over the bar, standing his ground.

"That's not why I'm here." I hold up my phone, showing the bartender Jaylen's hockey headshot. "I'm looking for this guy. Have you seen him?" I ask.

He laughs. "The comeback kid? Yeah, I've seen him." I eagerly search the bar top for Jaylen. "He's right here." The bartender points to the TV behind him. It's a replay of Jaylen's pregame on-ice interview. I thank the bartender and leave empty-handed.

I run up the street and barge into Trolls Bridge, a few locals turning as I come bursting through the door. None of them are Jaylen. I worry I'm too late, or worse, I've completely misunderstood him, and he's already forgotten all about me and the weirdest night of his life. I run to the final spot, faster and faster as if my pace can turn back time.

As I hurry up the road, I see him. He's slumped on the curb, staring at the tattoo shop across the street. There's a new thirteen sign dangling from the awning, only this time it's heavily reinforced with chains and screws.

"Your phone's off." My breathing is labored from the run. My heart doesn't let up as I slow my pace, approaching him. Jaylen still remembers that night—our night—yet I might be too late to make things right between us. As I get closer to him, I see it. A beard. Well, more like a patchy scruff. Still, he must be feeling miserable to let himself go like that. I sit on the curb next to him. "I like your new look. It's very Drake of you." I ease into conversation.

"It's a playoff beard. It will be gone tomorrow." Jaylen keeps his head hung.

*Oh, thank god.* I was really worried for a second. Beards are bangs for men; when they appear unprompted it's a cause for concern. "I tried to find you after the game, but everyone said you already left."

"I needed to get out of there. I could feel my chest getting tight." He rubs his hand across his chest like external compressions. His eyes still avoid mine as he stares ahead.

"Are you okay?" I want to touch him, but I'm not sure I'm allowed anymore.

"Shouldn't you be gone?" There's little emotion in Jaylen's voice, and even less in his face.

"I turned down the apprenticeship." I tuck my legs into my chest, staring across the street at the new sign. I can't believe he convinced me to steal it that night, and yet now there isn't much I wouldn't do for him.

So much has changed since the last time we were sitting on this curb together. I'm painting again. I've cut myself free from the expectations I had for my dad. I haven't even stolen anything in a while. But when I look at Jaylen, it's hard to believe any time has passed at all. I still want to follow him into the night and wind up tangled in his bed. I want him to whisper nice things into my ear, and this time I'll be sure to believe them.

"You did what?" He finally looks my way. There's just enough light from nearby streetlights to see his brows strain together as he searches for an explanation.

"Not because of you," I say, quickly blurting out the words. "Well, that's not completely true. You helped me realize that my infatuation with a tattoo apprenticeship was really an attempt to run away from old wounds. I should be painting. I am painting." I motion to my paint-smeared attire.

"Really? Good for you, then. I guess you'll have to find another way to tell your dad to go fuck himself." He fights a smile.

"Don't worry, I found a way. But I didn't come here to talk about my dad. I have something to show you. Will you come with me?"

"I don't know, Lucy. I'm beat."

I pull myself up off the curb. "I'll carry you on my back if I have to. Please," I say, looking down at him. My bottom lip droops and I hold out my hand. He reaches out, once again putting his trust in me.

I bring Jaylen to Brewed This Way, stopping him right in front of the giant mural I painted on the side of Cooper's café this afternoon. It was an ambitious undertaking considering the time constraint, and my wrist is still limp, but I need Jaylen to see how I feel about him. I want everyone to see how much I love him.

It's a collage in which I've included the infamous stolen thirteen sign, my thirteen heart tattoo, the Trolls Bridge glowing neon sign, Zuko and Katara from *Avatar*, a few other meaningful relics only we understand, and finally, a large portrait of Jaylen in the middle. Across the top the words "Can I have another shot?" are painted boldly.

"I usually paint houses for the people I love, but every time I tried to paint your apartment, I kept seeing your face. I think my Finding Home series is complete, because when I'm with you I feel like I've finally found it."

Staring up at the mural, he whispers, "It's beautiful."

"I'm so sorry, Jay. I've been running from the things I love for so long that when settling down was finally a possibility, I didn't know how to stop myself." A brisk breeze blows on the back of my neck, but I still feel flush.

"You really hurt me when you left." He turns away from me, looking down at his feet.

"I know. I was trying to hurt myself, but I took us both down instead." I reach for him, but my grasp slips.

"And now what?" He shrugs, sticking one hand in his pocket

while the other rubs across his face—doing anything to avoid eye contact. "Do you actually know what you want this time?"

"I want you. Real life could never measure up to a painting until you stepped onto my canvas. *I'm sorry* is not enough and I'll spend forever wishing you good luck and painting you murals if it makes you happy. If it means I can still know you."

Jaylen looks at me with the same patient eyes and the same longing as he did months ago when I first looked into them on a street corner not too far from here. "I've missed you. Not just your texts before my games, but I've missed you in my life."

"You have?" I can't hold back my eagerness as my body shakes with shameless desperation.

Jaylen nods, and there's a hint of an upturn to his lips. He grabs my hand and pulls me in close beside him. He lifts my hand to his mouth and kisses the thirteen tattoo on the inside of my wrist.

"Say you're my girlfriend," he says, holding my hand.

I smile, clinging to him with my fingers digging into the flesh of his hand. I can't let him slip out of my grasp again. "I'm your girlfriend."

Jaylen wraps his arm around my shoulders, and I lean into him as we look at the mural together. Two large security lights on the corners of the building illuminate the art like spotlights. "I can't believe Cooper let you paint this huge mural on the side of his building."

"It came at a price. I have to cover it with a mural of his face on Lady Gaga's body tomorrow."

Jaylen laughs softly. "Probably for the best. It's beautiful, but it also kind of looks like I died tragically and I'm worried people are going to start leaving flowers on the ground in front of it."

I cock my head to the side. "Oh god, it does. And the text is incredibly insensitive. I'm sorry, I haven't been sleeping much lately, and I only had a few hours to get this thing done."

Jaylen takes me into his arms and kisses my self-doubt away.

Under the dark indigo blue sky and glowing moon, his mouth parts and I wrap my hands around the back of his neck. I savor the kiss, internally battling between not wanting to ever pull away and wanting to immediately head back to Jaylen's apartment and crawl into bed with him.

Hand in hand we head down the street together. "I'm sorry you lost tonight," I say.

"It doesn't feel that way." He gives me a discreet wink. "So, you're really staying in Seattle?" He swings our hands back and forth in motion with our steps.

"Actually…"

Jaylen stops walking. "You're not?" Anchoring himself on my arm, I snag back to him.

"I was hoping your offer for the summer still stood. I've always wanted to visit the Art Institute of Chicago." I peer up at him, anxious for his reaction.

A welcoming smile engulfs his face. He quickly drops his grin and tries out an unfitting cool-guy act. "I might have room for my good-luck charm. You know, you're luckier than we thought. I'm signing long-term with the Rainiers," he says casually.

"You did it!" I jump into his arms, my interlocked fingers tethered to the back of his neck. "I knew you would. I'm so happy for you, Jay; you got everything you always wanted."

"If I've got you, I've got it all." He picks me up and we kiss under the streetlight.

# EPILOGUE

## Jaylen

*Two years later…*

What happens in Vegas, doesn't always stay in Vegas. It haunts your digital footprint for better, for worse, for richer, for poorer, in sickness and in health, to love and to cherish, until parted by death.

"What's a blood diamond? And why doesn't Lucy want one? They sound fancy," Lamber says, dragging his feet behind Wells and me as we quickly trek our way through the casino.

"It's like an unethical diamond or something. I'm not entirely sure, but I've heard that Jay-Z song. It doesn't matter right now," I shout back to Lamber, frazzled and overstimulated by the noises and lights in this place. I'm too busy to get into it with him because I'm frantically searching for Soko among the rows of slot machines in the bustling casino.

"Tell that to the kids in Africa," Wells says.

I'm stressing because Soko's typical flashy garb seamlessly blends into the backdrop of Vegas, making him unusually difficult to spot.

"There he is!" I point across the casino at Soko, like I'm about to yell *Seize him*. We all rush over. "Did you get it?" I impatiently look him over.

"Easy, easy, guys. Let's hit up the tables before we go." Soko attempts to grab a seat at one of the poker tables.

I grab his arm and lift him up out of the chair. "Soko, I'm getting married in thirty minutes. Please, give me the rings. I don't have time for this."

He reaches into his pocket and takes out a ring box. He starts to hand it over to me but pulls it back right at the last minute. "Lamber and I want to come." He holds the box hostage.

"Sure. Fine. Just don't do anything stupid." I snatch the box from his hand before he has time to list any other demands like requesting to be the flower girl.

"Can I *do* a bridesmaid?" Lamber's laugh is unreciprocated.

"The bridesmaids are a witty gay man and a very powerful lesbian. On second thought, sure, give it a try and see how that goes for you," I snap at him. I open the ring box, and suddenly, all my worries melt away. It finally hits me: I'm marrying the love of my life tonight.

Inside are two thick gold bands with the words Till Death engraved in Gothic font. I noticed Lucy looking at similar rings a few months ago on her phone late at night and I took a mental note. I'm surprised Soko was able to find them on such short notice, but then again it seems he has a lot of connections in Sin City.

I didn't formally propose to Lucy. Not because I didn't want to, but because she once went on a long-winded tangent about how it should be a decision two people make together. With no diamonds and no proposal, she was making it difficult to be romantic. Still, I couldn't argue with her logic, so I waited until she was ready to have the conversation about marriage. We've been toying with the idea for a few months now, but with the team winning the Stanley Cup a few weeks ago, our plan to have a serious talk about marriage kept getting pushed back.

My teammates and I are fresh off our wins at tonight's NHL

awards show. Soko took home the Hart Memorial Trophy, Lamber was nominated for the Norris Trophy, and Wells was invited to the festivities by the keeper of the Stanley Cup. I was awarded the King Clancy Memorial Trophy for my leadership on the ice as the Rainiers' captain and my tireless work with Cam's House.

In my acceptance speech I thanked Lucy, calling her the love of my life. I thought the recognition would have embarrassed her, but apparently, the public declaration of love sparked an idea. Somewhere among the pre-award show champagne, the Vegas weekend getaway with all our friends, and the three-week-long Stanley Cup celebration, we began feeling recklessly romantic.

When I slid back into my seat next to her after my acceptance speech, Lucy interlocked her hand in mine and leaned over. "Let's get married," she whispered to me.

Before the award show ended, I had an Uber waiting out front to take us to the Clark County Marriage Certificate Bureau for a marriage license.

A firm hand grabs my shoulder and gives me a shake. "Let's get you married, JJ!" Wells says, and the boys all holler like we've hit the jackpot. I snap the ring box shut and hand it to my best man for safekeeping.

## Lucy

"She needs something blue!" Cooper frantically shuffles around the casino gift shop in search of any blue accessory for my last-minute impromptu Vegas wedding.

"She's wearing a black minidress and fishnets. I think we can drop the traditions." Maya loafs around the store at a much more casual pace. She picks up a small souvenir shot glass but puts it back down after checking the price tag.

"I've never been a man of honor before. It's my duty to make sure everything is perfect for Lucy. You're not trying to mess with my duty, are you?" Cooper presses Maya, finger pointed and nostrils flared.

"Please, listen to yourself." Maya swats his finger out of her face and pivots to a sunglasses display to check her meticulously laid baby hairs in the small mirror.

I step in between them. "Cooper, I've already said this, you are both my bridesmaids."

"Yet only one of us is taking it seriously." Cooper huffs as he disappears in the gift shop again.

I take a long sip from my comically shaped casino-branded plastic cup, which has stained my lips scarlet from the red dye forty in the cocktail. The only thing I'm stressing over is missing our appointment at the twenty-four-hour wedding chapel.

It's been an incredible year. Not only for my painting business—which, after winning this year's Seattle Art Museum's prestigious award, is booked solid for the next year—but things with Jaylen have never been better. I can't wait to marry him, with or without my something blue.

Maya begins tearing at the black lace overlay of her maxi skirt, ruthlessly pulling off the front panel before I can stop her. She reaches into her purse, grabbing a bobby pin from the bottom of the bag. It doesn't take long for me to realize it's a makeshift veil.

"Is this my something borrowed?" I ask as she fastens it into my messy updo. I'm not sure how she will ever get it sewn back on her dress.

"It's your something used." She adjusts some rogue strands of hair and lays the veil delicately down my back. Maya sure does love a reduce-reuse-and-recycle moment. Her head tilts to the side as she looks me over lovingly. She grabs my hands and says, "I'm glad you finally realized you deserve good things."

"Me too. Thanks for the kick in the ass." I pull her in for a hug.

"It's a kickable ass."

"It is, isn't it?" I twist my back to get a look.

A shriek from across the store interrupts our moment. "Got it!" Cooper yells. Running over, he hands me a light blue lacy thong.

I hold it up at eye level. Bejeweled across the front are the words *Viva Las Vegas*. I giggle. I know Jaylen will get a kick out of them too. "It's perfect."

"Next!" The woman behind the front desk sounds like she swallowed a frog. The red lipstick stains on her teeth are the same glossy scarlet as her nails. She looks like the type of woman to call you "honey" and always have a light on hand.

Jaylen tugs on Wells's arm, spinning him around. "Where did Lamber and Soko go?"

Wells shrugs. "They said they needed to grab something and they would be right back."

I hand over our paperwork and I'm given a bouquet of weathered faux roses. "Get in line, lovebirds. Be sure to pick up your buy-one–get-one coupon for our strip-club breakfast buffet after the ceremony," the woman says, ushering our group into the chapel.

"This is the sanctity of marriage that homophobes are so pressed about preserving?" Cooper leans in to say to Maya. She giggles into her palm, but quickly pulls it together to shush him.

We file into the dingy chapel. The once-pristine white early-2000s wedding decor is now a time-stained pale yellow. An Elvis impersonator emerges from a side door and electric slides into place under the awning.

Cooper gasps. "This is so camp."

"It's so Lucy," Maya says.

It's gaudy and tacky—but to me, it's perfect. I know I will owe Jaylen something more traditional—something with all our friends and family—but I don't mind because this is exactly how I always pictured it. A little bit crazy, and a whole lot of love.

Suddenly, the back door bursts open. I jump, having expected some dramatic speak-now-or-forever-hold-your-peace moment with one of Jaylen's overzealous fans. Luckily it's only Soko and Lamber finally returning in time for the ceremony to start. Soko strolls in holding the Stanley Cup over his head like he's trying to air out his armpits, while Lamber is cradling one of those comically large bottles of champagne like it's a baby.

"Was the trophy really necessary?" I say to Jaylen. Soko sets the Stanley Cup in an empty chair in the front row.

"Did you steal that?" Jaylen asks.

Instead of getting a straight answer from either of them, Soko does a double-finger gun hand gesture and sits down in an empty chair beside Wells and Hannah.

"We're gathered here tonight to join Lucy and Jaylen in holy matrimony. All right, how 'bout some vows," Elvis says in character.

I pull out a crumpled piece of paper tucked between my boobs and unfold it in trembling hands. I shake my bangs out of my eyes as I steady my breath. "I only knew chaos before you. I didn't know life could be so calm. I didn't know love could be so comforting. You are so good at loving me, Jaylen. I showed you the darkest parts of me, and you still saw light. I promise to always search for that light in everything we do. I love you." As I begin to tear up, Elvis quickly pulls a tissue out of his oversize gold-and-diamond-encrusted belt buckle.

It's Jaylen's turn to say his vows and to my surprise, he doesn't pull a piece of paper out of his jacket pocket. Instead, he grabs both my hands and looks deep into my eyes. "I loved you at first sight, and I knew because I was terrified of you."

Our guests break out into a hum of giggles—myself included. Jaylen pulls me in closer.

He continues, "I knew right away that you were going to be someone who would change my life. And change is scary, even when it's good. It's been so good, by the way. I'm so happy I held on for all of this. When I met you, I was at a point in my life where I wasn't sure I would ever be happy again. I know I got through it to get to you because with you, I slowly started to believe that I deserved it, happiness and love and maybe even a bit of luck. It's you and me forever, and the rest is an added bonus." He starts choking up.

In that moment of silence, while Jaylen looks longingly into my eyes, Soko begins to sob violently. With all eyes on him, he cries out, "Even in the toughest battles, love is the only true victor."

"That was really touching, but you need to pull yourself together," Lamber says, taking Soko under his arm, where he sniffles into his chest.

Wells steps up and brings Jaylen two gold rings. I'm almost too distracted by the strobe lights reflecting off Elvis's sparkly outfit to notice that they are the same ones I saved on my phone months ago.

Jaylen repeats after the officiant, "With this ring, I take you, Lucy, to be my wife." He slips the ring on my finger, and I immediately pull it up to my face for a closer look. I do the same to his finger as we inch closer and closer together, impatiently waiting for the part where we can kiss.

The affiant declares, "By the power vested in me by the state of Nevada, I now pronounce you husband and wife!" Elvis hardly finishes his sentence before I'm grabbing Jaylen's face and kissing him. Jaylen takes me by the waist and dips me. We share a passionate kiss as our closest friends cheer and holler as we celebrate a life full of hockey, love, and lots of good luck.

★ ★ ★ ★ ★

# ACKNOWLEDGMENTS

I always say my life would be nothing without hockey. Even long before I began writing this book, the game has been so deeply embedded into my existence that it's a way of life. It was my escape as a kid, a way to connect with my family, it gave me my husband and my beautiful kids, and now the journey has led me to my debut novel—a beautiful love story between Lucy and Jaylen. Hockey has given me so much, and this is my small way to give back.

Please allow me to gush a bit more because it takes a team to release a novel and I've got some key players to thank.

I firmly believe that if you surround yourself with the right people, inspiration is abundant. My agent, Deidre Knight, is a force in the industry and with her in my corner championing my work, I began believing this dream of mine could hit the shelves. Thank you, Deidre, for your guidance, expertise, and friendship.

From the beginning my editor, Lynn Raposo, just got it— the story, the characters, my sense of humor, all of it. She saw me and, more important, she saw Lucy and Jaylen. Thank you, Lynn, for pushing me to my full potential, and for laughing at my jokes, which as far as I'm concerned is the nicest thing you can do for another person.

Everyone at Canary Street Press, even from the other side of the continent: I felt your support and encouragement throughout this entire process.

Debs, thank you for bringing Lucy and Jaylen to life. Your cover art is so cool that I hope people judge this book by its cover.

Thank you to my family, my all-time favorite team. To my husband, who fielded an onslaught of NHL-specific questions, forcing him to recall hotel locations, travel schedules, and pre-game routines because no detail was too small to not be NHL accurate. Writing about love is easy because you taught me so much about it.

To my kids, Lily and Booker, thank you for keeping me humble. It's them I have to thank for the violent stomach bug that ravaged my body the same day I was accepting my book deal. Not even vomiting (and worse!) could ruin my day as I replied to the best emails and calls a writer could ever receive. No one said parenting would be pretty, they said it would be worth it. And it is, every day I get to be your mama.

Last, thank you to the community of die-hard hockey fans who have wrapped me and my family up with love and support for more than a decade. Your cheers and passionate support are what made writing this so much fun. To the LGBTQ+ fans, the BIPOC fans, and anyone else who feels hockey doesn't love them the same way they love it, I see you and I'm happy you're here.